LONDON HOLIDAY

LONDON HOLIDAY

MIRANDA MACLEOD

London Holiday

Copyright © 2019 Miranda MacLeod

Find out more: www.mirandamacleod.com
Contact the author: miranda@mirandamacleod.com

ISBN-13: 9781798780121

Apple Blossom Press
PO Box 547
Bolton MA 01740

ONE

A DOZEN CHANDELIERS hung from the frescoed ceiling in long, neat rows, their twinkling lights turning the golden walls of the Kensington Palace ballroom into a fairy wonderland, but all Abby could focus on was her big toe. Specifically, the left one, which had been squeezed mercilessly into a shoe that was much too narrow to accommodate it, but which her stylist had assured her looked absolutely stunning with her gown. The royal stylist had said a lot of things, and Abby doubted the truth of most of them.

Handpicked by Countess Margaret, Abby's lady-in-waiting and chaperone for this trip—a woman who was contemporary in age to Abby's departed grandmother, and as equally out of touch as she was disapproving of anything that resembled a modern fashion trend—the royal stylist was a relic of a bygone era. The resulting look was a tragedy of Shakespearean proportion. The cut of Abby's gown was fussy and old-fashioned, her hairstyle so stiff it could double as a football helmet, and the tiara that topped it all off was as garish as it was pretentious. Abby felt, in short, like a ninety-year-old woman who was having an off day. The only redeeming item in the whole ensemble was the small, red evening bag that she clutched in one white-gloved hand, but even it was a disappointment since it was too small to hold her mobile phone. The fact that she'd accidentally trimmed her toenail short enough to draw blood earlier that afternoon just added to her woes.

Outside the massive arched windows, from the palace's second floor, Abby could see people from every walk of life strolling the manicured grounds of Kensington Gardens in the late afternoon sunshine. There was a man walking a small white dog on a leash and a mother helping her child to steady his wobbly bicycle as he pedaled. Scores of businesspeople power walked along the main path, dressed in suits but clearly eager to put the work week behind them as Friday evening approached. Some of the suit-clad women wore sneakers on their feet to ease their long commutes, and as ridiculous a sartorial choice as it was, Abby envied their practicality with every fiber of her being.

Just outside the public entrance to the palace, a group of women, all dressed in tacky, thrift-shop evening dresses and party-store plastic tiaras, huddled for photos around a woman wearing a large white sash that pronounced her the "bride-to-be." Abby sighed. Out there in the real world, people were being silly and having fun. Meanwhile, Abby was stuck in a stuffy reception with half the crowned heads of Europe, a dull affair that would stretch on for hours. What she wouldn't give for a walk in the park and a pair of comfortable shoes. Leaning wearily against the wall, she eased the back of her shoe away from her raw heel and winced as she wriggled the offending toe. She knew enough not to admit it publicly, but sometimes this so-called charmed life of hers seemed tremendously unfair. Cinderella had never had to deal with this kind of shit, or if she had, at least her shoes fit.

From across the room, a woman approached her with an effortless grace, her dark curls bouncing on her sun-kissed shoulders. The woman had recently become a duchess by marriage, and was the wife of Abby's third cousin once removed, or at least she was if Abby had interpreted the family tree correctly. She wasn't entirely sure she had. This royalty thing was still so new to her, and the ties between her father's royal family and all the other European royal families were so crisscrossed and tangled over the generations that there were a million ways to get it wrong.

The young duchess glanced at Abby's half-exposed, mangled foot and smiled sympathetically. "Next time," she whispered with a conspiratorial tone, "get them a size larger." The duchess raised the hem of her gown a few inches, enough to expose an almost comically roomy pair of heels. "You can be on your feet for hours in these things, and there's nothing worse than blisters."

Abby nodded gratefully at the advice and wondered, as the woman drifted off to continue her mingling, whether they'd have a chance to sit down privately later for a chat. What she wouldn't give to know that woman's secret. Like Abby, the duchess had begun her life as a commoner, a fellow American, no less, and yet she'd handled the transition to royal life like a pro. Meanwhile, this battle with ill-fitting shoes was just the latest example of lessons Abby—or Princess Abigail, as she was now known—was learning the hard way. Nothing in her laid-back California upbringing had prepared her for the turn her life had taken. Her, a princess? It still seemed absurd, yet the proof it was true was right there on top of her head, weighing about a million pounds. She massaged her fingers against her temple to relieve the pressure, and almost immediately Countess Margaret was at her side.

"Your Highness, are you quite all right?" The older woman's brow was creased in evident concern, and Abby feared she must look as out of sorts as she felt.

"It's nothing," Abby assured her. "It's only that this is my first official state function on my own, and my nerves are on edge." She looked around the room, which was packed with dignitaries and heads of state, and her stomach did a somersault. There were more people here than there'd been at her parents' wedding, or perhaps it was just that she'd been too distracted by the whirlwind nature of their courtship and marriage to be bothered by anything else. Little had she realized three months ago how completely the events of that day would ruin the rest of her life.

"Here. Take these." Countess Margaret held out a cupped hand with two white pills nestled in the palm.

Abby eyed them suspiciously. "What are they?"

"Just something your father's personal physician gave me for the trip. They'll help you relax."

Her face wore a stern expression that discouraged arguing. With a shrug, Abby pinched the pills between her fingers and popped them onto her tongue. What could it hurt? A waiter passed by with a silver tray laden with flutes of champagne, and she grabbed one to wash the medicine down. As she tilted her head back to drink, she could feel the tiara slipping. Abby poked at it with a finger, trying to straighten it out. "Do I really need to wear this thing? None of the other young, unmarried royals are wearing tiaras. I don't see why I have to."

"That *thing* is the Gamberini tiara. Protocol in this country may be different, but in *our* kingdom, the crown princess must always wear the Gamberini tiara when she is at a state function. It is a symbol of the authority of the royal family. It is non-negotiable. Now, come. You must meet Admiral Francisco and his wife."

Countess Margaret placed a hand on Abby's shoulder

to help her navigate the crowd. "Their son is with them, just a few years older than you. Very handsome, don't you think? And he has a promising career in our royal navy."

Abby snorted, and the champagne she'd just swallowed tickled the back of her nose. It wasn't the thought of her father's tiny, landlocked, and mountainous kingdom trying to support a full-blown navy that prompted this incredulous response. Since officially being named her kingdom's crown princess, Abby was fairly certain not a day had passed without at least one potential marriage match being brought to her attention. And while she had always been forthcoming with her family about her bisexuality, receiving numerous assurances that her newly-adopted country was very progressive, and that it wouldn't be a problem in the slightest should she someday choose to marry a woman, she couldn't help but notice that every suggested suitor had nonetheless been male. A quick glance revealed that this current specimen had a peculiarly thin face and the longest eyelashes she'd ever seen. Handsome? Frankly, he looked like a horse. "He'd be prettier as a girl. I don't suppose he has a sister?"

"Don't be rude," the countess admonished. "A royal wedding could be just what our little kingdom needs to raise its profile on the world stage. Just look what your cousins' weddings have done for the United Kingdom. Oh, and the babies! People do love babies."

"Yes, because no one had ever heard of this place before the queen's grandchildren started getting hitched and popping out kids."

"Your Highness. That's no way for a princess to speak."

Abby could nearly see her lady-in-waiting's veins throbbing beneath her wrinkled parchment of neck skin, and the visible proof of the agitation that her uncouth American personality was causing the woman filled her with a deep sense of satisfaction. "Anyway, our kingdom just had a royal wedding, or have you forgotten? Because *I* sure haven't."

The resentment that had grown inside Abby since her parents' marriage had been most unexpected. As someone who'd grown up with parents who had split up before she was even born, the prospect of her mother and father getting married and magically turning them into a real family should have been a dream come true. It was what she'd always wanted as a child. What she hadn't counted on was that, thanks to the laws of succession in her father's homeland, Abby had gone from being just some obscure, illegitimate daughter to the king's firstborn and heir apparent the exact moment the happy couple had said *I do*. No one had properly warned her about that part.

"Come, Princess." The countess took her by the elbow in a way that discouraged any further argument. "You have your duties to attend to."

Abby took a step and sucked in her breath as the

full weight of her body compressed her injured toe. "I'm not sure I can. I promise, I'm not just trying to be difficult this time. My foot is killing me."

"Here." Countess Margaret reached into her handbag and pulled out two more pills, oblong this time. "These will dull the pain."

Abby frowned. "Are you sure it's okay to take these so soon after I took those other ones?"

Countess Margaret hesitated a moment, then nodded decisively. "I'm sure it's fine. This is just a pain reliever. I don't see how it could hurt."

Too miserable to argue, Abby choked the medicine down with a second glass of champagne. "Can I just wait here until they kick in?"

The countess gave a curt bob of her head. "For a minute or two, but no more. You have people to meet."

So many people to meet. Abby squeezed her eyes shut. Would this be her life from now on, shaking hands with strangers, smiling and nodding, while her feet screamed in silent agony?

"Your Highness?"

Abby opened one eye at the unfamiliar voice. A young woman clothed in a servant's uniform made a quick curtsy. "The duchess wished for me to tell you that, if you'd like to follow me to her private quarters, you might find a more suitable pair of shoes."

"Oh, would I ever!" Abby gritted her teeth tightly as she hobbled behind the servant, until they reached a discreetly camouflaged door at the other end of the ballroom. Behind the door stretched a long, plain hallway that made up part of the maze of servant's passages that connected the many rooms and residences of the sprawling palace. As soon as she was out of sight of the other guests, Abby kicked off both high heels and curled her stocking-clad toes into the carpet. "Ah, bliss."

With the servant leading the way, they made several turns from one identical, unmarked corridor to another. As she went, Abby's head began to spin. *Perhaps*, she thought, *I should have eaten before getting here, if the champagne is already going to my head.* These formal affairs were murder for a healthy appetite like hers. She had yet to master the art of hunting down the people carrying those silver trays of appetizers in a way that didn't meet with Countess Margaret's disapproval, so she'd be lucky to score more than a bite or two during the reception. Dinner itself wouldn't be for hours, and it would probably be something pompously inedible. Was it likely that the servant would allow her to sneak a snack from her third cousin's pantry before returning to the party? And would they have potato chips? She loved potato chips.

Stopping in front of a door that was no different in appearance from every other door they had passed, the servant took out a set of keys and fiddled with the lock. "Here you are, Your Highness. The duchess's shoe closet is just through there, and she said you may choose whichever pair you'd like." She glanced anxiously down the hall in the direction from which they'd come. "Unless you require further assistance, I really must get back to my duties. You won't get lost finding your way back?"

"Of course not," Abby assured her, with much more confidence than she felt. "I was a Girl Scout. Direction finding is in my blood." This was very much not true. The closest she'd come to being a Girl Scout was buying a dozen boxes of cookies every spring in junior high school. And she'd only done that because it meant Rebecca Schwartz, the raven-haired goddess in the class above hers, would personally deliver them to her house.

As soon as the servant had retreated, Abby took a shaky step toward the aforementioned closet. The spinning in her head was growing worse by the second, and though she now had a strong craving for chocolate mint cookies, she was no longer convinced a simple snack was the solution. But if she tried to feign illness, Countess Margaret would have her head on a platter. She'd just have to make it through the night as best she could, perhaps with the help of a sensible pair of kitten heels.

Resolute, Abby inspected the shelves of shoes, which included dozens of demurely elegant styles, any one of which might suit her better than the torture devices she'd been wearing, but over and over, her eyes kept coming back to a pair of black-and-white Chuck

Taylor All-Star sneakers. God, they looked comfortable. She peeled off her gloves and picked them up, caressing the worn canvas, which might as well have been velvet beneath her fingertips. She stripped off her pantyhose, found a pair of ankle socks, then gingerly slid her mangled foot inside both sock and shoe and gave an audible sigh of relief. Protocol or not, Countess Margaret could pry these shoes off her cold, dead toes. If the businesswomen of London could wear sneakers with their suits, she sure as hell could wear them under her gown. Abby put on the second one, then let the shiny red satin skirt fall to the floor. She nodded with satisfaction at the way the folds obscured the sneakers. With any luck, no one would be the wiser.

Abby took a step back in the direction of the hallway door where she'd entered, but had to catch herself against the doorframe as the corners of her vision darkened, and the room began to sway. Her stomach lurched alarmingly. If she didn't get some food in it soon, she was going to lose what little it contained all over the prince and duchess's oriental rug. And knowing the way royals were, it was probably priceless. There'd be no living it down. She took a deep breath and moved deeper into the private residence, sliding her cheek along the cool wall as she walked.

The kitchen was homey and bright, a charmingly practical spot at odds with the grandeur of the rest of the apartment. Abby quickly found a piece of bread and spread it thickly with rich, yellow butter. The morsel was enough to settle the worst of her nausea, though even after eating, the room continued to move with a gentle rocking motion that gave Abby the impression of being at sea. She'd have to find her way back to Countess Margaret as soon as possible and see what could be done. Maybe she could give her a third type of pill to fix the damage done by the others? At this point, Abby was fairly certain that the medicine was to blame, and not the champagne. Or it might have been the combination of all of it. In any case, she should never have taken anything without knowing precisely what it was, no matter how scary the countess could be when crossed.

After a few wrong turns, Abby found her way back to the servants passages, but as soon as the door shut behind her, she was hopelessly lost. Every direction looked the same, and she found she had almost no memory of being led there in the first place. Eventually, she chose a direction at random and began to walk. She came to a staircase, which she suspected wasn't right, and yet her fuzzy-headedness left her without any better ideas than to follow it down two flights, to where it ended at a heavy steel door with a knob on the inside but only a keyhole on the other side. She emerged into a corridor, the door closing and locking behind her, and heard voices echoing from somewhere nearby. She followed the sound, and soon found herself in a brightly lit shop where a gaggle of women oohed and aahed over souvenir mugs and tea towels. Their cheap tiaras and garish gowns marked them as the same bachelorette party Abby had observed from the ballroom above.

"Closing time in two minutes!" The booming voice of the security guard made Abby jump, but she collected her wits enough to approach him, hoping for help getting back to the ballroom. Without a key, the way she'd come was a no-go.

"Excuse me," she said, "but I'm trying to find—"

"The rest of your party is over there, miss, at the exit. Hurry along, please." His tone was more bored than gruff, but his size alone told her that he'd be impossible to subdue. Her hand-to-hand combat skills were somewhat better than her direction-finding abilities, which is to say she'd taken a few courses in self-defense, but was that really what she wanted to pin her hopes to in this situation?

"No, you see—"

He wasn't listening. "Any last purchases need to be made over there."

Abby took a breath and tried again. "I don't have any purchases. I—"

"Then you'll need to head to the exit. Right over there." He placed a large hand on Abby's shoulder and gave her a gentle spin, which started the room rocking once more.

"No, but I'm supposed to be upstairs, in the ballroom!" She stumbled and looked back pleadingly, but his sardonic expression caught her short.

"Sure you are, love." He chuckled, looking pointedly at the ground, where the black-and-white Chuck Taylor All-Stars poked out from beneath her gown. Abby cursed her impulsive fashion choice, along with her family's stubborn insistence at keeping her photos out of the newspapers. It was obvious he didn't recognize her, and no one was going to believe she was a real princess dressed as she was. "Go on, now. Your friends are waiting out there." He held the door open as he gave her an encouraging nudge in the direction of the sunken garden, where members of the party had gathered. Before she could react further, the door behind her clicked shut, locking her out again.

Now what? The only accessible door was clear on the other side of the palace, flanked by a pair of military guards. Her personal bodyguard could have vouched for her, only he'd been given the night off, given the abundance of palace security and the fact that the distance she'd had to travel that evening from her family's private apartment, which was next to her country's embassy and across the street from the palace, was only a matter of yards. The only thing she had to prove her identity, in fact, was the old American passport that she'd slipped into her clutch. The reminder of her former identity was a security blanket of sorts, but she doubted her old name, Abigail Mallard, would get her very far. If the security guard hadn't been willing to hear her out, Abby despaired at the thought of making her case to someone holding a rifle.

The evening gown-clad women began to walk in an ambling line away from the palace, but as Abby watched them, feeling particularly small and lost all by herself, one turned and squinted against the fading light and waved to her. "Aren't you coming?"

"Me?" Even though she knew it was a case of mistaken identity, the invitation warmed Abby's insides.

"Of course, you. You're Mary's cousin, right? Let's get going, or we'll be late for the club!"

"Well, er..." Oh, how she wished she were Mary's cousin, with a night out on the town ahead of her instead of a humiliating encounter with armed guards and a possible international incident in her near future. Between her swimming head and the sudden warmth of inclusion, Abby couldn't get the word no to form on her lips.

"Or was it her niece? There's so many of us tonight, I can't keep track." The woman shrugged, clearly accepting her as a member of the party, whomever she happened to be. She stuck out her hand. "Pamela."

"Abby." For the past three months she'd been addressed as nothing but Princess Abigail, and so hearing the name she'd grown up with, the one her friends had called her back home, was almost a shock.

But just plain Abby was who she wanted to be right now. She grasped Pamela's hand tightly, giving it a firm, decidedly un-royal, shake.

"Come on, Abby." Pamela adjusted her plastic tiara with a grin. "Next stop, Café Diana! We're all princesses tonight, love."

What could go wrong? a little voice in her head urged, and so Abby followed. The lights from the ballroom in Kensington Palace blazed brightly behind her as she traipsed along the path toward the exit onto Bayswater Road. At the nearest traffic light, her newfound friends crossed the street, but Abby did not. Instead, she did her best to blend into the crowd as they disappeared from view. They could all be princesses tonight if they wanted, but Abby's heart leaped at the realization that, for just a few hours at least, *she* didn't have to be.

TWO

"YOU CAN'T BE SERIOUS." Jordan clutched her pen between her fingers, tapping it over and over against the hard, black cover of her tattered Moleskine notebook. She'd come to the office prepared to receive her next week's assignments from her boss, but instead, she'd been blindsided. "The Australian. You're sure?"

The editor of the *Londontown Crier* repositioned her thick tortoiseshell glasses higher on the bridge of her nose. The eyes behind the frames looked weary, the wrinkles at the corners more pronounced than Jordan was used to seeing. "I'm afraid so. Effective next week, the paper will be under new management."

"But...but...the *Australian?*" Jordan squeaked as she said it. She sucked in a breath and brushed a strand of dark, shoulder-length hair behind her ear. "Come on, Diane. All he knows is running tabloids. He has no idea what real journalism entails. He'll completely ruin the *Crier*'s integrity."

"I won't argue with you there. But the *Crier* is woefully behind the times and hasn't managed to turn a profit in years, as I'm sure you're aware, given how many times recently the payroll has been late. Like it or not, he knows how to make money in these changing times."

"Sure, by publishing flashy, trashy e-zines filled with scandalous fluff and royal gossip, and not a single piece of hard-hitting investigative journalism. It's a wonder he even bothers with reporters. He could just as easily employ a bunch of amateur bloggers to write the type of crap..." Jordan's voice trailed off at the sudden pinched look on her mentor's face.

"Again, I can't argue." Diane shut her eyes, her voice reduced in volume to just above a whisper. "Which is why, also effective next week, all the remaining assignment reporters will be made redundant."

"But," Jordan choked, then tried to swallow the lump that had formed in her throat with limited success. "But, Diane, I'm an assignment reporter."

"I'm so sorry, Jordan." After a moment of sullen silence, Diane's eyes brightened, her expression broadening into that familiar smile she so often wielded, the one that always accompanied one of her famous "buck up, little camper" pep talks, and Jordan groaned. "Try to see this as an opportunity."

"An opportunity?" Jordan scoffed. "Since when is unemployment such a golden opportunity?"

"You're a good reporter, Jordan. You were, by far, my best student during the time I spent mentoring at the University of Nebraska, and are far too talented for the likes of the *Crier*."

"Sure, now you tell me." Despite her sarcastic tone, Jordan's cheeks flushed with genuine pride at the praise.

"Well, I couldn't let on before. I needed you on my team here, and I couldn't very well afford to give you a raise if you got a swollen head and thought you could look elsewhere for a position, now could I?"

"Are you saying that you don't need me now?"

"It's not that I don't need you, Jordan. It's that I won't be staying."

"Where are you going?"

"I'm taking my own advice and looking at this development as an opportunity for a much-needed move to greener pastures. I'll be giving a series of lectures at a university up north in the fall. After that, I'm not certain. What I do know is I could never work for that blowhard from Down Under. Frankly I'm not sure he plans to keep me on, but I'm not going to give him the satisfaction of having a choice. I would take you with me if I could, but since I can't, my advice is for you to follow your heart."

"I'm a journalist, Diane. I'm not sure I have a heart. And that advice is well and good for you, but I'm here on a work visa. That means if I don't have a job, I don't have a visa. And you know what happens then."

A lead weight settled into Jordan's belly at the thought of being forced to retreat to her birthplace like a dog with its tail between its legs. From the moment the jet's wheels had lifted off the runway at Eppley Airfield in Omaha five years ago, she'd sworn she would never go back. But with no savings and no job prospects, where else could she turn but her childhood bedroom at her parents' home? "Greener pastures. Do you have any idea how limited the options are for an investigative journalist in corn country? The only pastures I'll find there are actual pastures, for livestock."

"Well, better an honest source of manure than the shite you'd have to produce if you stayed here. The only thing that loathsome Aussie cares about is sensational, once in a lifetime stories of the century. Which he wants his reporters to produce weekly, of course."

Diane gave a dismissive laugh, but Jordan's brow creased as she pondered her mentor's words. "What if I did, though."

"Did what?"

"Produced a sensational story, the kind he's looking for."

"Jordan," Diane admonished, "that's not your style. You're too good for that."

"Am I? I mean, it's not like I couldn't manage it." Jordan tapped her pencil in a rapid staccato rhythm against the notebook as she warmed to the idea. "I'm a professional, Diane. I can write whatever I need to write. I would do anything to stay in London. I would literally shovel horse shit every week if I had to. So, if I found a juicy enough story, would it save my job?"

"If you produced a tell-all, sensational story of the century by next week, would the new editor keep you on?" Diane frowned as her glasses slid down her nose. After a long pause, she looked at Jordan over the top of her frames. "It's possible. But this isn't a joke, Jordan. A story like that represents everything you hate about the business today. Even if you did get offered a job, are you sure it's what you really want?"

"It's a chance to stay in this country and continue working as a reporter. So, is it what I want? Um, yeah." Jordan laughed incredulously.

"I could put you in touch with colleagues from my time in the States who are at reputable news organizations. They may not have anything glamorous to offer you now, but it could be a stepping stone to something better down the road. How about Des Moines or Kansas City?"

"My life's here in London." Even as Jordan made the argument, she could hear a tiny, mocking voice in her head saying, *Yeah, right. Some life.* She worked long hours for low pay. No girlfriend. No pets. Plus, her dingy cave of a basement flat was so small that she slept on a bed that had to be folded into the wall if she wanted to have room for company. Not that she had much company either. So, fine, it wasn't much of a life, but it was hers, and it was a hell of a lot better than what she could expect in someplace like Des Moines or Kansas City. "I know it's not the ideal position for me, but for now it's my only hope."

Diane didn't argue. Instead, she studied her in silence with a look that expressed her understanding but also hinted at a disappointment that struck Jordan to her core.

Diane picked up a file from her desk and waved it at Jordan. "My final assignment for you. It's covering the London leg of the first European tour of Her Royal Highness, Princess Abigail."

"A princess?" Jordan's mood lifted slightly. Though not at all a royal watcher, Jordan nonetheless combed her memory for any pertinent details she may have retained. There wasn't much, not even a photo. "She's that American one who grew up as a commoner?"

Diane nodded as she cracked open the file and quickly scanned its contents. "Princess Abigail is twenty-six years old, born in California. Her mother, Colleen Mallard, was a waitress at a seaside resort when she met Prince Randolph of the House of Gamberini, who at the time was a bit of a notorious playboy. After a brief romance, they parted ways. He headed back to Europe, and about nine months later found out their little dalliance had made him a father. He accepted his responsibility to a certain degree, bought Ms. Mallard a house in a nice neighborhood, paid for private schooling, even visited every year or two throughout Abigail's childhood. All in all, the child had a pretty normal life."

"Sure, right up to the part where her father has his own kingdom, and she's going to inherit it."

"Yes, that had to have come as a shock. You see, while she may have known early on that her father was a prince, it didn't matter much in the grand scheme of things. Her parents hadn't been married when she was born, so she had no royal title and wasn't in the line of succession. Plus, she lived so far away that the media in her father's kingdom barely noticed her. Honestly, he kept them busy with plenty of scandals much closer to home, although no other babies. He did seem to have learned his lesson on that one."

"Am I remembering correctly," Jordan asked, "that her father wasn't even supposed to be king?"

"That's right. He had an older sister who was meant to inherit the throne. She was the very model of a crown princess, which is probably why Randolph got away with as much as he did. Everyone knew the kingdom was in good hands. Then, about two years ago, the queen and crown princess were both tragically killed in a car accident while on holiday in the south of France."

"That's terrible, even for a prince. Can you imagine losing your family like that?"

"It changed him, that's for certain. He'd always

avoided responsibility, and now he was expected to govern and heal a grieving nation. And I'm sure that his remaining family became a lot more valuable to him. Even though they weren't a couple, Colleen had always been a stabilizing force in his life, and with his mother and sister gone so suddenly, he reached out to her."

"And then King Randolph and Colleen decided to marry?"

"Not right away, but when they did, it was almost overnight. They announced their engagement in January and were married at the end of February. And because of their kingdom's laws, the moment they married, Abigail's birth was retroactively recognized as legitimate, and she became not only a princess but the heir to the throne."

"Lucky bitch," Jordan murmured. It wasn't that she had any desire to be a princess. Actually, it seemed like a terrible job to her with all the formal etiquette and public scrutiny, not to mention the whole having to marry a prince thing, which would be a total deal breaker for Jordan. But a plump, juicy royal allowance would sure be nice. Under her current circumstances, she'd settle for turning this into a story plump enough for her to keep her job. "So, is Her Highness a party girl? Heavy drinker, maybe?" Jordan asked hopefully.

"Afraid not. The princess has kept a low profile since her parents married, and prior to that she was pretty straight-laced." Jordan's shoulder slumped, but after a short pause, Diane added, "Actually, straight might not be quite the right word for her."

Jordan perked up immediately. "You mean... she isn't *straight?*" This was a revelation that was right down her alley.

"It's hard to say. There was virtually no media or tabloid interest in her until this past January. We know she graduated from Stanford with a business degree and was working at a public relations firm in Los Angeles. There are almost no details of her personal life, but a few rumors have surfaced from her university days that suggest she might be bisexual."

Jordan grinned. "Now, *that* would be a story."

"Jordan!" Diane scolded. "I'm surprised at you. I would have expected you to have a little more hesitation at the prospect of outing this poor woman in the tabloids."

Jordan squirmed in her seat, trying her best not to admit that her boss had a point. "Well, first, she's not a *poor* woman, is she? She's a rich, spoiled princess. It's always open season on princesses. And second, I'm not saying I would write a tabloid-style exposé. It could be a thoughtful piece of investigative journalism."

"Yes, but a thoughtful piece of investigative journalism isn't going to save your job."

"You know, you're the one who brought up the whole thing in the first place." Jordan tapped her pencil against her notebook, praying an idea would present itself to her, but none did. Finally, she sighed.

"It's no use. I don't even know where I'd begin. It would take months of research to do justice to the story."

"It would. And you have barely a week. Unless you decide to just raise your hand during her press conference and ask if she'd like to go out with you, I think this particular story angle is a bust."

Jordan sat in silence, her brain still mulling the possibilities but coming up empty at every turn. Finally, she scooted to the edge of her chair and started to stand. "Right, I'd better just drop by Janice's desk on the way out and pick up my paycheck."

The look on Diane's face made Jordan's blood run so cold that she felt frozen to the chair. "Oh, Jordan. I hate to be the bearer of more bad news, but about the payroll situation. I know the *Crier* owes you some back pay, plus your check for this week, but—"

"But, what?" Jordan could almost taste the panic that Diane's use of the word *but* had stirred up inside her belly.

"You'll get your money, don't worry. It's just that there's been a delay, what with transferring ownership and all. It could be a few weeks until the issue is resolved and the payments are disbursed. If you need some help in the meantime..."

"No, of course not. I'll be just fine," Jordan assured her, though she had no idea how. Her savings account had been depleted after weeks of not being paid, her checking account had barely enough left in it to cover the rent that was due this week, and because of several complications she'd run into as a foreigner trying to open a credit card, she'd never bothered to follow through on it. It had never mattered before. She was usually extremely frugal with her money, but the *Crier's* hard times had drained her own resources dry. The only thing she had left was her pride, and she had way too much of it to accept help from a woman whose respect meant everything to her. Something in her mentor's expression told her that she knew Jordan was lying, but wasn't going to press it.

"My offer stands; anytime you need it. Plane fare, a job recommendation, you just let me know. Here." Diane handed her the file on Princess Abigail, blinking back tears. "Take this; go to the press conference, and write a final story for the *Crier* that will make us both proud."

A ROW of perfectly trimmed shrubberies lined the pavement outside Jordan's favorite pub, where planters cascading with lush greenery flanked the rich wood-paneled exterior, and a portrait of Churchill gazed solemnly from beneath the Union Jack that flapped against its pole in the evening breeze. She peered through squares of leaded glass as she gave the shiny brass plate on the worn oak door a shove. Max was already there, his trademark wool cap of Royal Stewart tartan forming a brilliant red beacon beneath the glowing lamplight that bathed their usual spot in the corner. Jordan pushed Max's leather camera bag away from the legs of an empty armchair with her foot, then slid the chair back a few inches from the table, and plunked her body into its deep leather seat.

Without a word, Max motioned to the waiting pint of ale, refraining from speaking until she'd taken several generous gulps. "Who died?" he finally asked in his thick Scottish brogue.

Jordan took one more sip before setting the almost empty glass atop a cardboard coaster. "Journalistic integrity. The *Londontown Crier*. My career. Take your pick. The paper's been sold," she added when his only response was a confused stare. "Sold to a trashy tabloid hack from Australia. I have a week to prove I deserve to keep my job, or it's goodbye London, hello Omaha."

"A week?" Max gave a low whistle. "That's rough."

"Tell me about it."

"But won't your work at the *Crier* speak for itself? You've won awards, after all."

"If it were anyone else, I wouldn't be worried, but my style doesn't exactly mesh with the new owner's. If I can't produce a tell-all story of the century on someone rich and famous by next Friday, there's no way they'll keep me on."

Max stroked the patch of ginger whiskers on his chin thoughtfully. "So, you'll be looking for something new. Want me to check in with the news organizations I freelance for?"

"I appreciate the offer, but there's no time."

"So, it's back to the States, then."

"Oh, hell no."

Max's bushy red eyebrows shot up. "What's the plan?"

"To produce a tell-all story of the century on someone rich and famous by next Friday. Have you not been listening?"

His deep chuckle filled the space around them. "Come on, Jordan. That's not how you operate."

Jordan stiffened. "Why does everyone keep saying that? I'm a professional. I have the ability to write anything I need to write."

"But, tabloid hack? Really, Baxter?" His disappointment in her showed through as clearly as Diane's had, making Jordan bristle. And he'd used her last name, too. Never a good sign. "You're made for better than the likes of that."

"Yeah, well, it's easy for you to judge. Unless Scotland votes for independence one of these days, you're not the one facing deportation."

"I've told you before, there's always the marriage option. Just say the word, and we can elope to Gretna Green like they did in the old days."

"Thanks, Max, but you're not exactly my type," Jordan answered with a laugh. "Besides, I don't think Moira would put up with it. Speaking of Moira, when are you planning to make an honest woman of her, anyway?"

Max's cheeks flushed. "Soon. I've saved up nearly enough to buy the ring. I was thinking of proposing when we're in Paris later this summer."

"Max, you old devil!" Jordan clapped a hand on her friend's shoulder, grinning. "Paris? Jesus. I had no idea you were such a romantic."

Max stroked his chin some more, looking uncharacteristically hesitant. "You really think she'll like that? Enough to say yes?"

"Yes. Trust me, girls love that kind of thing."

Max shot her a doubtful look. "How would you know? I can't even remember the last time you went out with a girl."

Jordan blinked. "Max. Look at me. I *am* a girl."

"Barely." The corners of his mouth twitched as he took in her dark jeans and white T-shirt, topped with a straight-cut black blazer and rounded out with a pair of thick-soled, clunky black leather shoes on her feet. It certainly wasn't the most feminine of outfits, but it suited Jordan's no-nonsense style and on-the-go lifestyle.

Jordan rolled her eyes. "Look, buddy, I may not be the girliest of girls, but hell, if you took me to Paris and gave me a big shiny rock in front of the Eiffel Tower, even I might get caught up in the moment and say yes. Before coming to my senses, of course."

Max's cheeks deepened to a rich ruby red. "Well,

if Moira's a sure thing, I guess that marriage offer's off the table, then. Sorry."

"It's all right. I still have the option of writing a sensational celebrity gossip article worthy of the sleaziest tabloid. Lucky me. I don't suppose you've photographed any promising candidates, lately? Someone with a sordid past. Actually, a sordid present would be better."

"Can't think of anyone. But if I do, you'll be the first to know."

Jordan swigged down the last of her beer. "Thanks, mate. I appreciate it."

They headed out, Max turning right to walk in the direction of Kensington Gardens while Jordan contemplated her options for getting home. Though usually a night owl, this day had exhausted her, and somehow just imagining the effort that would be required to sustain her between the pub and the moment when she could collapse on the bed in her flat was almost too much for her to bear. But considering the news that had put her in this emotional state, shelling out money for a cab was out of the question. Judging by the crowd that had gathered at the stop, a bus would be along in a minute, but Jordan hated buses. They were crowded and smelly. It was a twenty-five minute walk to her flat on the far end of Portobello Road. Could she survive? Jordan took a deep breath and set off. She'd have to survive, both the walk and everything else the week ahead of her might hold. She had no choice.

The stretch of Portobello Road nearest to the pub was the posh end. It was the part most tourists knew, where antique vendors set up their stalls on market days, their tables overflowing with things no one on earth needed, like pearl-handled Edwardian grapefruit spoons and silver-plated candelabras. There were swank shops along this section that sold overpriced cups of the latest trendy drinks, like cold brewed coffee or flat whites with elaborate images of leaves and hearts formed in the foam.

This was not the area of Portobello Road that Jordan called home, where million-pound homes sported brightly colored doors that conjured up images of Julia Roberts romcoms. Rather, she occupied a dingy basement at the very far end of the road, on the other side of the highway overpass, where all of the quaint boutiques that sold hand-smocked children's clothing or novelty socks gave way to rows of flats that seemed perpetually to be undergoing maintenance. The buildings in her neighborhood were more often than not shrouded behind scaffolding and tarps, interspersed with storefronts where faded signs advertised utilitarian offerings ranging from pet grooming and mobile phones to traditional pies and mash. Tourists rarely made it as far as Jordan's part, and if they did, they were easy to spot by the frightened looks on their faces.

She continued on along the mostly deserted street. Everything was closed now. Though it was the end of

May and daytime temperatures had been pleasant, the night air was chilly, biting through her blazer with the damp, raw edge that London weather was known for at any time of year. Jordan wrapped her arms closer to her chest and quickened her pace, dreaming of the warm cup of tea she'd make when she finally reached home.

There were few bars or pubs along her route, with the exception of one, a bohemian sort of venue that served drinks and hosted live entertainment on weekends. Jordan was friendly with the owner and would sometimes drop in to write up a review of a new band for the *Crier* as a favor to him, but she hadn't been by in a while. As she approached the place tonight, Jordan noticed that a large crowd had gathered outside the entrance, where a light-up marquee announced the return of the Portobello Burlesque Club's "Princess Revue." Jordan slowed her pace. It wasn't exactly a room full of partying Kardashians, but on the other hand, a burlesque show seemed like the type of thing a certain Australian might find interesting. Besides, she'd be a fool to turn down a chance to see a stage filled with nearly naked princess look-alikes, right?

She checked the time on her phone and sighed. It was nearly nine o'clock. The show would be starting soon, and if she could talk Clive the bouncer into letting her in, she might at least snag an interview or two with the performers between acts. Despite the fact that being backstage at a burlesque show would make her the envy of hundreds, she looked longingly down the street. Her flat, with its promised mug of tea and comfortable bed, was so close, barely five minutes away, and yet Jordan knew she wouldn't see it until well into the early hours of morning. And for what? An interview with burlesque dancers wouldn't be enough to save her job. On the other hand, it was the only option on the table right now. At least she'd feel like she was trying.

Squaring her shoulders, Jordan moved briskly past the crowd, her eyes fixed on a nondescript door a little farther down, which she knew from experience led to the club's backstage. The door was open, and she could see the familiar outline of the bouncer's bald head, but he didn't see her yet. He was too busy carrying on an animated conversation with a woman who, judging by her getup, had to be one of the performers in the princess review. She wore a floor-length, red gown and was sporting a massive diamond tiara atop her blonde upswept hairdo. Most unexpectedly, a single black sneaker poked out from the hem of the gown, its white toe and laces reflecting the light from a nearby street-lamp. Intrigued, Jordan stepped closer and called out a greeting to her old friend Clive.

THREE

THE BALD MAN'S head seemed...*wobbly*. Abby blinked, but it did nothing to bring things into focus and instead resulted in the man having not one but two bald heads. This was not an improvement. Both of the heads stared angrily at her, and Abby swore she could feel her body physically shrinking under his scrutiny.

"I wasn't trying to sneak in," she assured him. At least, that's what she'd tried to say. What came out was more garbled than it should have been. Surely this couldn't still be the aftereffects of the champagne, could it? If so, her Kensington Palace cousins sure knew their bubbly. Her suspicions about the contents of those pills Countess Margaret had given her were growing.

"You pushed your way through the front door without a ticket," the bald man countered, his booming voice making her teeth hurt. "And then refused to buy one."

"An oversight, I obscure you." *Obscure? No. Azure?* That didn't sound right, either. "I told you, I have nothing in my purse. Countess Margaret controls my money."

"Right." Even in her current state, Abby couldn't fail to notice the man's sarcastic tone. "And Countess Margaret is who, exactly?"

"My lady-in-waiting." Abby steadied herself against the doorframe. Why was this so hard for the bald man to understand? At least it had gone back to there being just one of him. That was a relief. She'd been feeling outnumbered.

Before the man had a chance to reply, a woman's voice called out. "Hey, Clive!"

Abby swiveled her head toward the sound and regretted it immediately. Either a pair of identical twins was heading toward her, or the rapid movement had set off another round of dizzying double vision. Though she knew it was likely caused by the latter, as she took in the dark-haired beauty who was approaching her, she sent up a fervent wish for the twins scenario. Wouldn't *that* be lucky.

"Jordan!" The bald man, whose name had just been revealed to be Clive, flashed a grin at the stranger who, if Abby was following things correctly, seemed to be named Jordan. Names were hard.

"Clive. Jordan." Abby nodded solemnly from one

to the other, as if greeting them in a receiving line at the palace. "A pleasure to meet you both."

"You here for the show?" Clive asked Jordan, neither of them paying Abby even the slightest bit of attention.

"I thought I might check it out. Okay if I go in?"

"Of course, of course." Clive stepped away from the doorway to make room for Jordan to pass.

"Thank you, Clive," Jordan said as she stepped through the doorway.

"Thank you, Clive," Abby said, then ran directly into what felt like a brick wall but turned out to be one of Clive's beefy forearms.

"Hold it right there, princess."

How does he know I'm a princess? Then Abby giggled. *Oh, of course.* She reached up to straighten out her tiara, which had become lopsided on her head right around the time she'd been stopped in her tracks by Clive's hairy bare arm. She gave him a conspiratorial wink as she began to ramble. "I'm Abby, but when I was little the kids at school sometimes call me Ducky, on account of my last name being a type of duck. Wasn't that smart of them?"

"Right. Ducky. You still can't come in without a ticket."

"Hold on there, Clive." Jordan had made it a few feet down the narrow hallway, but then had turned to listen as their conversation played out. "What's going on with her?"

"You mean Ducky here? She tried to get through the front door without a ticket."

Abby puffed out her chest, indignant. "But, I didn't! Er, that is, not really. I—"

"Clive." Jordan gestured toward Abby, waving her hand up and down the length of her body in a way that sent a shiver down Abby's spine as an image formed in her brain of the woman's fingers traveling along her skin instead of the air that separated them. Naughty brain. "Have you not noticed what she's wearing?"

Clive frowned. "What she's wearing?"

"Yes, what I'm wearing, Clive," Abby repeated with all the authority she could muster, though she had no idea why what she was wearing had any relevance whatsoever to the situation.

"Isn't tonight the princess review?" Jordan prompted gently.

"Of course!" Clive smacked a meaty hand against his shiny brow. "And Jeremy was just here a few minutes ago looking for his final girl. I'm such an idiot."

"Oh, don't be too hard on yourself," Abby soothed, still uncertain what they were talking about but suddenly awash in emotions of both pity and affection for the bouncer that she couldn't explain but hoped would prove temporary. Her eyes misted up as she placed a hand on his shoulder. "I forgive you, Clive."

"Right. Well, thanks." The man's flushed cheeks were apparent even in the dimly lit doorway. He turned to Jordan with a pleading look. "Er, maybe she can follow you down to find Jeremy? I think I'd rather not explain it to him, if that's all right by you."

"Yeah, of course, mate," Jordan assured him. "Come on—Ducky, was it?"

"Yes, that's right. Because my name is a duck."

"Okay." By the look on Jordan's face, Abby got the feeling she hadn't done her best job at explaining the nickname this time, but trying again seemed way too complicated.

"And you're... Jor-Dan... Jooordan." Abby giggled as the name came out all wrong for a second time. "Nice to meet you."

"Uh, yeah." Jordan was giving her a quizzical look that made Abby giggle again as her body flushed with warmth. That woman's piercing brown eyes were to die for. How come the people Countess Margaret wanted her to meet never looked like her? "Nice to meet you, too, Ducky. But, are you sure you're okay for this evening's show?"

"The show?" *Show. Show. Isn't it funny how sometimes you can say a word over and over again until it stops sounding like a word? Show. Show. Show-show-show.* Abby's lips were starting to feel squishy, and based on the fact that Jordan was giving her that funny look again, she'd begun to wonder just how much of that she'd accidentally said aloud. Then she remembered the sign outside the club that had caught her attention in the first place. "Oh, right! The burlesque thing. Yeah, definitely okay for that. It looks fantastic, right?"

"Uh, sure. I mean, I guess you would know better than I would, being in it and all, but yeah." Jordan arched an eyebrow, and the gesture made Abby's knees start to wobble. *God, that was hot. I would definitely not kick her out of bed for looking at me like that.*

"Sorry, what?" There was that funny look again. Shit, had she used her outside voice that time, too? Abby held her breath but Jordan just laughed. "Come on, Ducky. Let's go find Jeremy."

"Okay, let's find Jeremy." Abby trotted down the hall behind Jordan like an eager puppy. "Who's Jeremy?"

Jordan stopped walking and turned abruptly, fast enough that Abby missed the cue and plowed directly into her chest. It was warm and very curvy, with a hint of spicy scent, and provided such a delightfully soft landing that Abby briefly considered staying right there and never moving again, but after a second or two of apparent shock, Jordan took a step back. "Jeremy, the stage manager. Seriously, are you sure you're up for this?"

"I ask you this, Jordan..." Abby paused for effect, her face beaming philosophically. "Who *isn't* up for a night of nearly naked women? I mean, truly. What could be better?"

"You have a point."

"Right?" Abby gave Jordan's shoulder a playful

slug. Jordan's eyebrow arched upward again, appraisingly this time. *Is she checking me out? I think she is. I think she likes me.* Abby nearly collapsed in a heap at her feet. As Jordan started down the hall again, it was all Abby could do to keep up.

Jordan stopped by an open door at the end of the long hall and tapped on the doorframe. "Jeremy?" she called. "I've got the girl you were looking for."

"It's about time!" A young, wiry-looking man, whose skin had a pallid appearance as if he hadn't seen sunlight for even longer than the average Englishman, spun around in his chair and Abby could feel his gaze land on the top of her head. "Nice tiara, princess."

Abby smiled politely at the man, though she was struck by a certain snide quality to his tone, and she couldn't shake the feeling that he was directing an unusually high amount of frustration in her direction. She couldn't imagine why. She'd never met him before, had she? Or maybe, it occurred to her to wonder; was it possible he worked with Countess Margaret? That could explain the hostile overtones she was picking up on. Still, ever since she'd begun her intensive training in royal protocol, it had been impressed upon her daily the importance of being courteous, and so she extended her hand toward the man. "How do you do?"

He snorted, and instead of taking her hand, he shoved a pile of fabric at her. "How do *I* do? How do you bloody well do, is more like. I don't know what the agency was thinking, but that gown is a frumpy nightmare."

"*Thank* you. Finally, someone who agrees with me. I've been saying it all night."

"Get these on." Jeremy gave the wadded-up clothing another shove, and Abby stared at what she now clutched in her hands and nodded mutely.

"This way, Ducky," Jordan said. It seemed clear that Jeremy wanted no further part of the interaction. Abby followed her to a door on the other side of the hallway that opened to a tiny room, no bigger than a closet. And not an enormous walk-in closet like the ones Abby had become accustomed to recently at her father's palace. No, this was more the size of what one would find in a modest three-bedroom tract home in Santa Barbara, where she'd grown up.

Abby put one foot inside, which was about all of her that was likely to fit, and looked helplessly at Jordan. "Now what?"

"Put on your costume." Jordan's lips twitched, like she was deciding whether to say something else, and Abby watched them, mesmerized, until Jordan spoke again. "Maybe after the show, we could sit down and... talk? Maybe have a drink. Wait, no. Alcohol might be a bad idea for you right now. How about coffee?"

Abby's heart skipped a beat. Jordan wanted to have coffee with her—like, a date? Granted, it had been a while since she'd been asked out, but she was fairly certain going for coffee was a move straight out of a *Dating for Dummies* manual. "I'd...uh, totally. I mean, yes," she corrected herself, remembering all of the lectures Margaret had given her about her use of what the older woman liked to call lazy American slang.

"Great!" Jordan grinned, and her teeth shone a dazzling white, though what really caught Abby's attention was the tiny mole just to the right of her lower lip. It was so delicate and alluring. Abby wondered if she'd be allowed to touch it, assuming their coffee date went well. Maybe with the tip of her tongue. She was still contemplating this as the dressing room door clicked shut and she found herself alone, clutching a pile of—what, exactly?

Abby held up the items in her hands, but try as she might, she couldn't make heads nor tails out of them. She'd been told to put them on, but there didn't appear to be quite enough of whatever they were in the pile to accomplish that. Were there pieces missing?

She cracked the door open and poked her head out. "Jordan?"

"Yes?" The woman's voice came from somewhere down the hall, and Abby soon heard footsteps heading back in her direction.

"I'm not sure what to do with this. Can you help?"

Jordan arched that single eyebrow again, and Abby clutched the doorframe to keep from swooning. *I could seriously watch her do that all day.* After several seconds were spent untangling bits of fringe and feather, Jordan held up two distinct garments, one in each hand.

"Top," she said, brandishing the first. "And bottom."

"I see," Abby said, and she did see, somewhat. One item was a corset-like thing, in a garish shade of pink satin with black lace over the top. It immediately conjured memories of the cheap saloon girl costumes they used to provide for dressing up at those old-time photo booths at her favorite Southern California amusement park growing up. The other item could possibly be described as a skirt, although Abby couldn't recall if she'd ever worn a skirt made entirely of feathers before. Or if she'd worn a corset, for that matter. And what she really couldn't see was why everyone seemed so intent on her wearing them both right now. She had clothes on already. And yet everyone kept telling her to change, and her head was still spinning, and she was finding it impossible to argue. "Can you help me put it on?"

Much to Abby's disappointment, Jordan shook her head. "I think that would be a little dangerous, under the circumstances. You'll do fine. Jeremy said to tell you there are stockings and shoes on the chair. Now I need to go and see if I can set up a few more interviews."

The door clicked shut again. This time Abby turned her attention to the zipper that ran down the back of her gown. Margaret had helped her into it earlier in the day, but after some interesting contortions, Abby managed to grasp the zipper-pull on her own and gave it a good yank. There was a sound that might have been the zipper opening, or might have been the entire back seam of the dress ripping apart. Either way, the dress loosened and Abby let it fall into a heap on the floor, which she quickly stepped out of without pausing to examine the extent of the damage. She didn't care anyway. It had been a horrible dress. She kicked off her sneakers, but retained the ankle socks.

The costume went on more easily than expected. The corset didn't lace, but just had a row of large metal hooks down the center front that Abby managed to fasten without incident. The skirt had an elastic waistband that slid on over the hips, and even in her very off-kilter state, Abby couldn't get *that* wrong. The only trouble was there wasn't a lot to it, and her bare legs were quickly turning to gooseflesh against the chilly air. Between the feathered skirt and the bumpy skin, Abby felt exactly like a chicken that had been left half-plucked.

Her eyes fell on the chair, where the aforementioned stockings and shoes resided. After a mere glance at the four-inch high stilettos, Abby tossed them into a corner. They were worse than the ones she'd worn to the reception, and there was no way in hell she'd subject her toes to that kind of torture again so soon. But stockings should be simple enough, and would provide a little bit of warmth. Biting down on her lower lip, Abby focused every last drop of concentration on sliding her pointed foot, into the sheer nylon toe without causing a snag. It was only after she'd rolled it all the way up that she realized two things. First, she was still wearing the socks, which showed clearly through the fleshy hosiery. Second, she was not putting on a pair of pantyhose as she'd assumed, but a single, thigh-high stocking. A stretchy bit of ribbon dangled from the bottom of the corset, with a fastener on one end.

A knock on the door made her jump. A man's voice bellowed, "Two minutes!"

Heart racing, Abby fumbled with the fastener, working it against the lace band of the stocking blindly until she felt it snap into place. She tried to repeat the process on her second leg, but with decidedly mixed results. No matter what she did, the fastener wouldn't close. But soon the sound of rapping knuckles against the door told her that her time was up, and so she stuffed her feet into her Chuck Taylors, which were possibly the only shoes she was ever willing to wear again, and emerged from the dressing room with her right hand clutching the top of the loose stocking to keep it from sliding down her leg.

Jeremy's mouth gaped, his skin becoming even more pale than before, if such a thing were possible. "What the hell is this?"

"I—I did what you said," Abby stammered. "Except the shoes."

"Jordan!" Jeremy's booming voice reverberated off the walls, and a second later Jordan's startled face emerged from a dressing room farther down the hallway. "Explain this!"

Jordan scurried toward them. "What's the problem, Jeremy? I told you before, I just wanted a few interviews." She stopped dead in her tracks as soon as she was close enough to catch an unobstructed view of Abby. She wore the same look of utter confusion on her face that Jeremy had, and Abby was beginning to suspect that she'd gotten something wrong.

"There's no way I'm letting this woman go on stage." He continued to bellow, even though both Jordan and Abby were just inches away from him at this point.

"No, I'd agree with you there," Jordan said, her tone calm and soothing. "She's in no condition to perform. I think she's drunk, or possibly high on something. Maybe both."

Jeremy's upper lip curled into a sneer. "You don't say."

At that moment, the sound of clicking heels echoed rapidly down the hall. "Mr. Winston?" A woman came into view, dressed in a tight-fitting corset and a floor-length, feathery skirt with a slit so high up her thigh that it afforded an unobstructed view of her perfectly fastened stocking garters. She was out of breath, but still managed to be stunningly sexy. "Is there a Jeremy Winston?"

"That's me." Jeremy looked from the newly arrived woman, to Abby, and back again. "Who are you?"

"Gretchen, from the agency. I'm so sorry I'm late."

"I'd say you're just in time." Jeremy pointed his finger at Abby, so close to her nose that she could feel her eyes cross. He glared at Jordan. "Get this walking disaster out of here before I have you both banned from backstage for life!"

"Me? Why should I be responsible for her?" Both of Jordan's eyebrows had shot up simultaneously, and Abby couldn't help but notice that the effect on her this time was more alarming than alluring. Whatever was going on, everyone seemed very upset with her. It wasn't nice.

"You brought her in here."

"So, what, that makes her my problem?"

"Yes, that's exactly what that makes her. Gretchen, love, will you follow me?" Jeremy held out his arm and escorted the exotic dancer toward the dressing room without another word, leaving Jordan alone in the deserted hallway with Abby.

Jordan looked her up and down, and her dismay was impossible not to see. She let out a loud sigh. "Okay, then. I have no idea who you are, or what you're doing here, but I guess I can call you a cab. Where are you supposed to be tonight, anyway?"

Abby cleared her throat, which had become dry in all the uproar. "Kensington Palace."

"Uh-huh." Jordan blinked. "Look, do you even have any money?"

Abby shook her head, which temporarily resulted in double vision again, but she didn't mind so much since it was two of Jordan that she got to enjoy. "Money? Never carry the stuff."

Jordan let out her breath in a low rush. "Great. And I'm down to my last fiver."

Abby clapped a hand to her mouth to stifle a yawn. "So sleepy."

"Well, we'd better figure out where your bed is, then, Sleeping Beauty."

"No, *you're* the beauty." Abby giggled, the pitch of her voice rising at least a full octave. It was suddenly extremely important that she convey to Jordan exactly how she felt. "Sooooo pretty. You really, really are. Really." *Yeah, that should win her over,* she thought, flashing a self-satisfied grin. *I've always been a smooth talker with the ladies.*

"Wow. You are really far gone." Jordan squeezed her eyes shut and made a sound that could best be described as a whimper. "I can't believe I'm doing this, but you better come with me."

As Jordan strode to the exit, Abby attempted to trot along behind her, but the spring had left her step, and she soon stumbled and grabbed on to Jordan's arm to steady herself. The arm was warm and strong, and attached to such an inviting shoulder that Abby snuggled against it before Jordan could say otherwise. She closed her eyes and allowed herself to be led, head still firmly against Jordan's shoulder, until they were out on the street.

"You really have no idea where you're supposed to be tonight?"

Abby rubbed her forehead back and forth against Jordan's armpit, an action that released a bewitching scent of cinnamon and blackberries, with just a hint of spicy amber, from somewhere beneath the woman's layers of clothing. It was as close as Abby could get to indicating that no, she really had no clue where she was supposed to be. Thinking had become difficult, and trying to think and walk at the same time was virtually impossible. Instead she focused her energy on placing one sneaker in front of the other until finally Jordan stopped in front of a narrow opening in a short iron fence that ran along the pavement in front of a building shrouded in blue plastic tarps.

"Home sweet home," Jordan announced.

Abby opened one eye cautiously and peered around in confusion. "There's no door."

"It's downstairs, silly. They call it a garden-level flat, but really it just means I live in the basement."

Abby opened the other eye and could just make out a narrow curving staircase that led down to a dark alcove. The door itself remained elusive, shrouded in shadows. "Down there?"

Jordan stepped away from Abby and gestured to the stairs. "After you." Unsupported, Abby took a single step but stumbled, and Jordan was quickly at her side again, propping her up. "On second thought, why don't I go first."

Jordan stepped down onto the first stair, her arm stretched out behind her to hold Abby's hand. She took another step, pulling Abby forward to the edge of the staircase. As Jordan took a third step, Abby lifted her foot, but as her weight shifted forward, everything around her went black.

FOUR

THE SUDDEN JOLT of a weight hitting her back pushed the air from Jordan's lungs and nearly sent her sprawling down the stairs. Fortunately, for both her and the woman who had slammed into her back unannounced, they had reached the part where the staircase took a sharp turn, and Jordan was able to steady herself with one hand against the wall before they both went tumbling to the bottom.

"Hey, do you mind?" Jordan admonished, but there was no response from the woman, whose full weight Jordan seemed to be supporting against her back and shoulders. "Hey, you. Ducky? You awake?"

Ducky, who was definitely not awake, simply looped her arms around Jordan's frame and nuzzled her face against Jordan's neck. Her lips were temptingly soft against Jordan's bare skin, her breath delightfully warm, and Jordan found herself thinking about all sorts of things that she really had no business thinking about, and especially not while supporting an unconscious woman while teetering halfway down a treacherously steep and narrow flight of stairs. Even so, there was no controlling the current of electricity that ran through her each time the woman exhaled, nor could she do much about the most inconvenient way her nether regions ignited in response. She'd been celibate for months without any issues. *Months?* There was no mistaking the mocking tone of the voice in her head. *Try years.* Fine. It *had* been at least a year, plenty of time to get used to the situation. So why did her body choose now, of all times, to register a protest?

"Right," she muttered. "Let's see if I can manage to get us safely to the bottom without my starved libido killing us both, shall we?"

By way of response, the passenger on her back tightened her grasp, and with one hand somehow landing directly on top of Jordan's left breast in the process, the chances of their surviving the rest of the way down the stairs diminished greatly.

Jordan groaned, doing her best to ignore the way the woman's hand brushed against her nipple as she hoisted her higher on her back and took a hesitant step. "Come on, princess."

"But I don't want to go to another ball, Countess Margaret," the woman whimpered. "Kindly send my regrets to the queen."

Jordan snorted. "I don't know what you were

drinking tonight, sweetheart, but I could sure use one." She took another few steps, stopped to draw several huffing breaths, then continued her descent, repeating this process until they finally reached the bottom. She straightened her back until her cargo's feet were planted firmly on the ground. The sensation of supporting her own weight seemed to rouse the woman back to a state of semi-consciousness, at least enough to keep herself upright when Jordan stepped away.

"Where am I?" she asked, not bothering to cover her mouth to disguise her yawn.

"My flat, remember?" Jordan replied. She jiggled the long, old-fashioned key in the lock, praying it would open without incident, which it only did about half of the time. Why the English were so intent on using keys that looked like something a Victorian ghost would rattle on a chain, in an old haunted mansion, was still a mystery to her. Try as she might, she could never get these vintage-style keys to line up properly, and even if she did, more often than not, she'd encounter a problem with the knob, which always seemed to turn the opposite direction from what she expected. In fact, her difficulty opening doors was somewhat legendary among her coworkers at the *Crier*, much to her chagrin. But luck was on her side tonight, as the door opened without any trouble, revealing the tiny square room that she called home. Jordan snapped on the flat's single overhead light, gestured for her guest to enter, and waited as the woman took one unsteady step inside.

"Is this the closet?" the woman asked, scanning the flat with eyes that failed to fully focus.

"No, this is *not* the closet," Jordan shot back, insulted by the comment even though she'd described it as exactly that more times than she could count. Still, it was different coming from someone else, especially when that someone else was an inebriated burlesque dancer that she'd just carried down the stairs on her back. Some gratitude *that* was. "I happen to live here."

"I see." As she said it, she had both of her eyes closed so that she could see nothing at all. The ridiculousness of the comment lightened Jordan's mood.

"I think I need a drink," Jordan announced.

Pushing past her guest, who stood rooted in place and showed no signs of moving any time soon, Jordan tossed her satchel next to her desk chair and made her way to the kitchenette along the left wall of the room. There was a small counter for food preparation, covered in a nondescript beige laminate and containing a miniature-scale stainless steel sink to one side. The refrigerator was underneath the counter, just large enough to hold a few days' worth of takeout containers and a carton of milk for her tea. It was currently stuffed to the brim with bags of kale, the reason for which was a very tedious story. It had a tiny freezer, too, but there was something wrong with the thermostat, and the space had been taken up by a frozen dinner trapped in a solid block of ice for a good six months. There was a stove just to the other side of the counter, but it was a rickety-looking thing, and Jordan wasn't certain if it even worked. The only purpose it served was to provide a flat surface to support her microwave.

She opened one of the cabinets that hung on the wall and pulled out a clear glass tumbler and a bottle of whiskey. After she'd poured a splash of the amber liquid into the glass and put the bottle back, she turned to find her guest watching her actions intently.

"Do I get one?"

Jordan raised an eyebrow as the woman, who was still dressed in a pink corset and feathered skirt, with one stocking pooled around the top of her black and white sneakers, began to trace a serpentine path across the tile floor.

"How about some coffee instead?" Jordan began rummaging in the cupboard again, pushing aside some canned goods of indeterminate age and content. "I don't drink the stuff myself anymore. Five years in the UK has won me over to tea for good. But I think I may have some packets of instant somewhere. Oh, here we go. Will this work?"

The woman nodded mutely, and Jordan swiped an electric kettle from its spot beside the toaster. There was also a blender, and these, along with the microwave, made up the whole of Jordan's kitchen appliance collection. As Jordan filled the kettle with water, her curious interloper wandered farther into the flat, exploring the room's few furnishings thoroughly with her hands as she went. Jordan didn't particularly care, as none of them belonged to her. She'd moved from flats several times in the past five years, a low rent being much more important to her than comfort or décor. This particular one had been furnished by the landlord, who presumably had acquired its contents from the estate of a very old and exceedingly color-blind relative.

There were two upholstered chairs, the type with the wings on each side that served no purpose that Jordan could think of other than to provide a barrier to making eye contact with the person sitting in the other chair. Not that Jordan was accustomed to having anyone else over to sit in the other chair. This wasn't that type of flat, and even she spent as little time there as possible, preferring to experience the sights and sounds of the city.

The chairs were the same general size and shape as one another, but they were not a set. To say that their upholstery didn't match was an understatement. It wasn't just that the patterns were different. With one a burnt orange and the other a slate blue, their color schemes didn't even inhabit the same universe. The burnt orange one came with an ottoman, whose tattered sides suggested it had once been the favorite domain of someone's pet cat. Between the chairs sat a battered old tea cart made of brass and glass that served as the only table in the room. It had wheels that squeaked when they rolled. It was a fact Jordan had never been aware of before that moment, but couldn't help but notice now as Abby pushed the cart back and forth repeatedly, as if mesmerized by the sound.

"Could you knock that off?" Jordan said through gritted teeth.

"Oh. Sorry." The woman jumped, and the tea cart's push-handle loosened with an even more alarming squeak than the wheels had produced. She let her hands drop from the cart, leaving the handle at a very unnatural angle. Almost immediately her fingers began to fidget with the feathers on her skirt.

Jordan approached with a mug of strong black coffee, eyeing the pile of pink, downy fluff that was forming on the floor around her. "You're molting, Ducky."

The shedding showgirl grasped the mug with both hands, which had the unintended but welcome side effect of stopping her from plucking the rest of her costume or destroying any of Jordan's remaining pieces of furniture. Jordan could live without a tea cart, but there was no telling what might occur if her guest got her hands on the desk or office chair.

"How did you know people used to call me Ducky?"

"Uh, you told me that was your name, back at the club." Jordan suppressed a laugh as the woman clearly struggled to recall.

"It's Abby, actually."

"You mean, your parents didn't really name you Ducky?" Jordan feigned shock. "How disappointing. Considering what you're wearing, I think the name Ducky suits you better."

Ducky, or Abby, as she now claimed her name was, took a sip of coffee, which seemed to steady her somewhat as she was able to place the mug on the tea cart without causing any disasters. "Thank you for this."

"Are you feeling better?"

Abby blinked slowly, as if considering. "My head. It's spinning. And I'm so sleepy." As if to demonstrate, Abby stepped toward Jordan and rested her head on her shoulder. The moment she exhaled, the fresh infusion of warm breath against Jordan's skin sent a new wave of tingles coursing through her body. "So comfortable."

Jordan agreed. The feel of Abby's body against hers brought her a sense of comfort she'd rarely experienced. Abby's arms circled her waist, and instinctively, Jordan did the same, holding her close enough to smell the blend of industrial-strength hairspray with undertones of clean citrus scent that emanated from the top of her head, where her off-kilter tiara twinkled merrily.

The experience was almost intoxicating, which was a poor choice of word, because as soon as she'd thought it, Jordan was all too aware of Abby's compromised mental state. Taking advantage of a drunk woman was not Jordan's style. Reluctantly, but firmly, Jordan placed her hands on Abby's shoulders and gently pushed her away. "Time for bed."

Abby's face scrunched in disappointment. "More coffee first?"

"I'm down to the last packet, so this will have to be it." Jordan retrieved Abby's mug from the glass surface of the tea cart.

As Jordan ran more water into the kettle, Abby moved toward a set of double doors that were just to one side of the armchairs. "Is this the bedroom?"

"No, wait!"

But before Jordan could finish her warning, Abby had turned both knobs and yanked the doors open. Her face froze in astonishment as a mattress sprung from inside the wall and descended rapidly toward her. She landed with a thud on the floor, feathers flying, and her dislodged tiara skittered across the tile as the bed came to rest on her head. "Wh...what just happened?"

Jordan sprang across the room to Abby's aid. "It's a Murphy bed," she explained as she raised the device enough for Abby to slide out from underneath. Jordan held the bed upright with her shoulder while she offered a hand to help Abby back onto her feet. "It gets stored in a compartment in the wall during the day so the room doesn't feel so small."

"Clever," Abby replied, her voice as shaky as the hands she used to dust herself off, an action which sent yet another cloud of pink feathers billowing into the air.

"This one's a little temperamental." After making sure that Abby was far away from the bed, Jordan lowered the mattress into position and straightened the covers. "There we go. I'll push the chairs together to make another bed and we'll be ready for the night. Let me go get some extra sheets. And maybe some pajamas for you to change into," she added, watching the last bits of fluff fall to the floor. While oddly sexy in a campy sort of way, that burlesque getup wasn't exactly suitable for sleeping.

Jordan crossed back through the kitchen and slipped through the door that led to the bathroom. There was a closet just inside with a set of built-in drawers beneath it where Jordan stored her underwear and pajamas, plus her extra sheets and towels, and pretty much anything else she owned, plus a few things that had been abandoned there by previous tenants. She scoured it thoroughly for the items she needed. With a pillow and sheets tucked under her arm, Jordan reemerged. She'd only been gone for a minute, but it was long enough for Abby to have stretched herself out across the bed and fallen fast asleep.

With the occasional roll of the eyes in the direction of her unexpected houseguest, Jordan quickly pushed the two arm chairs together into a makeshift sleeping place, with the ottoman in between them to provide a little more length. It could hardly be referred to as a bed, but judging by the woman's hearty snores, Abby would probably never notice. Whatever that woman had been drinking throughout the evening, it would keep her sleeping soundly until morning, for sure. Besides, studying her body where it lay stretched out across the mattress, Jordan could see just how tiny a frame she had. Unlike Jordan's tall and lanky body, this petite scrap of a woman would fit perfectly in the little nest she'd made. Jordan plumped the pillow one last time for good measure, then turned her attention to moving Abby into position.

She'd placed the chairs beside the mattress, so the easiest thing to do would be to give her a good roll and see where she landed. But when Jordan placed her hand on Abby's side, she couldn't help but notice the hard metal boning of the corset. Passed out or not, Jordan didn't feel right about leaving her in it. Then again, given the tingling she felt between her legs at the prospect of stripping it off her, she didn't feel entirely right about not leaving her in it, either.

Jordan paced back and forth, as much as the narrow space beside the bed would allow. *What is it about this woman?* she wondered, trying to remember the last time another human being had made her feel like this. But no one came to mind, and she wasn't convinced she'd ever felt like this before. Attraction, sure. She hadn't always been in a dry spell. She'd had her share of pretty women she'd enjoyed taking to bed. But though Abby was physically good-looking, what she was experiencing went beyond that. Jordan was consumed with the desire to take care of Abby, to protect her. That wasn't something she'd ever wanted to do for a woman before.

Jordan raked her fingers across her scalp as she studied Abby closely. Her corset looked stiff, the feathered skirt itchy. If it were her, she'd be dying to get out of that horrible getup. She went back to the cupboard in the bathroom and retrieved a pair of cotton drawstring pants and a faded T-shirt, from a beer festival she'd attended a few years before. When she returned to the main room, she cleared her throat loudly and Abby whimpered.

Cautiously, Jordan nudged Abby's shoulder. "Abby?" Abby groaned. She rolled from her side to her back but didn't open her eyes. Jordan tried again to rouse her. "Hey, Ducky, time to get up and put your pajamas on." This seemed to get her attention.

"Pajamas?" Abby smiled, one eye opening the slightest hint of a crack. "I *love* pajamas. Margaret never lets me wear them. She says I have to wear nightgowns."

"Oh, does she?" Jordan gave a loud sniff. The existence of this Margaret person rubbed her wrong in all sorts of ways. "Well, this Margaret of yours sounds like a bossy bitch. I wouldn't take that from a girlfriend if I were you."

Abby's eyes opened most of the way and she struggled to raise herself on her elbows. "No, no. Margaret's not..."

"Let's not worry about Margaret right now, okay?" Jordan soothed. "Come on, sit up all the way, now. That's a good girl."

Abby made it to a sitting position. Jordan handed her the T-shirt and pants, but Abby just held on to them and blinked her eyelids sleepily. When nothing else happened for several more seconds, Jordan took the T-shirt and eased it over Abby's head, bringing it to rest like a bulky Elizabethan collar around her neck.

"There you go," Jordan told her. "Now you just need to get that corset off and put the shirt the rest of the way on, okay? You've got this."

Abby grasped the corset in the middle, and in a single movement like Clark Kent opening his shirt to reveal his Superman suit beneath, she tugged the garment open with both hands at once. The cheap metal hooks gave way without a fight, and revealed not a large red letter S, but an expanse of milky white chest, with the delicate outline of collar bone beneath her slender neck, elegantly sloping shoulders, and two extraordinarily perky breasts, completely unencumbered by any sort of covering. She continued to hold the corset wide, looking eagerly to Jordan for approval. "Like that?"

Jordan tried to focus on Abby's face, with its dark brown eyes and pixie-like features, or the helmet of blonde hair that had loosened here and there to form a spun sugar cloud around her head, but it was a losing proposition. Jordan's eyes kept slipping down the narrow bridge of Abby's nose, past her full, pink lips, then jumping from her pointed chin and landing, repeatedly, right back on that bare chest. Eventually, even Jordan, master of self-discipline, gave up trying and allowed her eyes to become glued to Abby's nipples. They were small but taut, a delicate shade of pink that was somewhat darker than the inside of a seashell but not as bright as a piece of bubble gum. They were definitely two of the nicest nipples Jordan had ever had the pleasure of seeing. And continue to see them she did, for quite some time, as she found that she couldn't turn her head away, or even blink. They were so perfectly pert and round, she could almost feel the way they would slide across her lips as she took one into her mouth.

As she touched the tip of her tongue to her lower lip, alarm bells sounded in Jordan's head. *I'm salivating over a drunk burlesque dancer's nipples. Averting her eyes, Jordan reached out and tugged the T-shirt down far enough to obscure the view before prying the corset from Abby's hands.*

"Put your arms in, okay?" Jordan's voice was

brusque, almost scolding, but Abby just giggled, and the sound of it was enough to reignite Jordan's desire in a most unwelcome way. She gritted her teeth. "Here are the bottoms. *I'm turning around now, and when I turn back, I expect that you will have figured out how to get them on properly, by yourself.*"

From behind her, Jordan could hear huffing and puffing, and the squeaking of bedsprings as Abby attempted to do as she'd been told. When the ruckus died down, Jordan turned back around, half prepared to find the woman completely naked, but to her relief, Abby had managed to put the new clothing on, and even appeared to have gotten all of her limbs into the correct holes. Jordan gave an approving nod. "Good job. Now let's get you into your bed."

Abby frowned, looking with confusion at the mattress beneath her. "But, I'm already in bed."

"No, no, no. That's not your bed. You will be sleeping on those chairs right over there. That's *my* bed."

"It's okay. I don't mind sharing." Abby reached out and grabbed hold of Jordan's shirt. She pulled on the hem, hard, and Jordan felt her footing slip. She toppled forward, and landed on top of Abby, pinning the woman to the mattress, which groaned and bounced in warning.

"Careful!" Jordan tried to right herself, but Abby clung tightly, wrapping her legs around Jordan's hips for good measure. "Abby, let me up."

Abby did not let her up. Instead, she took a moment to nibble on Jordan's ear before answering. "Do you still want me to let you up?"

"Yes." Jordan's reply was muffled, as Abby had inadvertently pressed her face into the pillow beneath them in her attempt to gain access to Jordan's earlobe. Abby loosened her grip and Jordan sat up quickly, gulping in air. "Do you hear all of that squeaking? This bed isn't strong enough for that kind of horsing around."

Abby propped herself onto her elbows and stared at Jordan, dumbfounded. "You have a bed you can't have sex on? Why?"

Jordan stiffened defensively. "It wasn't my choice. It came with the flat."

"Huh." Abby continued to stare. "You're American, right?"

"What?" Jordan ran a hand through her hair, letting out an exasperated breath. "What does that have to do with anything?"

"It's just, you're American, like me, right? But you use words like flat instead of apartment, and you drink tea instead of coffee. It's weird."

"I've lived here a while," Jordan answered with a shrug. "I guess I've learned to blend into my surroundings."

Abby sighed. "You're lucky. I'm not very good at blending in."

"I've noticed," Jordan said with a chuckle. "Look,

Abby, I've had a crap day, and while I'm flattered by your attention, I'm exhausted. I'd like to go to bed. Alone. So, if you could just scoot yourself over onto those chairs there while I get ready, I'd really appreciate it."

"Absolutely, I understand." Abby's expression radiated sympathy, and possibly a hint of increased sobriety. "It's just...well, I'm very grateful."

"You are?" Jordan arched a brow. She hadn't expected her to be so coherent.

"I am. You came to my rescue tonight. I don't know what I would have done without you."

"Well, that's very nice, but you don't have to sleep with me to say thanks. I'd settle for having my bed back."

Abby giggled. "You've got it, Jordan. I'll just scoot right onto those chairs like you said. But I owe you one."

With a yawn, Jordan headed to the bathroom to brush her teeth and change into her own pajamas, a mix-match set of cotton drawstring bottoms and a well-worn T-shirt similar to the one she'd loaned to Abby, with the exception that, instead of a beer festival, this shirt announced that if history repeated itself, she was going to get a dinosaur. That one always made her laugh. Jordan had a whole stack of novelty shirts emblazoned with snarky sayings, and when she wasn't dressed in her blazer and jeans for going into the office, she considered them to be her de facto work uniform for writing at home in her flat.

When Jordan made it back into the main room, Abby was not on the chairs as she had promised, but was sound asleep in the middle of the Murphy bed, snug as a bug beneath the pile of blankets that kept Jordan from freezing in her often-damp basement room. Having had it with the entire day, and without further ceremony, Jordan attempted to roll Abby's sleeping body onto the makeshift bed. It was harder than she'd anticipated.

Every time she got Abby rolling in one direction, the woman would roll just so far before stretching out and then curling up in a fetal position facing the opposite way. Sometimes, she kicked, and for such a small body, it turned out that Abby had surprisingly large and powerful feet. After an extended struggle, Jordan's muscles ached and she'd worked up a sheen of sweat on her brow, but Abby was right back in the middle of the Murphy bed.

Jordan sighed wearily. Though usually up for any challenge, sometimes even Jordan had to admit defeat. This was one of those times. Once more, this inconvenient sense of propriety that had suddenly taken root inside of her stopped her from climbing into bed alongside Abby, but she had to get some sleep, and the armchair nest wasn't going to cut it. Instead, she grabbed the pillow she'd set aside for Abby and put it at the foot of the bed, then wrapped herself in her last remaining blanket and lowered herself onto the bed.

Her intention was to sleep on top of the covers, with her head at the wrong end near Abby's feet. The Murphy bed, however, had other ideas. As soon as she'd transferred her full weight to the mattress, there came a groaning from somewhere underneath, a terrible noise of rusty springs accompanied by a lurching, buckling feeling of the bed itself. Jordan jumped up in alarm. The last thing she needed was to end up trapped inside it with a snoring burlesque dancer. The armchair bed, however, looked just as impossible for her to fit in as when she'd first made it.

"I'm not going to sleep at all tonight, am I?" she muttered. Abby replied with a sound that was half snort, half snore, and Jordan was fairly certain she could see a puddle of drool on the pillow. For no comprehensible reason, she found this adorable.

Resigned to the long night ahead of her, Jordan scooted through the narrow gap between the edge of the mattress and her desk. The utter lack of space was the reason she continued to tolerate the Murphy bed instead of replacing it with something sturdier, but if she twisted herself exactly right, she could just manage to slide into her office chair. She did so now, opening her laptop so that the light from the screen provided a faint illumination of the space, which was too small for even a clip-on desk lamp. She opened a new document, then remembered that she had no idea what she would write. Aside from the single assignment Diane had given her to cover the state visit of some entitled royal brat, Jordan was fresh out of story leads.

Jordan sighed. "Might as well start researching that story for Diane."

She rummaged beneath her desk and pulled out her satchel, where she had stored the file on the royal visit that Diane had given her at the end of their meeting. She pulled out the folder, and for the first time, gave the contents a good, long look. As she did, her breath caught in her throat. There on the top of the first page was a photograph of a beautiful young woman with pixie-like features, her blonde hair swept high on her head and topped with a sparkling diamond tiara. Jordan knew in an instant that she had seen both the tiara and its owner before. How had she not realized?

Jordan wracked her memory, but she couldn't recall ever seeing a photo of the princess before. She paid no attention to royals anyway, and the woman was notoriously reclusive with the media. But as her eyes darted between the file in her hands and the woman in her bed, there was little room for doubt.

Swiping around with her foot, Jordan soon heard the scrape of metal on tile. She curled her toes around the item she'd been searching for, pulled it closer, then reached down and came back up with a tiara. Not just *a* tiara, but *the* tiara. With its five perfect diamonds, each larger than a robin's egg, surrounded by laurel wreaths of platinum and even more shimmering diamonds, there was no doubt that it was the one from the photograph in her file. Jordan was holding the famed Gamberini tiara, the exact same one that had flown off her houseguest's head not long before. It was a wonder Ducky's neck hadn't snapped while wearing it. The thing seemed to weigh a hundred pounds.

Ducky. Jordan chortled as she searched for that line in the file. Her Royal Highness Princess Abigail of the House of Gamberini, who had once been Abigail Mallard, of Santa Barbara, California. Mallard. The nickname made perfect sense to her now.

"Princess Abigail?" Jordan whispered, just to confirm what she already knew. She cleared her throat and the woman stirred. Jordan continued in a slightly louder voice, "Your Royal Highness?"

"Hmm? What is it, Countess Margaret?" Abby muttered, then flopped over and buried her face into Jordan's pillow. The late-night silence was soon replaced by a steady, low snore. Jordan smiled at her with affection, but then doubt crept in. *What are you doing, Jordan?* Her smile faded as she obeyed the voice in her head. Sleeping like she was, Abby looked barely older than a child, so innocent and vulnerable. *And you're going to betray her, just like that?*

Jordan balled her fists, breathing in deep. It wasn't fair! That tell-all story of the century on someone rich and famous, the one she needed to save her career? It had just fallen in her lap like a gift from the heavens, and her conscience was about to wreck it. Stupid conscience. It had been nothing but trouble tonight. Why had she ended up stuck babysitting a drunk burlesque dancer in the first place? Her conscience. Why was she not getting laid tonight by that very same sexy woman? Her conscience.

But come on. What reasonable person would pass up an opportunity like this? Was there a single colleague at the *Crier* who wouldn't jump at this story if they were in her shoes? Hell, how many of them would have passed up having sex with the princess right now if they'd been in her shoes? Yeah, not many. And yet here she was, letting her conscience ruin everything. Which is why next week they would all have jobs with the new management, and she would be halfway to corn country.

On the other hand, she was a professional. She would treat the princess fairly, with all the integrity she always brought to her work. When a princess went out for a night on the town, *someone* was going to get the story. Why shouldn't it be her? Honestly, it was lucky for Abby that Jordan had found her, and not some tabloid paparazzi.

And hadn't Abby just said she owed her one?

Yes. Yes, she had.

That settles it, Jordan thought. *This story is mine!*

Jordan bit her lip, trying to stifle the laugh that bubbled up in her chest. This was it. This was her one chance to save her career, and she was going to get it right. But not without sleep. Quietly, and oh so carefully, Jordan moved to the edge of the bed where Princess Abigail slumbered. This time, she was able to ease herself onto the mattress without it threatening to spring into the wall, and she settled in quickly with her head on a pillow near Abby's feet. She closed her eyes, but was too excited to sleep. She had big plans for the morning.

FIVE

ABBY'S EYES were still closed, but even in her half-awake state, she was keenly aware of two things. The first was the pleasantly warm sensation of tired muscles coming back to life after a full night of rest. The second was the heady and somewhat familiar smell of cinnamon and blackberries, which filled her with a general sense of well-being and seemed to assure her that today would be an excellent day.

Abby rolled languidly from her side to her back, and the lovely scent grew stronger with the shifting of the blankets that surrounded her. She burrowed her face into them and took a deep, relaxing breath that filled her lungs with more of that deliciously spicy aroma. With eyes still closed, she stretched her arms out wide to each side and pointed her toes, smiling at the satisfying crackle and pop as countless joints and sinews along the length of her body released their tension. With a swift motion she flung her legs out to match the width of her arms, and was met by something unexpectedly hard, and even more surprising, capable of speech.

"Ouch!" it cried out.

Abby's eyes flew open, but instead of the rich velvet folds of the canopy bed, that for some mysterious reason she had expected to see above her head, the cracks of a plain white ceiling came into focus, along with a rusty water stain that looked amazingly like an upside-down version of Alfred Hitchcock's silhouette. Her heart pounded as the realization struck that she had no idea where she was. She bolted upright in bed and was met by the sight of a woman's dark head poking out of the covers at the opposite end of the bed, one hand gingerly massaging the spot where Abby's foot had no doubt made contact seconds before.

"Who the hell are you?" Abby demanded, her rising panic giving an edge to her words.

The woman slowly raised herself into a sitting position and stared at her with a look that seemed to indicate more bemusement than anger. "That's a fine way to say good morning, considering."

Considering? She might not know exactly who she was, where she was, or how she'd come to be there, but there was one thing that seemed immediately obvious to her as she studied the woman with whom she was sharing the bed. With her piercing dark eyes and chiseled jaw, the attraction was undeniable. This woman was definitely her type. *You don't think it's possible we...* Abby swallowed nervously. Her mind raced to locate any details of the night before but came up empty. "Considering...what, exactly?"

"Considering I lugged your drunk ass down the stairs last night and gave you a safe place to sleep it off."

"Sleep it off. Is that all?"

"Is that all?" The woman's left eyebrow shot up, and Abby experienced a sudden tightening just below her belly. It wasn't the fluttering of nervousness, but something altogether different, more primal. It left her feeling hot and bothered, and not at all sure whether she'd rather the answer to that question ended up being yes or no.

"Um, well..."

"Do you know how hard it is to carry an unconscious woman on your back down a flight of stairs? I'd think that would be plenty. But as it happens, I also shared my bed with you."

"You carried me down the stairs?" Abby frowned. "Why don't I remember that?"

The woman's expression softened with a hint of sympathy. "You were pretty bad off. I don't know how much you had to drink last night, but it definitely got the better of you."

Abby blinked as flashes of memory tickled her hippocampus, like scenes from a long-forgotten movie.

The swirl of formal dresses. A glass of champagne. A stab of pain in her toe. She shook her head as a tiny but important sliver of a detail emerged. "I wasn't drunk. I think I remember, I'd taken some pills. Not the illegal kind of pills," she added at the sudden look of alarm on the woman's face. "I don't take drugs. I'm almost positive of that. These were prescription, I think, but I must have gotten mixed up and taken too much, because I don't remember a thing after that. I know this sounds terrible, but I don't even remember your name."

"Well, that's a bit of a blow for a woman's ego the morning after."

The morning after? Abby's eyes widened at the use of that phrase. *Something* must have happened between them after all. "Oh God. I'm so sorry. I didn't think...that is to say, I'm sure last night was really great. I just..."

"I was just messing with you. Nothing happened between us last night, so relax, Ducky."

Ducky. It wasn't her name, but at the same time it rang with the comforting tone of familiarity. It felt right, and told her that this woman, whose name she still didn't know, clearly knew her. "Really?"

"Yes, really. What kind of a person do you think I am?"

"What do you mean?" Abby bit her lip, uncertain what to make of the question. What kind of a person... Was she trying to say she wasn't interested in women?

Or was it more personal than that? "Are you saying I'm not your type?"

"What? No. That's not it at all. Of course you are. But you were completely shit-faced last night, with no place to go. I'd have to be a pretty awful person to take advantage of the situation, don't you think?"

"Yes, I suppose so." Abby paused. "But, wait. Are you saying I *am* your type, then?"

"Seriously, are you my type? You can't remember an entire night of your life, have no idea what the name of the woman you wake up next to is, or how you got here, and *that's* the question you get stuck on?"

Abby dug her front teeth deeper into the flesh of her bottom lip as the truth of the woman's assessment sank in. Aside from swallowing those pills, and being certain that she found the woman across the bed from her wickedly attractive, and being somewhat hazy about a canopy bed that may or may not belong to her, very few other details about her personal life had come back to her. "You're right. I have no idea where we met, or how I got here. And I still don't know your name."

"Jordan," the woman replied. She swung her legs to the side of the bed and stood, and as she did so the mattress beneath them jiggled alarmingly. It was the final proof Abby needed that there had been nothing physical between them last night. A bed this loud and unsteady would never have allowed it. She stuck out her hand, and Abby responded by giving it a tentative shake. "Jordan Baxter. We met at the club down the road from here, where you were working. You weren't feeling well and had nowhere to go, so I brought you home."

"So, I work at a club." Abby pondered this new information, trying to make sense of it, but it didn't fit. What type of job would she have in a club? She had no idea. Almost every detail of her life was murky. Finally, she hazarded her best guess. "I suppose I must be a bartender."

"No." Jordan waited a beat. "A burlesque dancer."

"*Excuse* me?" She'd barely been able to imagine herself slinging cocktails all night, but this news was beyond anything she could have imagined. "You mean, I'm a *stripper*?"

"Common misconception. Burlesque isn't stripping. It's an art form, really. And you keep your costume on the whole time." Jordan bent down to retrieve something from the floor, reemerging with an armful of what appeared to be the tattered carcass of a hot-pink goose. "See? Here's the costume you wore last night."

Abby poked at the pile of feathers that Jordan tossed on the bed with a mixture of awe and revulsion. "I actually wore this? What was I supposed to be, exactly? A duck?"

"Is that not why you call yourself Ducky?" Jordan chuckled, and Abby felt her cheeks tingle but in a way that wasn't unpleasant. "Although you still haven't told me your real name."

"I still haven't remembered my real name. So why was I dressed in feathers?"

"Last night was the princess review."

"Princess?" For some reason, the word sparked an uneasiness within Abby's belly, a recognition that was just beyond her grasp. She pushed her hand farther into the feathers and brushed up against something hard and cold. Her pulse quickened. Hidden within the tacky princess costume was a very sparkling, and very genuine-looking, tiara. Abby drew a sharp breath as the pieces of the puzzle shifted into place. She'd worn this tiara the night before, all right, and not to dance in some burlesque review.

Oh my God! I'm Princess Abigail.

She remembered it all now, the state visit and the reception, and Countess Margaret with those damned pills. And Abby wasn't 100 percent certain, but if her memory was truly firing correctly, there was a good possibility that she was on the run. A dull worry was gnawing at her insides at the trouble she must be getting herself into back at the embassy. She was new to this line of work, but still pretty sure that runaway princesses were frowned upon. "I'm so sorry, Jordan. I'm going to need to go."

"What's the rush? Is it that girlfriend you told me about last night? Margaret?"

"Margaret? Oh, no. She is definitely *not* my girl-friend." Abby shuddered at the thought.

"I see."

"I don't have a girlfriend," Abby added, it seeming extremely urgent that they were perfectly clear on that point. "I'm very single."

Jordan's lips twisted in that unnatural way that sometimes happened when a person was trying desperately to keep from laughing. "I sort of gathered that last night."

Abby searched her memories, but the file labeled Last Night was completely empty. She shook her head slowly. "What did I do?"

"Nothing to worry about. You were just a little...forward."

"Me? Forward?" Forward was a word that had never been used to describe her before, not even after she'd had several drinks. Abby simply wasn't a forward sort of a person. It just wasn't in her. She was about to inform Jordan as much, but she stopped short. That file labeled Last Night wasn't completely empty, after all. There was a single memory, hazy but unmistakably there, of her biting down on Jordan's earlobe and giving it a good nibble. She touched her index finger to her teeth, feeling weak. What else had she tried to do?

Abby glanced toward the curtained windows and could just make out the base of a small staircase in the cement courtyard beyond. Though the light was dim, Abby was fairly sure it was already morning. Countess

Margaret would be frantic that she was missing. They'd have scoured the palace already, and the embassy, plus the private apartments next door to it where she was meant to be residing during her visit. The entire embassy staff had probably been placed on high alert. Abby's blood suddenly ran cold. Had they called her parents? That would be some real trouble. There was nothing she could do but head back immediately, and pray her mother and father didn't know yet. She grasped at the first excuse that popped into her head. "I'll be late for work."

Jordan chuckled. "It's Saturday morning. I know it's a more demanding job than most people realize, but I don't think burlesque dancers have to get to work this early."

"Oh." Burlesque dancers might have the luxury of sleeping in on the weekend, but princesses rarely did. Abby's lips twitched with the desire to spill the truth, but instantly she decided against it. Jordan would never believe her if she said she needed to be back at the palace for a press conference at noon. She stifled a laugh. *She'd think I was out of my mind.*

"Why don't you stay a bit longer," Jordan suggested, her tone both soothing and convincing in a way that was as tempting as a brownie sundae. "You still seem out of sorts. Would you like some breakfast?"

Abby's stomach gurgled loudly at the suggestion. She couldn't remember the last time she'd eaten, and considering the size of her remarkably un-princess-like appetite, experience told her this could quickly escalate into a very uncomfortable situation. "I am pretty hungry," she admitted.

"There you go, then," Jordan said with a decisive nod, as if the matter was settled. You drank the last of my coffee last night, but I'll run out and grab something from the place across the street. It's new, and about the fanciest thing on the block. Would you like a bath?"

Abby nodded silently. Despite knowing she needed to get back as soon as possible, a bath sounded heavenly.

"Perfect. I'll get the water running and set out some towels before I go. Do you prefer coffee or tea?"

"Coffee, please. With a little bit of milk."

"Sure thing." Jordan made her way to the other side of the room and disappeared through a darkened doorway. A light snapped on, and soon there was a series of loud squeaks, followed by the sound of running water. Jordan reemerged and shrugged on a light jacket over her T-shirt, not bothering to change out of her plaid pajama bottoms, before slipping on a pair of shoes. She snapped a mock salute. "Coffee with milk, coming up. Just one thing, though."

"What's that?"

"You still haven't told me your name."

"It's Abby." She fidgeted with the hem of her T-shirt, uncertain whether she should use her real name.

She decided against it, and grasped at the first alias that popped into her head. "Abby Duckworth."

"That explains the nickname. Nice to meet you, Abby Duckworth. I'll be right back."

Left on her own in the basement flat, a thousand thoughts swirled in Abby's brain. Her memory was clearer now, and she could picture herself walking along the hallway that led from her cousin's apartment, then emerging from the stairwell into the palace gift shop. She remembered the brusque security guard, and the raucous bachelorette party, too. But what she couldn't quite put her finger on was what had possessed her to leave the palace with them instead of returning upstairs where she belonged.

But deep down, Abby knew the answer without having to put it clearly into words. She knew, because for the first time in months the ever-present anxiety that had been humming inside of her had gone still. In fact, it had all but disappeared the moment she'd broken away from the group of tiara-wearing women and set off by herself along Bayswater Road. With the pressure of royal life gone, she'd been able to breathe freely again. Abby shut her eyes, reveling in the peacefulness inside her. She'd forgotten what it felt like, but now that she remembered, how could she ever give it up again?

The sound of running water brought her back to the present. Abby rose and went to check the tub, dipping her fingers in to check the water. Satisfied with its warmth, she stripped off her borrowed pajamas as she headed back into the main room to retrieve her clothing. She paused just long enough to twist the lock on the front door until it was engaged. Judging by her surroundings, this didn't seem like the best of neighborhoods, and the last thing she needed was a stranger walking in on her bath.

The sight of the feathered costume caught her up short. Where was her gown, that absolute travesty of fashion that her stylist had spent weeks tracking down? She swiveled her head, but it was nowhere to be found. Instead, all that was in view was that burlesque monstrosity she'd worn on the walk home with Jordan last night, which meant that with the exception of the pair of Chuck Taylors that sat beside the bed, and the priceless tiara that sparkled on top of the covers, she didn't have a single thing to wear that she could call her own.

Abby let out a heavy sigh at her latest predicament as she flung her body lengthwise onto the bed. She landed with a plop, and a moment too late did she realize her error, as the gentle bob of the mattress quickly turned into something much bouncier, which was accompanied by a loud springing noise followed by a terrifying snap. Before she could do anything about it, Abby found her body flying through the air, the world flipping upside down as the Murphy bed folded itself back into its cupboard in the wall, with her inside.

SIX

"DIANE? IT'S JORDAN." Jordan tapped her foot on the pavement as she stood at the top of the stairs that led up from her flat. Her arms were crossed against the morning breeze as she held her phone to her ear.

"It's Saturday morning, Jordan." Her boss's voice sounded sleepy, and Jordan thought she'd detected a yawn partway through. It occurred to her that she hadn't bothered to check the time before calling, but it was too late to worry about it now. "This better be good."

"Well, I'm not sure," Jordan bluffed, knowing exactly how good it was. This very moment, Princess Abigail was sitting on the bed in her apartment, waiting for a bath. Oh, how she wished she could tell Diane in person, just to see her face when she heard this news. "What if I said I could get an all-access, tell-all exclusive with Princess Abigail? Would that qualify as good?"

"An exclusive interview with Princess Abigail. Like, *the* Princess Abigail, newly-minted crown princess of the House of Gamberini and notorious media recluse?"

"That's the one. And not just an interview, Diane. No, I'm thinking bigger. Much bigger." Jordan grinned triumphantly as she imagined Diane's mouth dropping open. Even the most serious journalist wouldn't be able to stop themselves from salivating over an opportunity such as this. "I'm thinking a full day in the life kind of thing. What she's thinking, her hopes and dreams. Everything."

"Hopes and...That would be a very valuable story, indeed, if you could get it." Diane's measured response made it obvious she thought Jordan was pulling her leg. "But I'm not certain how you're going to do that as word just came from the embassy that the princess has canceled all of her appointments today due to illness."

Interesting, So that's the cover story. "You just leave it to me how I'll get it. If I do, is it worth enough to save my job?"

"I think you know it would be, Jordan, especially given that Princess Abigail has, thus far, managed to stay out of the spotlight almost completely since her parents' marriage. A story like that would be worth a fortune to just about any news organization on the planet."

Jordan didn't care about every news organization on the planet. She only needed one to be interested. "So, if I can deliver this by next Friday, I can keep my job at the *Crier* and stay in London?"

"Let's be real for a moment. Exactly how do you think you're going to go about doing that?"

Jordan glanced down the stairwell to where her houseguest was, probably at this very moment stepping into a steaming tub, completely unsuspecting that her identity had been discovered. She looked away quickly, ignoring the inconvenient twinge of guilt in her gut. It was always open season on princesses, and guilt was a luxury she couldn't afford. "Never mind how, Diane. Just promise me that if I can deliver this story, I'll have a job. I need it in writing."

"You'll need photos. Candid ones, not those perfectly composed portraits they like to release."

"Not a problem. I know someone." Relief flooded over Jordan. This type of nuts-and-bolts detail planning meant that Diane was taking her proposal seriously. "So, we have a deal?"

On the other end of the line, Diane chuckled. "I'll have to run it past the new management first, but even if there's no way in hell you're likely to deliver, they'd be fools to pass it up on the off chance you do. I should be able to send over a contract later today."

After ending the call, Jordan hesitated before putting the phone in her pocket. Diane wanted photos, and if anyone could deliver the perfect candid shots, discreetly and from a safe distance, it was Max. He spent most of his time these days running high-end fashion shoots for magazines, but like most artists, there'd been lean times when he'd had to supplement his income with some good old-fashioned, paparazzi-style celebrity stalking. He was certain to have the gear and skills she needed, but would he agree to accept payment in the form of IOUs at the pub? There was only one way to find out. She dashed off a text, then crossed the street to the coffee place.

"One latte, please," Jordan told the woman behind the counter. "And one of whatever that is," she added, pointing to a flaky creation in the pastry case with a fancy French name she could never hope to pronounce.

Whatever its name was, it looked like the type of thing a princess would eat. The grumbling in her stomach made Jordan wish she could add one for herself, but the handful of coins she'd rescued from the depths of her backpack to pay for this extravagance reminded her how wishful that thinking was. If she were really lucky, there might be a smashed granola bar hiding in the same pocket where the change had been. With a princess to entertain, she couldn't afford to be picky about her own breakfast. As she handed over payment, it occurred to Jordan to wonder, exactly how much was it going to cost to keep a princess enter-tained for an entire day, anyway?

She glanced at her phone. No response yet from

Max, but time was ticking and considering her empty wallet, she knew she had another favor to ask of him, so she took the unusual step of dialing his number as she waited for her order to be ready.

"Max, I've been trying to reach you!"

"Yes. For one whole minute." Far from being sleepy, his voice gave every indication that he'd been out all night and had yet to go to sleep. "Your text just arrived. What's the emergency?"

"Remember those cameras you used to use when you would hide behind bushes and snapshots of the young royals in Soho?"

"I never hid behind bushes." Max paused. "Okay, maybe that once."

"I think it was more than once. Point is, do you still have them?"

"Have what, the scars from being scratched by the shrubbery? No, I think they've all healed."

"The cameras, Max. The one with the super tele-photo lenses, and those little ones that don't look like cameras that you can use right in front of someone and they'd never know."

"Yeah, I...Look, what's this about, Jordan?"

"Remember how I told you last night I needed to come up with a major scoop to keep my job?"

"And I said how I'd heard that Omaha's pretty nice in early summer? Yes, I recall."

"Well, I did it."

"Booked the flight to Omaha? Smart girl."

"No. I found the scoop. And it's a big one. Huge."

"I'm listening."

Jordan took a breath and held it a moment, knowing how this was going to sound. "If I tell you, Max, you have to promise not to judge."

"Spill it, Baxter."

Yikes. The last-name treatment again. "Fine. On my way home from the Churchill last night, I dropped into that place on Portobello. You know, the one that does those burlesque reviews."

"Are you trying to take naughty photos in the dressing rooms? Because I can't condone that. Besides, the pay for that kind of thing isn't what it used to be, believe me."

"Of course that's not what I'm doing, and I don't even want to know why you know how much it pays. No, I met someone backstage at the club."

"A dancer?" Doubt colored his tone. "I guess that could be a good story, if you had the right angle."

"Not a dancer, Max. A princess. Princess Abigail."

Silence radiated from the other end of the phone, until finally Max cleared his throat. "A dancer who looks like Princess Abigail?"

"No, the real one. She'd been—I don't know—drinking, maybe? She was definitely disoriented. Long story short, I got stuck with her. She's at my flat right now."

"She's at..." Max's voice trailed off, words failing him.

"My flat. Having a bath. At least, I think that's what she's doing. I stepped across the street to get her a coffee and a pastry."

"As one does when royalty pops by," Max spluttered. "Jordan, have you lost your mind?"

Jordan bit down on her lip, her eyes scrunching closed as she considered. "It's possible. But what was I supposed to do, Max? She was incapacitated. I couldn't just leave her there. Something terrible could've happened to her! And to be fair, I didn't realize who she was until after I'd gotten her home. As far as I knew, she was a damsel in distress. And you know how I feel about those."

"Yeah. A regular knight in shining armor, you are. So now you're going to do what, exactly? Ask her for an interview?"

"I was thinking more of a day in the life kind of a thing. Look, it's pretty obvious she's run away. And from the little time I've spent with her, it's also clear she's in no big hurry to get back. So, I thought I'd tempt her with a day on the town, an incognito princess, and get you to take some pictures."

"That's it, just a day on the town?" Max asked, oozing suspicion. "No compromising situations?"

"What?" Jordan gaped, taken aback. "Of course not! What kind of person do you think I am?"

"I don't know, Jordan. It's just, with the new management at the *Crier*, I wasn't sure."

"Well, you can be sure. I'm just looking for an

exclusive angle, not a scandal." Although, as the memory of the young princess's flirtations came back to her, Jordan realized that she did, indeed, have the makings of a scandal on her hands if she wasn't careful. She shook her head resolutely. She would be very, very careful. "Absolutely no tabloid trash."

On the other end of the line, Jordan could hear Max suck in a breath, then let it out again. "Okay."

Jordan let out a squeal. "You'll do it?"

"Yeah. Give me some time to change clothes and dig out the equipment. I can be there in about thirty minutes."

"Thank you so much, mate." Jordan glanced up as her name was called, and the sight of the woman behind the counter holding out a paper bag and a takeout coffee cup to her reminded her of a pesky detail. "There's just one other thing. It's hardly worth mentioning, but—"

"Spill it, Baxter."

"I'm totally broke. I didn't get my paycheck again this week, and every penny in the bank right now is earmarked for bills. So, I don't suppose you could spot me some cash?"

"How much?" There was that suspicious tone again.

"A hundred quid?" she asked hopefully.

"A hundred...Jordan! I'm not made of money, either."

"Yeah, but I know you have it. You said yourself you've been saving up."

"For Moira's engagement ring!"

"I know, I know. But I'm good for it, Max. This story is worth a fortune. I'm not talking about just keeping my job. There's going to be a bonus for something this big. I wouldn't be surprised if I got ten grand. I'll pay you back the hundred and split the bonus, fifty-fifty."

"But, a hundred quid?" The pain that figure brought to the frugal Scotsman was unmistakable.

She made a face at the pricey pastry and coffee clutched in her right hand. "Princesses are expensive, Max. Maybe we should say two fifty, to be safe."

"Two..." Anything else he might have tried to say disappeared into a choking cough.

"Come on, mate. Ten grand. Fifty-fifty."

"Fine," he grumbled when he'd recovered the ability to speak. "See you soon."

Jordan nearly skipped her way back across the street, showing just enough restraint to keep from spilling a single drop of what might as well have been liquid gold for what it cost her. She glided down the stairs and paused in front of her door. Clutching the bag and cup tightly, she reached out with her free hand and gave it a push, but it didn't budge. Jordan squinted at it. *Odd,* she thought, *I know I left it unlocked.* Setting the cup and bag beside her on the ground, Jordan grasped the knob with both hands and gave it a good rattling, but no luck. The door remained firmly in place.

A scowl on her face, Jordan turned to survey the single window that led into the front room of her flat. It was too high to reach from the ground, but she knew from experience she could just manage it if she climbed three steps up and gave a good jump. She also knew from experience that the window didn't lock properly, and with a few firm shakes, she'd have it opened wide enough to climb through. As for the drop from the top of the window to the floor, sadly, Jordan had experience with that, too, and the best she could say for it was that at least gravity would make it quick.

Pausing long enough to mutter "I don't want to do this" half a dozen times under her breath, Jordan set to work on her plan, and about a minute later she landed with a thud onto the floor of her flat. She picked herself up and dusted off her backside, then looked around. The room was empty, but from the direction of the bathroom, Jordan could hear the sound of running water. She frowned. The bathtub, not unlike the rest of her flat, wasn't particularly large. Surely it should have been full by now?

"Abby?" Jordan called out from just beyond the bathroom door. There was no answer. "Abby? Don't be alarmed by that crashing noise. It's just me." Still there was no answer, and Jordan's pulse ticked rapidly as a sudden vision formed in her head of Princess Abigail drowning in her bathtub. *Ludicrous,* she thought, *but just in case...*

She gave the door a hard shove and burst inside, but the apology she'd readied for her guest died on her lips the moment she was in the room. The brimming bathtub was unoccupied, excess water pouring into the overflow drain as rapidly as it flowed from the spout. Jordan quickly turned off the spigots as her brain struggled to comprehend a terrible truth. The princess—and her ticket to job security—was gone.

"No. No, no, no..." Jordan backed out of the bathroom, then swept her gaze across the empty flat. There was no sign of Abby, save the remnant of feathers that fluttered across the expanse of white tile floor. Jordan frowned. Was she imagining things, or was this a lot more floor than had been there when she'd left? A muffled squeak drew her attention to the closed doors of her Murphy bed, and her eyes grew wide.

"Abby?" She sprinted to the wall and pulled the cupboard doors wide. As she did so, the muffled sound grew more distinct. With a firm yank, she pulled the top of the bed frame until it unfolded with a groan to reveal a very startled Princess Abigail sprawled across the mattress. Correction, a very startled, very *naked* Princess Abigail.

Her earlier impression had been that the woman was tiny, and she was, but in all her naked glory Jordan could see now that Abigail was small but not at all childlike in her shape. Jordan's eyes skimmed her body, noting how her breasts were rounded, her waist narrow, and her hips full. It was clear that Abby worked out. Her muscles were toned, and her calves looked like sculpted marble. Jordan's eyes traveled upward along her thighs until they rested on a perfectly groomed patch of blonde hair between her legs. *Jordan,* that helpful voice inside her head informed her, *you are staring at Princess Abigail's pussy. Stop it immediately!*

Cheeks ablaze, Jordan averted her eyes. "Are you okay?"

"I...I was..." Abby's whole body shook as she tried and failed to form a coherent sentence. "I..."

"Stay right there." Jordan's own hands trembled as she dashed to the front door, opening it just long enough to grab the coffee and pastry that she'd left on the welcome mat. She handed the still-warm cup to Abby, who grasped it eagerly. "Drink that. It'll help settle you down. And there's some breakfast in the bag."

The princess tipped her head back and chugged, a dribble of milky foam soon escaping from the corner of her lip. The droplet made its way down her chin before landing to form a tiny dark spot between her bare breasts. The spot grew larger as a second drop landed, and Jordan couldn't help but notice the contrast between the creamy tan color of the latte foam and the more rosy shading of Abby's nipples that she'd admired so thoroughly the night before.

No, not Abby. This was Princess Abigail she was ogling, the subject of her soon-to-be, career-making, tell-all article. *Journalistic integrity, Jordan,* she chided herself as she forced her eyes to look away. Without a word, Jordan rose and strode to the bathroom, grabbing a thick terry-cloth robe from the hook behind the door. She held it out in front of her when she returned, using the ample fabric to block the woman's naked form from view. "Here. Put this on."

Mutely, Abby shrugged the robe onto her shoulders, then stood unsteadily long enough to wrap it around herself and tie the belt tightly at her waist before sinking back down onto the bed. "I think I need to go."

"Of course." The look on her face signaled to Jordan that it was pointless to argue. It didn't matter. Ever resourceful, Jordan was already formulating a plan.

"It's just, they'll be..." Abby poked at the sad pile of feathers beside her on the bed that remained of her clothing. "Only, I don't have..."

"I think I can help."

As she rummaged through her scant supply of clean clothing in the cupboard, Jordan's brain kicked into overdrive. The woman was shaken, and understandably so, but that didn't mean she had to give up on her plans to spend the day with the princess quite yet. It was market day on Portobello Road, and if she played her cards right, Jordan was fairly sure she could use that to her advantage. True, Abby's expression when she'd said she had to leave had been resolute, but there had also been regret deep in the woman's eyes. Jordan was willing to bet that once her nerves had calmed, Abby would be in no hurry to let her brief taste of freedom come to an end. She just needed to give that rebellious streak a little encouragement.

Jordan pushed a pile of folded T-shirts on the top shelf aside and reached way into the back, her hand closing around a small box. Her emergency stash. She brought it down and opened the lid, her spirits falling at the sight of the single, crumpled, twenty-pound note that it contained. *That's one pathetic emergency stash, Jordan Baxter.* With an odd assortment of garments tucked under one arm, and the last of her life savings clutched firmly in her fingers, Jordan returned to the front room.

"Here," she said, handing the clothing to Abby. "It's nothing stylish, but you should be able to find something to put on that won't get you arrested. But why don't you have a bath first. The water's already been run, and then some."

Abby took the clothing with a grateful smile. "You know, I think I will."

As soon as the bathroom door was closed, Jordan stepped outside and called Max. "Slight change of plans, mate."

"You don't need my two hundred and fifty quid?" The relief in his voice was clear.

"Nice try. How close are you?"

"About twenty minutes?"

"Perfect. Look, she's going to be leaving the flat soon, unaccompanied. Can you tail her? She'll be in gray sweats and a blue hoodie."

"No problem, mate."

After her bath, Abby emerged from the bathroom dressed exactly as Jordan had described in gray sweatpants, a green T-shirt, and a blue hoodie that was zipped to the top, and with her sneakers on her feet. Her hair, which had been a massive helmet before, was now clean and combed out straight, and she'd pulled it, still damp, into a no-nonsense ponytail. She stood beside the front door. "I guess this is it. Thank you for letting me stay." She sighed as she said it, her fingers resting on the knob. The small, regretful sound was almost imperceptible, but it was enough to raise Jordan's hopes that her plan would work. It had to.

"Of course. Don't forget your pastry," Jordan told her, joining her at the door. "And take this, too." As she handed Abby the crumpled bill, she tried not to allow too pained of an expression to mar her face, but it was clear she hadn't entirely succeeded when Abby shook her head.

"I couldn't. You've done enough already."

"I insist." In fact, it was integral to Jordan's plan. In addition to being all the money she had to offer, Jordan sensed that twenty quid was exactly the right amount to buy herself the time she needed. Though too little to pay for a black taxi back to the palace, it was just enough to tempt the princess to browse the tables and carts in the crowded market as she made her way back to Kensington Palace on foot. A slower pace would make it easier for Jordan to follow her, and arrange for their paths to cross at just the right moment.

"Thank you." Abby tucked the money into the small red clutch that she'd carried the night before. "I'll arrange to have the money sent back to you. What's the address?"

"No, don't be silly." Jordan waved her hand as if to show how little something like twenty quid mattered to her. "You just take care of yourself. No more burlesque clubs."

Laughing, Abby began to climb the winding metal stairs. She turned at the top and lifted her hand in a silent wave before heading down Portobello Road. She was out of Jordan's sight quickly, but wouldn't be for long.

Jordan raised her phone to her ear as she stepped back inside the flat. "Max? What's your ETA?"

"Just passing the food stalls." In the background, Jordan could hear a reggae band. "About five minutes away."

"She's headed your way."

"Gray sweats...oh, yeah, there. I see her at the end of the block."

"Perfect." Jordan cradled the phone against her ear as she rummaged through her closet. Surely she had to have one clean outfit that was suitable to wear for a day on the town with a princess? *Ha! Success!* She grabbed a pair of black trousers and a pale pink silk blouse, both of which she'd pushed to the back because they required dry cleaning and she was, therefore, usually too cheap to wear them in the first place. She topped off the outfit with a ubiquitous blazer, grabbed her satchel and shoes, and was ready to roll. "Keep her in your sights until I get there, okay? I'm on my way."

SEVEN

I MUST GET BACK *to the embassy.* Abby repeated this mantra with each step, but as the initial panic that had engulfed her when she'd been trapped in the Murphy bed subsided, the urgency of the message faded as well. Though it was early on a Saturday morning, she saw a thin stream of people on both sides of the street that grew denser as she walked. Excitement replaced worry. It was market day on the famed Portobello Road, and this was her first time in London, after all. Didn't she deserve a little fun?

What would be really fun, a little voice in her head told her, *is to turn around and get Jordan to come with you.* Abby stopped, swiveling in place to look in the direction from which she'd just come. Part of her knew that she shouldn't listen to that little voice. It was the same one that had assured her nothing could go wrong by sneaking out of the palace in the first place. And look how that had turned out. She'd nearly ended up on stage in a burlesque review. But Jordan had come to her rescue.

Jordan. Details of their time together flooded back, more than she'd recalled before, so that Abby could almost feel the silkiness of the woman's dark hair against her cheek as she'd carried her down the stairs on her back, and the memory of her spicy scent made her flush with warmth inside. *No. It's too complicated,* she chided herself, tamping down a swell of regret. The last thing a nice woman like Jordan needed was to get tangled up in the mess of royal life: the schedules, and expectations, and complete lack of privacy. It could be a nightmare, and wasn't that the real reason Abby felt so ambivalent about returning home? She pivoted in place, her body once again facing in the direction of the market. No, dragging Jordan into what awaited her return wouldn't be fair, but even without a companion, was there any reason she couldn't take a few extra minutes to take her time and enjoy the journey?

Having granted herself permission to dillydally, there was a bounce in Abby's step as she came to the first few tables set up on the street corner. They were simple booths, no more than a few plastic folding tables strewn with what looked like the contents of someone's grandmother's jewelry box. Abby poked through one of the piles and smiled.

Abby's grandmother on her mother's side had had

a box like that, filled with cheap beaded necklaces and gaudy rhinestone rings. She'd loved to pour the contents out on her grandmother's floral bedspread and try them on when she was little. It was the highlight of every sleepover. She'd never met her grandmother on her father's side, but she doubted a sleepover with her would have been as much fun. All of her jewels were kept in a vault surrounded by palace guards.

Leaving the jewelry tables behind, Abby continued walking. Soon the rhythmic beat of a reggae band greeted her, along with the delicious smells of hot foods from every imaginable region on earth. Her mouth watered, and she reached into the pocket of her borrowed hoodie, pinching the twenty-pound note Jordan had given her between her fingers. It wasn't much, she knew, but it was the first time in quite a while that Abby had carried her own money, and she felt for all the world like a millionaire. She breathed deeply of the spice-laden air. Should she get a curry? Or maybe a donut? For someone who had gone so many months without choices, the selection was overwhelming.

Though her taste buds were tempted, the pastry and coffee she'd been given that morning were still doing a decent job of filling up her belly, so with some reluctance she decided to continue exploring all the market had to offer before making a decision. There were fresh flowers in the next section, rows and rows of blossoms in every color and shade. There were more flowers than she'd seen anywhere, just sitting in buckets in the street, and when she closed her eyes, the smell of roses and lilies surrounded her with more intensity than even her father's royal gardens.

Somewhere in the distance, a church bell tolled nine times. Abby's stomach tightened a little more at each successive bell. Was it really that late? She'd been gone more than fourteen hours. Her disappearance had to have been noticed by now. Was Countess Margaret worried? *Livid, more likely,* Abby thought. But she was almost certain her disappearance was being kept quiet, at least for now. The countess and the embassy staff enjoyed their employment too much to bring anyone else into the loop just yet. Most likely her bodyguard knew, but if they let on to the police, or heaven forbid, her parents, that they'd allowed a crown princess to go missing on their watch; heads would roll. Not literally. At least, Abby was pretty sure that lopping off heads wasn't something that modern-day monarchs could do. She swallowed and touched a hand to her throat. It might be a good idea to quicken her pace a little, just in case. After all, didn't she have a press conference she was expected to attend at noon?

But by this time the market was in full swing, and Abby was in the heart of it. Walking quickly was a relative term, and even in the middle of the street her speed options mostly ranged from a slow shuffle to a dead stop where bottlenecks had formed in front of the most popular booths. It was frustrating at first, but when she reached the section of the market with vintage-clothing stalls, all thoughts of rushing flew right out of her head. There were few things Abby enjoyed more than rummaging through the clothing styles of previous decades and centuries.

A sizable crowd had gathered around a short man with a booming voice who was hawking a selection of ancient furs and old Soviet military coats at what he claimed were unbeatable prices. Abby had little interest in these, especially as it had turned into a pleasantly mild spring day once the first chill of morning had burned away. No, what caught her attention was a smaller stall just past this one, where half a dozen full-skirted dresses hung from a pop-up canopy, fluttering in the breeze like extras on the set of an Audrey Hepburn movie.

Abby unzipped her hoodie and cringed at the T-shirt underneath. It was bright green with a picture printed in white of some type of heavy construction equipment. Emblazoned across the chest were the words "UA Local 798 Annual Picnic" along with the assurance that "Nothing's Finer Than a Tulsa Pipeliner!" *So not my style. Is it anyone's?* And yet she smiled despite herself as she pictured Jordan handing her the shirt. The woman had muttered a brief apology as she'd done so, explaining that she'd rescued it from the lost and found at a gym in Omaha back in college. Abby couldn't imagine why she'd kept it all these years, and yet she guessed that somehow on Jordan, the shirt would look cute. *But not on me.* That white dress with the brown polka dots, hanging in the middle, though, with the sweet shawl neckline, had Abby's name written all over it. She stepped closer, running a finger along the smooth rayon fabric. She smiled as the saleswoman approached. "How much is this one?"

"Fifty," the woman replied.

"Pounds? Fifty pounds?" Abby's face fell as her spirits plummeted. She'd foolishly assumed that prices at an outdoor market would be low, and while in her normal life she'd consider this dress a bargain at twice the price, the twenty quid in her pocket wasn't going to get her very far. "Oh well. Thank you anyway."

"Wait," the saleswoman urged as Abby turned to go. She shot the commemorative T-shirt a look that was somewhere between sympathetic and appalled, and Abby could feel the color race to her cheeks. "I have a few dresses in the back. The waistlines are small, and not many customers can wear them, but you're such a tiny bird, they just might fit. And they've been steeply discounted."

"I..." Abby wasn't sure whether to be offended by the bird comparison or thrilled over the prospect of a new dress. After a second of hesitation, and after catching another glimpse of her secondhand shirt, she chose the latter. "Thank you. I would love to have a look."

Pushing between two racks that bowed under the

weight of every possible variety of midcentury garment, Abby followed the woman to a trunk at the back of the tent that had been stuffed full of odds and ends. The woman knelt down and rummaged around, her hands emerging with a bit of cheerful yellow fabric clutched between them. She stood and unfurled it, revealing a 1950's dress of fine cotton lawn. It was the brilliantly warm shade of fresh lemon curd and had bunches of dainty cherries embroidered across it to form neat rows of stripes. Abby took it from her and held it up to her chest, glancing dubiously at the thin belt of red leather that circled an impossibly narrow waist. "I'm not sure..."

"Try it on," the saleswoman urged. She pulled aside a bedsheet that hung from an overhead pole to form a private changing space, motioning Abby inside with an encouraging smile. In truth, it didn't take much convincing for Abby to strip off and discard her borrowed clothing. After a brief moment of disappointment with a stuck zipper, followed by a valiant effort of sucking in her pastry-filled tummy, she emerged in a dress that could have been made for her. The saleswoman clapped her hands together and grinned. "It's perfect."

Abby returned her smile as she twirled in front of the mirror. "It is really nice."

The saleswoman came up behind her, her arms raised close to Abby's head. "May I?"

Abby caught sight of the disheveled ponytail she'd left Jordan's flat with and cringed. "Please."

With a comb and some hair pins from her pocket, the woman soon smoothed Abby's mess of blonde tresses into a sweet and simple chignon at the base of her neck. She even managed to get the stubbornly unruly hair in front trained into a graceful curl on Abby's forehead. Abby marveled at her reflection. It was completely transformative. She looked and felt like a new person, a happier person. Abby most often felt uncomfortable and overdone when her stylist dressed her for royal duties, yet somehow this street vendor had hit upon a look that suited her to a T.

"I hate to take it off," she said with a sigh. "I never want to look any other way."

"Why take it off? It's like it was meant for you!"

"I didn't leave the house prepared to shop, I'm afraid. All I have is a twenty." Abby stifled a laugh as she held up her little purse and considered just how ill-prepared she'd been when she wandered out of the palace. If it hadn't been for Jordan's generosity, she would have nothing at all. Her heart fluttered at the thought of the woman's name. *Jordan. I wonder what she's doing right now...*

"Sold!"

Abby blinked, emerging from her daydream. "Wait, what?"

"This one was marked down, remember? Not quite so low, but I can't imagine anyone else will fit into it half as well. Twenty pounds and it's yours, my dear."

Abby's eyes shot to the pile of discarded clothing on the dressing room floor. How she hated the thought of putting them back on, even if the remaining walk to Embassy Row wasn't very far. Besides, in sweatpants and that awful T-shirt the guards would never let her close enough to the gates to prove who she really was.

But twenty pounds, Abby, whispered the voice in her head that hadn't always been a princess. *That's all the money you have!* Abby smoothed her hand down one side of her hip, running her fingers across the voluminous yellow skirt. It was a beautiful dress, fit for royalty, really. And the fact was, Abby truly *was* a princess, and it was only another twenty minutes to the embassy, at most. What possible use would she have for that twenty pounds in her pocket between now and then? She grinned. "Okay. Sold."

She bent to retrieve her battered shoes, and snatched up the hoodie, too, in case the air outside the tent still held a chill. But the saleswoman tsk'd as Abby shoved her foot into the shoe. "That won't do." The woman went back to the trunk. "Here, will these work?"

Abby reached for the pair of red ballet flats the woman held out. "I think they might." She slid them on with the ease of the proverbial princess with a glass slipper. "Perfect. But I can't pay for them."

"I'll trade you for these," the saleswoman offered,

pointing to the black-and-white Chuck Taylor's. "They're very popular with some of my customers, and they'll more than cover the cost. You may as well take this, too. It completes the ensemble. They even match your handbag, so it was clearly meant to be." She held out a thin cotton cardigan the same cherry shade as the shoes.

Abby put the cardigan on and gazed on her reflection in the mirror with satisfaction. If she felt a twinge of guilt at trading a pair of shoes that didn't belong to her, it only lasted a moment. The duchess had a lot of shoes. She might never notice they were missing. "Thank you. This is exactly the new look I've been needing. In fact, I feel more like myself than I have in a while."

When Abby stepped out of the tent, the press from even more shoppers who'd packed into the narrow street meant that movement had all but stopped. Mindful of the time, she stepped up onto the sidewalk where she could maintain a somewhat brisker pace, and as she walked she couldn't help but glance from time to time at the reflection of her skirt swinging cheerfully from shop window to shop window. The saleswoman had been a miracle worker, doing more for her in a few minutes than her stylist had ever done in her life. She touched her fingertips to the chignon, so elegantly retro, and wondered how the style would look paired with a tiara for a state dinner.

Abby gasped. *The Gamberini tiara!* Her heart

began to race, pumping so fast and hard that she was convinced if she looked down she would see it bursting from her chest. She'd worn the tiara out of the palace last night, and now it was gone.

She ducked into a narrow passageway between two buildings, away from the throng, and leaned against a brightly painted wall as she struggled to catch her breath. *You've lost your grandmother's tiara.* The pounding of the blood in her ears drowned out all the noise that surrounded her, yet even so she could hear the voice in her head above it, loud and clear. The priceless symbol of her father's kingdom, entrusted to her as the heir to his throne, and she'd left it in a basement flat somewhere on Portobello Road. She didn't even have the exact address. She rested her forehead against her palm and groaned. Countess Margaret was going to kill her.

Think, Abby. Think. All you need to do is retrace your steps.

Squaring her shoulders, Abby turned toward Portobello Road, but it only took one look for her to know that she would never manage to fight her way back to Jordan's apartment, wherever exactly that might be, at the height of market day—at least, not if she hoped to make it back in time to avoid starting World War Three on account of her disappearance. It was a miracle there wasn't an army of black helicopters circling above her head right now, searching her out. If she were going to retrieve the tiara, she'd have to do it quickly. Her best bet was to find a street that ran parallel, and hope to save some time.

Turning her back to the main road, she walked in the opposite direction until the passageway opened onto a residential street. One of the lush private gardens that the Notting Hill neighborhood of London was famous for stood in the center, surrounded by tall hedges and a wrought-iron fence. There was a single gated entrance just across the street, and as it came into view, she heard several loud barking sounds, followed by a shout. Just on the other side of the gate, an elderly woman struggled to gain control of an unruly Labrador.

"Excuse me," the woman called out to Abby, "but could you lend a hand with the gate?"

Abby darted across the street and gave the gate a tug, but it was locked. "I'm sorry. I can't get it open."

"Marcus, sit!" The woman shouted, but the overgrown pup showed little inclination to sit, and instead strained even harder against his leash with all the determination of a dog who has caught sight of a plump and tasty squirrel. "I've dropped my key, just there. If you could be a dear and reach it, you could unlock the gate."

Abby spotted a small silver key on the ground, tied with a long loop of red ribbon. She reached through the iron bars to retrieve it, then opened the gate. She held it open wide as the woman struggled to convince Marcus to exit. It took some effort, but once the

Labrador got it into his mind to leave the park, he did so with the same enthusiasm that he'd shown earlier for running in exactly the opposite direction. "Don't forget your key!" Abby called out as the gate banged shut, but the woman was too busy being dragged along by her gentle giant of a dog to pay any attention.

Alone in front of the gate, Abby turned the key in her hand. Though she knew she should be on her way to find Jordan, the serenity of the fenced-off park beckoned. Her head throbbed, a situation most likely attributed to the rumbling of her stomach. Her small breakfast was wearing off quickly. Just steps inside the garden was a bench beneath a shady tree. Abby considered the key for a moment, then fitted it into the lock, opened the gate, and tucked the key inside her clutch. She'd seen the movies, so she knew that private gardens were notoriously hard to get into, and she felt a curiosity about the space that drove her almost as much as her desire to sit and rest. What other chance was she likely to get to explore the secluded world beyond the gate, at least not without an entourage and all the public scrutiny that would entail?

A gravel path led from the entrance in a graceful arch, and though her initial goal had been the bench, once inside she heard the bubbling of water coming from somewhere inside a patch of shrubberies. She walked toward the sound and spotted a small stone fountain, droplets of water splashing merrily as they fell from the top into a shallow basin. As she got closer,

Abby saw the shimmer of coins in the bottom. At the same moment, her stomach rumbled with increased ferocity.

If I hadn't spent all of my money on this dress, she thought, *I could buy a donut.* She'd seen them at a stand on Portobello Road: giant puffs of fried dough rolled in sugar and filled with hazelnut cream, offered at the bargain price of two for a pound. The coins sparkled, just an inch of water at most separating them from her fingers. Abby gave a surreptitious glance in the direction of the garden path, but it was empty. A most un-princess-like growling noise came from her midsection. It was all the encouragement she needed. She plunged her hand into the cool water, emerging with a handful of dripping coins.

She shook off the excess water and did her best to remember what each coin was worth as she counted her haul. *Twenty, plus another twenty, plus...wait, what's this one again? Ten?* Not quite enough. She'd need to try again. At the other side of the fountain, she saw a two-pound coin with its telltale band of gold encircling an inner disc of silver. *Jackpot!* She'd just stretched herself out as far as she could, one foot off the ground and her hand up to her wrist in the water, when a sound caught her up short.

"Ducky?"

Abby froze.

"Ducky, is that you?"

Still clutching her treasured coin, Abby removed

her hand from the fountain and hoisted herself upright. Heat pricked her cheeks as she turned to face the owner of a very familiar voice. She stuffed the wet coins into her clutch as surreptitiously as she could.

"Jordan. How nice to see you again."

EIGHT

JORDAN BIT BACK A LAUGH. She'd been watching from a distance for quite some time, long enough to see Abby dip her hand into the water once, then stretch out along the edge of the fountain, her skirt riding high up to reveal her very shapely legs as she maneuvered to reach a different section of the water before plunging her hand in again. Was the princess really trying to pretend she hadn't just been caught fishing out a handful of coins? *Fine,* she thought. *I'll play along.* "What a lovely new dress. I almost didn't recognize you."

Of course, she'd recognized her just fine. Thanks to Max's expert spying, she'd even known to look for a woman in a yellow frock and red cardigan, heading in the direction of Ladbroke Square Garden. What she hadn't expected, after scaling a section of fencing that Max had assured her provided relatively easy access to the private space, was to find the princess sprawled out, arm immersed in water in the act of committing petty larceny. She patted a hand to her trouser pocket, grateful that she'd had enough time to snap some pictures with her phone before slipping it out of sight.

"Jordan, what a coincidence. I was just coming to find you."

"What, here?" Jordan blinked. It's not like this upscale part of Notting Hill was one of her regular haunts, though she could hardly explain that to Abby without letting on about the part where she'd climbed over the wrought-iron railing to break in. Her lips twitched with amusement. *Aren't we a fine pair of criminals?*

"No. I was just looking for a shortcut back up to your flat. I..." Abby paused, her expression becoming nervous. "Did I happen to leave something at your place this morning?"

"You mean that monstrosity of a costume? I think there were a few feathers left, yes. I suppose you have to get it back to the club?"

"Oh, yeah. That, too." Abby frowned. "And the, uh...tiara? Is that with it?"

It had come as quite a shock to Jordan as she'd prepared to leave the flat to discover that her houseguest had left behind a priceless piece of her country's crown jewels. She'd forgotten all about the tiara until she'd gone to close the Murphy bed and found it tangled in the sheets. Clearly Abby had experienced a similar memory lapse. "Yes, it's back at my place. Do you want me to just drop it off at the club along with the costume? I owe Jeremy an explanation about last night."

"No!" Abby's face lit up in alarm. "That is, I should probably bring it back. To explain."

Jordan stifled a laugh at the woman's lie. "Good luck with that. I'm afraid you're probably out of a job, anyway, so there's really no reason for you to put yourself through the hassle."

"Yeah." Abby scuffed the toe of her shoe along the dirt. "Actually, I have a confession."

Jordan's eyebrows shot up. This could be interesting. "Yes?"

"The truth is, I'm not really a burlesque dancer. It was all a bit of a misunderstanding. You see..." Abby swallowed so hard that Jordan could hear her from several feet away. "I was at a party last night. That's why I was dressed up the way I was when you saw me at the entrance to the club."

"I see. If you don't mind me asking, what type of party were you at that required a tiara?"

Abby bit her lip and glanced away from Jordan's gaze. "It was silly, really. It was one of those—oh, what do they call them here? At home we call them bachelorette parties."

"They call them hen parties, but I know what a bachelorette party is. I'm American, too, remember?"

"I keep forgetting. Your accent is all over the place."

"Is it?" Jordan's cheeks tingled. This is why she could never go back to the Midwest. She would never fit in.

"Anyway, you see, a...uh, coworker was having this party, and we were all supposed to wear tiaras. It wouldn't be a big deal, really, except I borrowed mine, and I kind of need to give it back."

"Interesting," Jordan replied, impressed at the woman's ability to spin a quick story. "So, the company you work for, it's in London?"

"Um, no. It's sort of a public relations position? I work in a lot of places. I just happen to be in London right now. It's actually my first time here." Abby smiled brightly, and Jordan's insides fluttered. Damn, that woman had a sexy smile.

"Oh well, that's nice." Jordan fumbled for words, unnerved by the sudden rush of attraction. This would never do if she was going to get this story. "How are you liking the city so far?"

Abby's smile faded. "I haven't seen very much of it. Almost nothing, in fact. I just go from one stuffy meeting to another. In fact, I'm supposed to be on my way to another one at noon."

"On a Saturday?" Jordan whistled, knowing full well that the princess had been scheduled to give a press conference at noon, since she'd been slated to attend it on behalf of the *Crier*. It had been canceled, but Jordan wasn't sure if Abby knew this. "That's rough."

"It is." Abby's lips formed into an adorable pout. "I don't suppose you could skip it?"

"Skip it?" A spark of something like rebellion sparked in Abby's eyes and shone for a moment before fading away. "No, I really couldn't."

"Oh, come on," Jordan pressed. "You won't lose your job over one missed meeting, will you?"

"No, I suppose not. But—"

"Besides, we need to head back to my flat if you're going to get your tiara back. You'll never make it there and to a meeting by noon."

The temptation Abby was experiencing was palpable. "I mean, I guess—"

"We could get lunch first. You must be starving."

"I am. In fact, I'd been planning to get a donut with the...oh, never mind." Abby pressed a hand to her stomach. "I don't have any money. I have to confess, I spent what you gave me on this dress."

"Money well spent. And lunch would be my treat. In fact, anything you want to do today, anywhere in the city, it's on me. It would be my pleasure to show you around the city."

"Oh goodness." Temptation and flattery were having the desired effect, and Jordan could see Abby waver and then fold. "You know, why not? You're right. I need to get the tiara back, and I'm starving. I don't know about all day, but one missed appointment won't be the end of the world."

"Excellent. I know just the place with platters of fish and chips as big as your head. Do you like fish and chips?" Jordan gestured for Abby to go ahead of her as she rambled on about the offerings at the pub. As they chatted, she retrieved her phone from her pocket and dashed off a quick text to Max with the location of the pub. If she were going to pay for this promised lunch, and God only knew what else, she was going to need the loan they'd arranged, pronto.

<hr>

THE SMELL of food hit Abby's nostrils even before they'd walked through the door of the pub, making her mouth water in response. Though it had only been a few hours since she'd eaten the pastry Jordan bought for her, she was ravenous. The last of her reservations over playing hooky from her royal duties dissipated at the prospect of a hot plate of simple, unpretentious food. This was definitely the right call.

It was a little before noon, and so the lunch crowd was still light enough that Jordan was able to lead them through the main room and to an open-air patio in the back where several tables stood empty. They found a seat off to one corner, and as soon as they were off their feet, Abby eagerly perused the menu.

"So, what do you say?" Jordan said after a quick

glance at the printed card in front of her. "The fish and chips here are the best in London, hands down."

Abby continued to scan the choices, the tip of her tongue tracing an outline along the edge of her lips as she read. As she looked up, Jordan quickly looked away, but not so fast that Abby missed the interest with which her companion had been studying her mouth. She giggled, and Jordan's cheeks flushed scarlet. "I'm not sure about the fish. It's tempting, but this surf and turf special looks amazing."

Jordan looked down at her own menu, and Abby thought she detected the woman's eyes growing a bit wider when she arrived at the correct line. "Yeah, I should hope so," she muttered.

Abby frowned. "What was that?" Her companion had mumbled something at the end, but it had been hard to make out.

Jordan looked up and smiled. "What? No, it was nothing."

"Are you sure?" Abby couldn't help but detect the sudden grumpiness of her new friend's demeanor. "I can order the fish and chips."

"No, absolutely not." Jordan made a valiant effort to smile. "Order whatever you'd like. Can I get you a drink? Beer, wine, prosecco? Anything you want."

"Prosecco, please. And I think I *will* have the surf and turf." Abby returned her eyes to the menu, already eager to look at the dessert options. She felt a pang of guilt at not having the money to pay for herself. *But*

Jordan had said to order what she wanted, she reasoned, *and she wouldn't have said that if she didn't mean it, right?*

A few minutes later, Jordan returned to the table with a glass of prosecco in one hand and a pint of beer in the other. Behind her trailed a ginger-haired man with the unruliest facial hair she'd had ever seen. Abby gave him a quizzical look.

"This is my friend Max. I ran into him at the bar and thought I'd invite him to join us. Max, this is Ducky—I mean, Abby."

"Abby Duckworth." Abby stuck out her hand. "How do you do?"

"Abby, so nice to meet you."

"Please, call me Ducky. Everyone does." Of course, no one actually did, but she was starting to enjoy it. It made her feel like she was undercover.

"So, Jordan says you're in town for business?" Max asked, giving her hand a firm shake.

"Yes, that's right." Abby took a swig of her drink, hoping to shore up her strength to continue her pretenses. The more she said, the harder it would become to keep her story straight. "I work in PR."

He smiled amiably. "I can tell from your accent that you're an American, like Jordan."

She nodded. "California, originally, but I'm mostly, uh, working in Europe these days. In public relations." *Crap. I already said that part.* She laughed lightheartedly, hoping neither of them would sense the nervousness that lay beneath. "So, what do you two do, anyway? Sorry, Jordan. I realize now that I never asked."

"Oh, yes." It was Jordan's turn to look uncomfortable, and Abby wondered why. "I'm in the fertilizer business, actually."

"Fertilizer?" She wasn't certain what she'd expected, but it wasn't that. "You mean like cow sh—"

"No, no." Jordan interrupted quickly. "Like chemicals. For farms. I'm from Nebraska," she added with a shrug, as if that should make it all clear.

"And I'm in, um, advertising, I guess you could say," added Max.

"Oh. Well, that's nice." Abby smiled, but couldn't help feeling that something was a little off with her new friends. "Chemicals, though. Really?"

Jordan shrugged again. "Family business. You know how that goes."

Abby nodded. "Do I ever. They always expect you're going to follow in their footsteps, no matter what else you might have in mind."

"Sounds like you know a lot about it," Jordan prompted.

"Yeah, I do." As Abby recognized true interest in Jordan's dark brown eyes, all the frustration she'd felt during the past few months bubbled to the surface. "You see, my dad has sort of a family business, too, and ever since he and my mom got married, everyone has expected me to be thrilled to take over for him someday."

"So, this is your stepdad?" Max interjected.

"No, no. He's my real dad. It's just that he and my mom weren't married when I was born. That's the problem. They reconnected under unfortunate circumstances, and my mother reached out to him to offer her support. Eventually they fell in love again, and now that they've made it all legal, there are all of these new...expectations," she finished somewhat lamely, unable to go into more detail without revealing who she was, which is something Abby found herself unwilling to do. She was enjoying her time as a normal person too much to give it up just yet.

"That sounds rough." There was real sympathy in Jordan's tone, and Abby's insides grew warm and toasty in response. In fact, she was filled with the urge to confide some more.

"It is. The problem is, and this is something no one really knows about outside the family, but my dad has been having some health problems lately. It's part of the reason he and my mom decided to get married when they did. He's going to be okay, but it's making me think a lot about the future."

"You mean, having to take over the, uh, family business?" Jordan asked.

Abby nodded slowly, her eyes downcast. What she'd left unsaid was that her father had had a minor stroke, and even though he had the best doctors in the world at his disposal, and her mom by his side constantly, she worried—about him, and about what it would mean for her if he were gone.

Max raised his pint glass. "Well, here's to his health."

Abby chuckled as she raised her own glass in response to this variation on her national toast. "It's funny. That's what a lot of people say." She drained the rest of the glass and set it down. "Does anyone know where the restroom is?"

"You mean the loo?" Jordan asked. "It's inside, past the bar."

"The *loo*. There you go again, sounding all British." Abby stood. "I'll be right back."

Inside the pub, a large television hung above the bar. It was set to a news station, and as Abby walked past, she stopped in her tracks when her own face flashed onto the screen. Above it was a banner with a headline that read "Crown Princess Abigail Taken Ill." The story scrolled below, explaining that all of the visiting dignitary's engagements had been canceled for the day due to a sudden illness. *So that's how they're playing it,* Abby thought, uncertain what to make of this revelation.

A large man who was standing at the bar turned his head from the screen and stared at her, unblinking. "Hey!" he shouted, without breaking eye contact. Abby's stomach lurched. Surely he'd just recognized her as the same woman who was on the screen. She braced herself, breath held, for her identity to be broadcast across the crowded pub. "Hey!" he shouted again, louder this time, and several heads at the bar swiveled to stare at her. "Can someone change the channel on the telly? The match is about to start."

Abby let out her breath in a rush as a barkeeper, who'd been walking right behind her, grabbed the remote, and seconds later her face was replaced by a soccer game on the screen. She scurried into the restroom and closed the door, twisting the lock to secure it in place. Her entire body shook. That had been a close call. She'd been certain her secret was going to be announced to the entire room, and she had no clue what she would have done if it had happened.

Outside the pub, Abby heard a cheer erupt, most likely from an exciting play in the game. She could hear laughter, too, and the sounds of people talking. Everywhere around her, average people were enjoying a normal Saturday afternoon, thinking nothing of it as they took their freedom to do so for granted. She knew what that was like. She'd been one of them herself not so long ago. But now, everywhere she went she was watched. Every outfit she wore was judged, every minute of her day planned, every person she spent time with carefully vetted in advance. If Countess Margaret had her way, they'd choose her spouse for her, too. And if it was this bad now, could she even begin to imagine what it would be like someday when her father was no longer around, or became too sick to rule, and she was crowned queen? *This might be the last normal day of my entire life.* The thought sent a chill to Abby's core. These stolen moments with Jordan and Max before returning to the embassy might be the very last time she had the freedom to order pub food and watch a soccer match, or stroll down a busy street on market day without people giving her a second glance. Panic rose to a crescendo in her brain. *How can I make this normal life last just a little bit longer?* But try as she might, there was no way out that she could find. Supporting herself on the edge of the toilet seat, Abby cradled her head in her hands and wept at the hopelessness of her plight.

"Abby," Jordan said when she finally reemerged several minutes later and made her way back to the table. "I was just about to come after you. Is everything okay?"

"Fine," Abby replied, settling into her seat and giving the steak and prawns on the plate that had been delivered in her absence a long and appreciative sniff before digging in. "I can't wait to eat."

Max cleared his throat. "So, Jordan, I'd better be going, but before I forget, here's that money I owed you." He set a wad of cash on the table, a pinched expression on his face as Jordan scooped it into the pocket of her blazer.

"Max isn't eating with us?" Abby followed him with her eyes as far as the door.

"No. He had some other things to do. It's just you and me. What do you say after lunch we go grab that tiara and then head out to see some sights?"

Jordan grinned, which had the immediate effect of starting Abby's body tingling in all sorts of hidden places deep within. But just as quickly, her heart sank. "I can't. I've been away too long already, and I missed my noon appointment. I'm going to be in so much trouble."

"Oh, come on, Ducky! You work for your family's business. It's not like they can fire you for skipping one day. Just promise you'll think about it while you eat, okay? The offer still stands that anything you want to do today, anything at all, is on me."

Abby nodded. "I'll think about it." She knew the answer would have to be no, but she didn't want to be the reason Jordan's mood was ruined. At least not yet. They hadn't even ordered dessert.

Why now? Abby wondered as she tucked into her lunch, savoring each bite all the more because of the fleeting taste of freedom it contained. Why now, when her life was not hers to control, did she finally meet exactly the kind of attractive, intelligent, funny, and sweet person she'd tried for years to find with no luck? It was so unfair, but what could she do?

NINE

AFTER A QUICK STOP by Jordan's flat, she and Abby were once again walking in the direction of Kensington Gardens along a busy thoroughfare. The sound of traffic was constant, making conversation difficult. It was a grittier, more urban route without the charm of Portobello Road, but also without the market day crowds, so Jordan was able to set a brisk pace. Abby walked beside her, the priceless tiara they'd gone back to retrieve wrapped in several layers of toilet paper and stuffed into a plastic grocery bag that she clutched tightly in a fist.

Jordan snuck a glance across the street to where a man in a tan coat and baseball cap was rifling through a stack of odds and ends on a table in front of a shop. Only the telltale red of his beard let her know that it was Max. Though he was an excellent photographer, he could just as easily have made his living as a PI, or an international spy. He'd been born for this sort of undercover work. In fact, as much as he had tried to give her a hard time about it during the few minutes when they were alone at the table before lunch, it had been clear that deep down he was relishing the challenge that surveilling the princess would entail. Jordan looked away from Max, and would likely not check again. She knew she needn't worry. Even if she lost sight of him, which she most likely would no matter how hard she tried not to, he'd be following at a safe distance, and the shots he'd capture would be amazing. Max knew how to do his job. Now Jordan needed to focus on hers.

"So, have you given it some thought?" Jordan asked when a break in traffic gave her the opportunity to speak.

"Given what thought?" Abby's face scrunched in confusion.

Jordan put a hand over her heart. "You wound me. Have you already forgotten your promise to consider spending the rest of the day sightseeing with me? I must be losing my charm."

"You're plenty charming." Abby's cheeks took on a pink flush, and the half smile on her lips gave Jordan all the evidence she needed to believe the woman's statement was true. "It's not that I don't want to, but I really do need to get back."

Jordan resisted the urge to groan. She'd pegged the princess as being desperate for a good time away from her royal duties, and Jordan still believed her assessment to be true, but the woman was proving much more difficult to persuade than she'd expected. This intrigued her. A big part of Jordan's job as an investigative reporter was being able to read people accurately, and she was rarely wrong. She was certain, for instance, that Abby was genuinely attracted to her, beyond just the clumsy, intoxication-fueled display from the night before. This wasn't her vanity speaking. It was just a fact that she'd picked up on. Blushing, stuttering, coy looks—all the signs were there. Under the circumstances, it should have made it that much easier to convince the runaway princess to play hooky from her duties for a few more hours. So why was this so hard?

"Is it your family? You're worried about your dad, I'm guessing. Are you close?" It was Jordan's best guess. The expression of concern on Abby's face when she'd talked about her father's health had spoken volumes.

"We are close, now. We haven't always been. When I was younger, he lived far away. I didn't see him much. But remember those unfortunate circumstances I mentioned? A couple years ago there was a death in my father's family. Two, actually. His mother and his older sister were killed in a car accident."

"That's terrible. You lost your grandmother and your aunt at the same time?" Jordan realized as she said it that she'd already known this fact from Diane's briefing, yet it felt so much more poignant talking to Abby about it face-to-face. These weren't celebrities or public media figures to her, but family members.

"Yes. I never had the chance to meet them, but when it happened, my father was really shaken up. He called, and my mom and I ended up flying out to see him. We stayed with him for several weeks, and that's how they reconnected and started to fall in love again."

"It sounds like you're close to them."

"Yeah, I really am. I mean, they're family, so by definition they're totally infuriating sometimes, but I love them and don't want to hurt them. Which is the problem." Abby closed her eyes and took a deep breath before continuing. "I sort of didn't tell anyone I was leaving the...hotel. They must be so worried."

"Could you send a text or something?"

Abby laughed as she held up her little red purse. "No room for a phone. I've got my passport and some lipstick, and that's it."

"You can borrow mine." It was a sincere offer, and only partially motivated by how valuable Jordan knew it would be to have the private number of someone in the royal household in her list of contacts. Mostly, she just hoped to ease Abby's mind so she would agree to spend the rest of the afternoon with her.

"This is going to sound ridiculous, but I don't know the number." Abby fidgeted with her fingers, avoiding eye contact, and Jordan could sense she was embarrassed.

"Hey, who bothers to remember numbers these days, right?" Jordan responded lightheartedly. "But you're a grown woman. I'm sure they know you can handle being by yourself for a few hours."

"You'd think so, right?" There was a bitter edge to Abby's voice, and immediately Jordan seized on it.

"What are you, twenty-six? Twenty-seven?" She knew the answer, of course. She'd read Abby's file and committed it to memory the night before.

"Twenty-six."

"My family was the same way. That's why I had to move." Though Jordan had an ulterior motive for sharing this tidbit, it wasn't a lie.

"You moved all the way from Nebraska to London?"

"Yeah. I got the chance after grad school. I was almost the same age as you at the time, twenty-five. That was five years ago. It was difficult and really scary to leave behind everything familiar like that, but I knew if I didn't, I'd never be able to achieve my dreams."

"Of becoming a fertilizer saleswoman?"

"What?" She looked at Abby in surprise and was met with a quizzical stare.

"Those big dreams you were pursuing. Working for your family's chemical company?"

"Oh, that." Jordan had thrown the cover story out there without a lot of thought. In fact, it was an old joke, how working as a journalist, especially under the direction of someone like the *Crier*'s new management, was a lot like being a fertilizer salesperson. Both peddled in bullshit. But she couldn't tell Abby that. "Yeah, we were expanding into Europe. Very exciting. But no, that wasn't the dream I was talking about. It was moving away, living in a big city, in another country. I knew I had one shot at something different, something exciting, and if I didn't take it, I'd live the rest of my life in Omaha."

"Hmm." Abby chewed her lip thoughtfully. "I guess we always want what we don't have."

"What do you mean?"

"Well, I was kind of forced into what a lot of people would consider an exciting life, doing a lot of travel, and sometimes all I can think about is how much I want to go back and live that quiet, normal existence that I used to think I would have. Sometimes I really miss going to an office and sitting in a cubicle all day, having lunch with a few coworkers, then battling the rush-hour traffic to get home."

They were almost to the gardens now, walking along Bayswater Road. About a block ahead, on the opposite side of the street from where Jordan and Abby were walking, a crowd had gathered on the sidewalk, holding signs and chanting loudly. The crowd was directly across from a gate that had a guard booth on either side, and where several dark, unmarked cars had been parked to block access to the road beyond. Down this road could be found, Jordan knew, the heavily fortified back entrance to the residences at Kensington Palace, along with many private apartments belonging to foreign dignitaries, and the embassies of several countries, including the one whose crown princess Jordan happened to be walking beside. The closer they got to this road, the more nervous Abby seemed to become.

"Jordan do you think we should cross?"

"And get caught up in that mess?" Jordan looked askance at the protesters. They were always there, yelling in the direction of the Russian Embassy on the corner. As far as she could tell, it didn't have much of an effect on foreign policy, but it did make it hard to reach the corner without bumping into them. "I'd rather not. Why?"

"No reason," Abby replied in a way that left little doubt that she did, indeed, have a reason. And Jordan didn't really need to be told what it was. She'd walked past this stretch of Embassy Row enough times to know that the presence of that many unmarked cars at one time was highly unusual. There was clearly something going on in one of the high-profile residences along the street, and considering her present company, it didn't take much of a guess on Jordan's part to figure out that a missing princess was the most likely explanation.

"So, where is this hotel of yours, anyway?" Jordan asked, curious what cover story Abby would try to spin.

"Near Kensington Gardens."

"Yes, well, we are near Kensington Gardens right now. It's just up there. So, if I'm going to get you back to your *real* life all safe and sound, I'm going to need a more specific address."

Abby's pace slowed, and the turmoil she was experiencing inside played out across her features. Jordan held her breath, hoping that the extra emphasis she'd placed on the word "real" would have the desired effect. It had to. She was running out of time.

Abby stopped, turning her back to the guard booth that was by now only several yards away. "About that. Does your sightseeing offer still stand?"

Jordan grinned. "Of course. What did you have in mind?"

"I do need to get back, but it's such a nice day, and I haven't had the chance to see much of the park. Maybe we could take a walk?"

"I have an idea. Do you know how to ride a bicycle?"

Abby gave her an incredulous look. "Of course I know how to ride a bike. But I don't have one on me. Do you?"

"Sort of." Jordan winked. "All around the city are bikes that you can rent for as long as you need. I happen to know there's a rack of them just another block from here. Can you ride in that dress?"

Abby considered for a moment, pinching the fabric between her fingers and holding it out to judge the fullness of the skirt. Finally, she nodded. "It should be fine. So, where are these bikes? Do we need to cross the street?"

Abby's backward glance at the guard booth underscored her nervousness, and Jordan reached out for her hand. She gave it a little tug, pulling Abby closer to the curb. "You know what? We probably should. I think we can make it across now if we're quick."

They sprinted across and pushed their way through the group of chanting people holding signs. Only when they were well past the guards did Jordan have them return to the other side of the road. They entered Kensington Gardens through the closest gate, and found the rack of rental bicycles just where Jordan had recalled them being. Next to the rack was the docking station terminal for making the payment. It required a debit card, but since she had an annual subscription, they would get the first thirty minutes free, and pay 50p each thirty minutes after that. Unless Abby decided she wanted to ride until midnight, Jordan was fairly certain she could cover the couple of pounds it might end up costing. Probably.

She fished a hand in her pocket, pulled out her wallet, and extracted the blue debit card for her checking account. She slid it into the machine and was issued a slip of paper with the code needed to unlock one bicycle. She handed it to Abby. "Here, take this and choose a bike. Why don't you hand me your bag and I can put it in my satchel?"

Abby bit her lip, holding the plastic bag that contained her tiara and clearly weighing her options thoroughly before handing it over. "Okay."

Jordan stuffed the tiara into her bag. "I'll only be a minute. I just need to rent one for myself."

Jordan turned back to the machine, but as she did so she caught her knuckles against the side of the metal box, which sent her wallet flying. It landed several feet away, its contents scattering in the dirt. Jordan knelt to gather up the array of cards, brushing off dust and doing her best to fit them back into the slots in some semblance of order. When she'd straightened up and made it back, her transaction had timed out. "Damn it," she muttered. She retrieved the blue card from her wallet again and slid it into the machine.

Meanwhile, Abby had freed one of the bicycles from the rack and wheeled it to the pavement. She mounted it gingerly, being careful to tuck in the excess folds of her skirt to keep the fabric from the spokes. Despite her frustration, Jordan couldn't help but smile at the sight of her practicing a series of slow figure eights. Catching her eye, Abby took a hand off the handlebars and waved, putting it back quickly as she began to wobble from side to side. "It's been a while," she called out to Jordan with a sheepish grin.

"They say you never forget," Jordan replied, then frowned at the terminal. Despite her having put the card in at least ten seconds earlier, the screen remained unchanged. She pulled the card out and tried again.

"Jordan, I'm going to ride down that way, okay?"

"Yeah. Just don't go so far that I can't catch up." She didn't look up from the screen, which now informed her that it had failed to read her card. "What the hell!"

She removed the card and was about to try a third time when out of the corner of her eye Jordan caught a glimpse of Abby pedaling down a pathway where she knew that bicycles were not allowed. From past experience, Jordan was also aware that the police in Kensington Gardens took infractions like that extremely seriously. In part they did so for public safety, as this was a popular place for families and children, but it was also due in large part to the garden's close proximity to the residences of several prominent members of the British royal family. She tried to call out a warning, but the distance was too great and the noise level on a busy Saturday afternoon too high for Abby to hear her.

"Crap."

Wallet in one hand and debit card in the other, Jordan raced after Abby on foot, but before she could come anywhere close to catching up, she heard the gallop of hooves. Two policewomen on horseback whooshed past her. By the time she reached Abby, the princess had come to a full stop, her feet planted on the ground one on each side of the bicycle. Her neck was craned upward to make eye contact with the policewomen, who were both still seated in their saddles, and they appeared to be deep in conversation. Jordan's stomach tightened. If the situation escalated, Abby could be facing more than just a fine. If they thought she was a threat in any way—and heaven forbid she share with them what would no doubt be received as a completely insane notion that she was a runaway princess—the officers were well within their rights to haul her off to jail.

Jordan approached the scene cautiously, and as she did so she flipped her wallet open to reach for her press credential. She would use it only as a last resort, but if she were able to explain who she was, it might let them both off the hook. Sure, she wanted to get her scoop and save her job, but Jordan also preferred not to be at the center of a major international incident. The debit card was still in her other hand, only Jordan realized now why it hadn't worked before. It wasn't her debit card after all, but her Tesco Clubcard, the one she swiped to earn points at her local supermarket, which happened to be the same shade of blue as her debit card. All this trouble because she hadn't bothered to look at what she was doing.

"Abby?" Jordan waited until she was close enough so that she didn't need to shout. One of the officers turned to look at her, giving her a curt nod when Jordan made a motion with her hand indicating that she wanted to approach. The two horses were massive and took up much of the path. Jordan swallowed hard as she skirted past, pulling her arms close to her body so she wouldn't accidentally brush against one of the muscular creatures.

Jordan had expected Abby to be terrified, or at least to show half the discomfort that she herself felt in the presence of these two imposing women and their giant steeds, but instead Abby looked perfectly at ease. In fact, she flashed Jordan a brilliant smile, the type usually reserved for advertisements from dentist's offices and commercials for chewing gum.

"Jordan, darling! There you are."

Jordan's jaw went slack. Had Abby just called her darling? "I...uh, yes. Here I am. What's going on?"

"I was just explaining to these very nice officers the reason that I was in such a rush that I didn't see the sign saying that bicycles aren't allowed on this path."

"Oh, okay. And the reason was...what?"

Abby giggled, as if Jordan had told the funniest joke. She held out her arm, and as Jordan took a step closer, she pulled her in close. "My silly girl. Obviously, it's because we don't want to be late. To our wedding."

"Our...right!" Abby had punctuated each of those last three words heavily, but even so it took half a second for the meaning to sink in. Once it did, she did her best to play along, her eyes wide and innocent as she looked from one officer to the other. "Yes. God, can you imagine how embarrassing that would be?"

"I could take you both into the station right now,

you know," said one of the officers, who looked like she had been born without the capacity for humor.

But the other woman's face softened a little, and there was something about the sudden shift in her demeanor that made Jordan wonder if she might not have a wife of her own waiting for her back home. "Ah, come on, Jackie. There's no need to be such a hard-ass all the time."

Officer Jackie stiffened. "It's a serious offense, Rosie. There are rules for a reason."

"Yeah, but they weren't really doing any harm. And it's their wedding day." Officer Rosie turned her attention back to Jordan and Abby. "So, where are you two lovebirds getting married?"

"St. Paul's Cathedral," Abby offered, not missing a beat. She snuggled closer to Jordan, whose eyes involuntarily fluttered shut, temporarily powerless against the wave of sweetness that washed over her.

Unmoved by the spectacle, Officer Jackie raised an incredulous eyebrow. "St. Paul's? My, aren't we fancy."

Snapping back to her senses, Jordan resisted the urge to glower at her supposed wife-to-be. *Oh, Abby, did you have to choose St. Paul's Cathedral, of all places? Who but a princess would come up with that* for a wedding venue? But before she had time to react, Abby once again came to the rescue.

"I didn't want to make a big deal of it before, but Jordan's father is a diplomat with the American embassy. That's how we were able to secure it. Just the crypt, of course, not the main part upstairs. I mean, it's not like we're royalty." She laughed heartily.

Officer Jackie still looked skeptical, but Officer Rosie nodded thoughtfully. "I had a cousin who got married there, actually. On my mum's side. Her fiancé's uncle was an MP."

"That figures," Officer Jackie said with a harrumph. "Fine. Look, ladies, I guess we can let you go with a warning this time."

Abby squealed and flung her other arm around Jordan, enveloping her in what Jordan thought was meant to be a hug. She thought it, in fact, right up to the moment when their lips met. If she'd had to put into words what she was feeling, the closest she could have come to imagine it was like a tsunami of honey, covering her from head to toe in sweetness. It rooted her in place, and if given the choice, she would have been happy to stay stuck in the moment forever.

Whether the kiss was intentional or just an accident, Jordan didn't know. If the circumstances had been different, she might have tried to figure out what Abby was thinking, kissing her like that in the middle of a public space, with two mounted police looking on, as well as a small crowd of bystanders that had started to form around them. Was it just part of the act, and if so, exactly how much of a response on her part would be appropriate to play along without the risk of anyone getting the wrong idea? Any of these questions would have been reasonable for a seasoned investigative journalist to ask, but that wasn't where Jordan's brain was. Not even close.

From the moment the kiss began, Jordan forfeited all power of thought and reason, and became instead lost to sensation and emotion. All that mattered was the feel of Abby's lips, soft and full against her, the sweet taste of her mouth as her lips parted to allow room for Jordan's tongue, and the sudden knowledge that never before had anyone's mouth fit so perfectly with hers. She would gladly drown in this kiss, lost in the scent of Abby's skin, a heady blend of soap and natural musk that had been warmed beneath the midday sun. The tiny murmuring sound that Abby made as Jordan brushed her fingers along the exposed skin at the nape of her neck was like a song composed just for her, one that soothed her fears and made her body want to dance. For sight, she had only her memory of Abby's beauty, as Jordan's eyes were firmly shut, but the light that filtered through her lids formed starburst patterns like fireworks inside her head. It was like a celebration of everything Jordan had never realized she needed until this moment.

When they broke apart, there was a smattering of applause from the onlookers, and Officer Rosie looked misty eyed. Officer Jackie just rolled her eyes. "Go on, now. Off with you. And keep off the pathways!"

Breathless and woozy, Jordan followed their instructions in a daze. What had just happened? Her body felt fizzy, expansive, like a bottle of seltzer that someone had shaken and then left on the shelf for the pressure to build without release. She kept her eyes glued to the gravel at her feet, afraid that if she looked at Abby, she might burst. She'd never felt quite like this before, and she doubted whether she would ever feel normal again.

You've got to get it together, she urged herself. *You're messing it all up, losing your objectivity.* She breathed in deeply, forcing herself to think about what was at stake. She had one shot at the story of a lifetime. Her career, her visa, her entire financial well-being was at risk. Whatever feelings she might think she had for Abby, she had to put them aside. Abby was a nice girl, but they'd only just met. She was fun, and smart, and had amazing nipples, but so did a lot of women. Jordan could search out someone with similar qualities another time, when her entire life as she knew it wasn't in jeopardy. There was exactly one thing that made Abby *The One,* and it had nothing to do with romance. It was that she was Her Royal Highness Princess Abigail of the House of Gamberini, heir to her father's throne, and that for the rest of the afternoon, Jordan had exclusive access to her like no other journalist on the planet.

And you'd better not forget it.

TEN

WITH THE MOUNTED policewomen still in sight, they walked along the forbidden pathway, Abby pushing the bicycle so as not to break the rules again. Her lips tingled and her insides fluttered with the remembered feel of Jordan's mouth against hers, but she avoided looking at her companion for fear that the same elation might not be showing on her face. What had come over her back there? It wasn't just that she'd initiated such a passionate, public kiss that shocked her, although it definitely did, but the way she'd handled herself the whole time. Perhaps it had been the adrenaline that kicked in at the sound of those approaching hoofbeats, but as she'd stared up at the riders seated astride their massive horses, it was like she'd been possessed by a much more clever and quick-witted version of herself, one that she'd never known existed until that moment.

As for the kiss, the impulse to it had been so spontaneous and natural that she hadn't stopped to think. Only now that she had, she was terrified to face the consequences of her lack of control. What must Jordan be thinking? Here she'd taken pity on an incapacitated stranger the night before, invited her into her home, and how had Abby repaid her kindness? By throwing herself at her. Repeatedly.

Though she still didn't remember every detail of how she'd behaved the night before, she'd pieced together enough of it to know that it had been appalling. There'd been nibbling, for certain, and possibly groping, though she wasn't sure. And that was *before* she'd tried her best to consume Jordan's face in front of two police officers and several dozen innocent bystanders, all of whom were simply trying to enjoy a nice day in one of London's lovely royal parks and certainly had not planned to get caught up in some sort of lesbian melodrama. The heat of embarrassment overwhelmed her to the point that Abby thought her body might spontaneously combust.

She drew in a shaky breath, composing her *mea culpa*. "Jordan, look, I'm really sorry..."

But to her surprise, Jordan let out a jocular laugh. "That was amazing! That Officer Jackie was a real ball breaker. I can't believe you got us out of that with nothing but a warning."

Abby laughed, too. The awkwardness of the kiss that hung between them momentarily diminished, if not entirely forgotten. "I'm just as astounded as you are. I have no idea where any of that came from."

"So, you're not a habitual liar, then?"

"Not usually, no." Abby bit down on her lower lip in uncertainty as she counted up all the lies she'd told in the past twenty-four hours.

Jordan stopped walking. "Well, you're a natural."

Jordan had said it admiringly, not accusingly, but even so, Abby knew it wasn't true. She was terrible at pretending to be something she wasn't, which is why she'd struggled so much with the royal turn her life had taken. Whatever was happening to her now, whomever this person was that she was becoming—this person who could think on her feet and boldly kiss women she'd just met for the whole world to see—there was something genuine at the core of this transformation. And the more she thought about it, the more she had an inkling of what it could be.

She slowed to a stop just in front of Jordan and turned to face her. "I couldn't have done it without you. Any of it. You followed my lead beautifully."

"You made it easy." Jordan pressed her lips together, and the sudden rush of color to her cheeks gave Abby a hint as to which part of their performance in particular she had in mind. Her expression shifted as she changed topics. "You still up for that sightseeing I promised you? It's only just past two o'clock, and if we grab up another bike, we'll easily make up for lost time."

Abby nodded. "That would be nice. I have a lot of excess energy in me after that adventure, and I think I'd rather burn some it off before I have to face my family."

They stopped at the bike stand, and Jordan quickly checked out a second bicycle. "Where to?"

"St. Paul's, of course. Or have you forgotten our wedding already?" Abby grinned, even as she surprised herself by how at ease she felt teasing Jordan in this way. "I guess I won't hold you to it, given that you only went along with the plan out of a desire not to get arrested."

"Don't sell yourself short. It was a tempting offer, although I don't think St. Paul's takes walk-ins like they're some wedding chapel on the Vegas strip."

"No, probably not."

"It's true that they do weddings in the crypt, though. How did you know about that?"

"I saw something about it on television once. To be honest, I wouldn't mind having a look at the cathedral. No wedding required. Is it far?"

"Maybe thirty minutes by bike. Can you manage that?"

Abby shot her a look. "Thirty minutes? I've taken longer Zumba classes. Lead the way."

Jordan laughed. "Yes, ma'am. I know a route that will take us past some of the best sites in London. Might as well see it all, since this is your first visit."

The pedaled through Kensington Gardens, purely

by way of approved pathways this time out of an abundance of caution, until they reached South Carriage Drive. It was a wide path with leafy trees on either side, evenly spaced in near-military precision. A sign pointed the way to Hyde Park Corner, and they rode in that direction, side by side in companionable silence. The route took them past Wellington Arch and through Green Park, and they went slowly and stopped now and then so that Jordan could point out something of interest or give Abby a tidbit of the history that surrounded them.

"How do you know so much about everything?" Abby asked.

"I like stories," Jordan replied. "London is full of stories. I love it here."

"So, no plans to return to the States?"

The briefest of shadows clouded Jordan's face. "Not if I can help it. What about you?"

"I can't deny it. Sometimes I miss California so much. But I'm afraid my family business will keep me in Europe for the foreseeable future."

They left the park and merged onto Constitution Hill, which quickly went from a tree-lined boulevard to a wide-open street where an imposing gate of black wrought iron, tipped in gold, came into view on their right. Behind it was a hulking building made of stone. Despite herself, Abby felt her hands clench the handle bars of her bike. "What's that?"

"Buckingham Palace, of course."

Of course. She should have known by the tightness in her belly that it had something to do with royalty. Upon closer inspection, the gate was strikingly similar to the one that surrounded her father's palace, too. "It's a little over the top, isn't it? I mean, who needs gold-tipped spears to keep the bad guys out? Wouldn't plain black ones be just as pokey?"

"Yes, but less regal. And one thing about the British royal family, they know how to put on the whole show. Speaking of, you really should make it back over to the palace for the changing of the guard sometime. It's past the time for it today, but it's really a spectacle."

If Abby remembered her schedule correctly, she was expected back at Buckingham Palace in a few weeks' time, but instead of viewing a simple changing of the guard, she would be a special guest of Her Majesty the Queen at the Trooping the Colour ceremony. From what she gathered, this was a long and boring public ceremony that the poor woman had to endure each June as part of the official celebration of her birthday, and worst of all, there was no cake. Abby didn't see the point of birthday festivities that didn't feature cake prominently. Was this the type of thing she had to look forward to someday when she became a monarch? Because frankly, it seemed cruel.

Abby smiled weakly. "I'll keep it in mind. Let's keep going, shall we?"

Jordan looked at her in surprise. "Are you sure? We have time to look around if you'd like."

"Nah. If you've seen one palace, you've seen 'em all."

There were people everywhere along the pathways as they continued along the edge of St. James's Park. Children laughed and played in the sunshine, chasing birds across the grass. There were even more people as they approached Parliament Square, and for a time, both Jordan and Abby hopped off their bikes and walked alongside to avoid running over pedestrians, many of whom were clearly tourists with no idea what side of the road to expect traffic to come from.

Though she'd felt nervous at the sight of the queen's residence, Abby stopped to take in the beauty of the Palace of Westminster, where the Houses of Parliament resided. "Now I feel like I'm really in London."

Jordan followed her gaze to the face of the giant clock tower. "It's too bad the chimes have been stopped."

"Have they?"

Jordan nodded. "Big Ben needed some maintenance. You'll have to come back in another few years to really get the full London experience."

"Only if you promise to show me around when I do," Abby said with a wink. It surprised her how good it felt to do that. Had she ever been the winking type before Jordan had come along? She didn't think so. But now that she'd tried it, she liked it, and she didn't think she wanted to stop.

When they reached Victoria Embankment, they were once again able to ride, and this time their view was the River Thames, its water sparkling in the sun. Every so often, a bridge crossed the expanse, and as they rode beneath, Abby couldn't help but admire the intricate detail of each marvel of nineteenth-century engineering. That was one thing that Europe had where California couldn't compare. She might miss the beaches and palm trees, especially when she was back in her father's mountainous kingdom, but she'd also discovered a deep appreciation for the beauty and rich history of the Old World that she'd never experienced when she was strictly an American.

"There's the London Eye." Jordan removed a hand from the handle bar long enough to point across the water to where the famous giant wheel turned at an almost imperceptibly slow speed. "It's easier to get to the top of the Eye than the top of St. Paul's, but I think the dome offers a better view. Are you up for it?"

"Of course. I love a challenge."

"You may change your mind when you get there. It has over five hundred steps."

"Is that all?" Abby rolled her eyes dismissively. "That's not so bad. I used to do twice that many at the gym next to my old office, at least three times a week."

"StairMaster and Zumba. You do like your workouts." Jordan laughed, but it was hard for Abby to know for certain if it was in admiration or teasing. "But I'll warn you, it feels a little different when you're climbing three hundred and sixty-five feet to the observation deck."

Abby lifted her chin defiantly. "Like I said, I love a challenge."

"Yeah, and like I said, we'll see."

Until that moment, they'd been traveling at a leisurely pace, but in addition to her mocking retort, Jordan now seemed to be pedaling faster, and was soon several yards ahead. Abby pushed her own pedals harder to catch up, but as soon as she inched up close, Jordan pulled out in front again. It was obvious the woman was trying to start a race. Abby hunkered down over the handle bars, her eyes narrowing. *If she thinks she can beat me, she has another thing coming.*

Bits of stray hair that had come loose from her chignon fluttered around Abby's face as she picked up speed. She paid them no attention. She whizzed past one ornate lamppost after another, the bobbing and swooping of seagulls as they dove toward the water barely registering as she focused on her goal of beating her companion. They were neck and neck for a while, but then Abby pulled ahead in a rush of triumph. It took several more seconds before she realized that she was riding alone. When she turned around, Jordan was stopped, waving at her and not even trying to hide her smirk. "We're going this way!" she shouted.

"You cheated," Abby informed her as she pulled her bike alongside.

"How did I cheat?"

"Because you know where you're going and I don't."

"I see." Jordan laughed. "Impeccable logic. No more racing, though. The rest of the way, you'll want to stay close. The streets are narrow, and on a Saturday, it can get pretty busy."

They left the Embankment to travel down a street called Puddle Dock, a name which immediately made Abby think of the Beatrix Potter stories her mother had read to her as a child. She half expected to see a rabbit wearing a velvet jacket crossing the road, but it turned out to be a perfectly normal street, which led into the heart of the city. The formerly wide thoroughfares and modern architecture gave way to narrow lanes and ancient bricks, until at last they turned a nondescript corner, and Abby found herself staring at St. Paul's massive dome.

"Wow."

"Yes, exactly," Jordan agreed. "Wow."

There was a bike stand nearby so they returned their borrowed rides and went the rest of the short distance on foot, Abby staring at the giant edifice the entire time with a growing sense of awe. "So that landing there," she said, pointing to the widest part of the dome, which was ringed with giant columns, "that's where we're climbing to?"

Jordan snorted, grabbing her hand and lifting it so that her extended index finger pointed significantly higher. "Uh, no. There."

"I don't see anything." Abby squinted, and after a moment, a tiny balcony came into view, way up toward the top of the dome. "You don't mean up there, do you?"

"Want to rethink this?"

Abby's eyes narrowed. "Absolutely not."

They entered the cathedral through the main doors, and when they emerged from the ticket area and walked along the black-and-white checkered floors into the nave, Abby was momentarily dumbstruck. The sheer scale of the place was overwhelming, and its overall appearance unlike other European cathedrals she had visited. In her father's kingdom, there was a medieval cathedral built of gray stone, with narrow aisles and vaulted arches, and dim light that filtered in from jewel-tone windows high above. But St. Paul's was altogether different. The interior was bright white, almost blindingly so, with accents of pure gold. The aisles were wide, the space almost cavernous, and yet despite the size and the large number of people milling around while they listened to their tour headsets, her main impression was of silence. She scooted closer to Jordan, feeling suddenly very small and insignificant.

"Isn't it spectacular?" Jordan whispered, not seeming to mind her close proximity but instead leaning in closer so that her lips hovered just outside

Abby's ear. "The original burned down in the Great Fire, you know. Well, not the original, original. There were a few others. But the one before this one. Did that make sense?"

Abby nodded, but the truth was she hadn't caught much, if anything, of what Jordan had said. She'd been too busy concentrating on the way the woman's warm breath tickled the tiny hairs inside her ear and sent sparks of electricity shooting from the base of her neck to her tailbone. She had no idea what Jordan was talking about, but neither did she want her to stop. "Uh-huh."

"The dome's this way," Jordan said, placing her hand on the small of Abby's back to usher her in the correct direction and setting off another round of sparks in the process, along with some thoughts that weren't, strictly speaking, appropriate for church.

Solid square columns drew the eyes skyward, where the ceiling was painted with intricate frescoes, highlighted in yet more gold. Simple chandeliers of shining brass were suspended above the chairs where worshippers would sit, but which were now mostly empty except for a person here or there who sat with head bent in prayer. Abby's red shoes with their leather soles fell silently on the tile as she walked. Though she was there as a tourist, she couldn't help but be impacted by a sense of reverence in the space.

In the center of the cathedral was the dome, the real showstopper of this architectural masterpiece. A gallery was directly above, ringing the base of the dome, and while people walked in a constant circle around it, they were barely recognizable as such, dwarfed as they were by the soaring structure above. Neatly spaced windows, each the height of a multi-story building, let in light all around, and the artwork on the top of the dome was so high up that Abby could barely see it.

Abby's pulse ticked higher as she took it all in, a cold anxiety settling in the pit of her stomach. This was no mere church, but a cathedral built for kings and queens. It had been the setting for royal weddings and funerals, with the eyes of the world watching what otherwise would have been an intensely private moment. It made her uneasy, as did the grandeur that surrounded her. Who would want to get married here, to mourn here, to live every second of their lives with everyone watching? And if she barely felt comfortable as a tourist in such a place, how would she ever succeed in the role her family and country expected of her?

"Are you ready?" Jordan asked.

Abby's first impulse was to scream no, no she wasn't ready at all. But then she realized that Jordan didn't mean was she ready to rule a kingdom. They were standing next to a sign that pointed the way to the staircase that led to the upstairs galleries. "Um, sure," she answered, hoping that some exercise would set her mind at ease.

The way up was a spiral staircase that wrapped itself around a seemingly never-ending column of stone. They took the first few steps side by side, but soon it became clear that this was an impractical approach, as group after group of tourists descending the staircase bumped into them. No matter which side they chose, it seemed that the crowds were incapable of avoiding them, so they settled for Jordan taking the lead and Abby following closely behind. The stairs coiled and climbed forever, and Abby's thighs burned hotter with every step.

"You okay?" Jordan called back to her, and Abby smiled smugly to hear the breathiness of her companion's voice. Clearly the stairs weren't any easier for her than they were for Abby.

"Yes, doing just fine," she lied. No amount of Zumba or StairMaster could have prepared her for the claustrophobic nature of this climb, with its constant barrage of people walking the wrong direction.

Jordan reached her hand back, and at first Abby thought that she was trying to get something from the satchel that she'd been wearing slung across her back since the bike ride, but then she extended it farther, wiggling her fingers. "Take my hand. I don't want us to get separated in this crowd."

It was as much a practical gesture as a romantic one, but as Abby felt Jordan's fingers curl around hers, her heart, which was already pounding from the exertion of the climb, skipped at least three beats. At last they reached the top, and Abby had a chance to catch her breath as they took a slow turn around the Whispering Gallery. Though the crowd was no longer an issue, somehow neither she nor Jordan thought to let go, and so they walked slowly around the circular platform hand in hand, enjoying the view of the people below, who looked as tiny from her perspective looking down as the people on the gallery had been when she looked up. It was only when they'd made it the full way around that they finally allowed their hands to drift apart. Though it was warm in the cathedral, Abby keenly felt the chill against her fingers where Jordan's hand had been.

"Shall we keep going?" Jordan asked as they reached the door that led to next staircase. "We have two more sets to go."

"Absolutely!" Her unbridled cheerfulness was mostly for show. Though she would never admit out loud that Jordan had been right; this was a lot harder than she'd thought it was going to be.

The second set of stairs was narrower than the first, the pain in her muscles that much more intense. When they reached the Stone Gallery, Jordan paused beside the wooden door that led to the outside observation area. "Do you want to just go and look at the view from here?" she asked.

"Are we at the top yet?" Abby countered.

"No."

"Then no."

They continued up the final staircase, a rickety set of metal stairs that twisted so sharply Abby's head spun as she climbed. The only thing that kept her moving for the last fifty steps was the knowledge that if she stopped, Jordan, who was a few steps behind her, would know that something was wrong. When they reached the door to the Golden Gallery, Abby's knees were shaking and her breath coming in short spurts. She would never complain about Zumba again for as long as she lived.

Her discomfort, however, was forgotten when they stepped outside onto the narrow balcony that seemed to float just inches below the clouds. Giddiness filled her instead as she leaned against the railing and looked at all of London stretching out below her as far as she could see. "It's stunning."

"I told you the view would be worth it."

Abby stared out wistfully at the array of winding streets and miniature buildings. It would take a lifetime to explore it all. And this was just one city. There were so many others. "I wish I could see everything," she said, the weight of that impossibility lending a melancholy tone to her words.

Jordan leaned beside her on the railing, studying her face with a thoughtful expression. "What else do you wish?"

The earnest interest with which she asked made Abby smile. It had been so long since anyone had asked her what she wanted. She thought long and hard before answering. "I want to dance."

"Dance?" Jordan's eyebrows had pulled together, and it was clear that she hadn't been expecting that response. "You want to be a dancer? Like, ballet?"

"No, silly. Like, just regular dancing, with music and people and everyone having fun and not caring about tomorrow."

"In that case, your wish is my command." A smile teased Jordan's lips, and sent Abby's stomach into a loop. "I know just the place."

She hadn't forgotten the need to return to the palace, but the longer she was away, the harder she'd begun to hope that she could stay away just a little longer. Just for one more day. More than anything, Abby didn't want to think about tomorrow, when she would surely be back at the embassy, her moment of freedom behind her and the woman whose company she was so enjoying just a fading memory. How unfair her life was. She would take the sweetness of Jordan's smile over Countess Margaret's scowl, a thousand times over. But that was a choice she'd never be allowed to make.

ELEVEN

THEIR DESTINATION WAS NOT YET in sight, but Jordan could already hear the rhythmic beat of music as she and Abby approached the stretch of Regent's Canal that was nearest to Paddington Station. It was early Saturday evening, and the streets were beginning to fill with people, mostly couples, dressed for date night in the area's many restaurants and night clubs. They were headed toward one of Jordan's favorite spots, a hidden gem where live music of every variety could be heard for free many evenings. *Free* was the key word on this particular night, for while there were many venues throughout the city to go dancing, the wad of cash Max had given her only a few hours before had grown alarmingly thin. A day in London with a princess had been a lot more expensive than she'd imagined it would be.

"I know we had a big lunch, but I'm hungry," Abby

informed her, perhaps prompted by the delightful scent of something cooking somewhere nearby. "Are you hungry?"

"Not very," Jordan lied as her own stomach rumbled. She slipped her hand into her pocket and tried to estimate how much money she had left. Enough for a small bite? Yes, but it would be best if they avoided anywhere fancy enough to have a waiter who came to the table to take your order. "How about that café over there?" she suggested, pointing to a narrow canal boat that was permanently docked several yards ahead, with a sign outside that announced good food at fair prices. *God, I hope they're not kidding,* she thought.

"It looks cute," Abby replied with an eager nod.

The boat was painted a deep brick red, with flowers spilling out of containers on the roof and flowing down its sides in a profusion of red and pink blooms. A dozen or so small tables were set up on the walkway, and through the windows Jordan could see additional seating inside. A few steps led down to the door, and Jordan took these just ahead of Abby so she could open the door.

"Let me get that for you," she said, turning the handle and pulling on the door. It remained shut. She tried again, her efforts yielding the same result. Through the window, Jordan could see people at the counter placing orders, and diners at tables eating their meals. They must be open, and yet the door wouldn't budge.

"Here." Abby reached for the door. "Let me give it a try."

The door swung open without issue, and as Abby gave her a puzzled look, Jordan realized that she'd repeatedly pulled despite the fairly large bronze sign above the handle that directed her to push. "Must have been stuck," she muttered.

A stack of printed menus sat on the counter, and Jordan grabbed up two, handing one to Abby and breathing a silent sigh of relief as a quick scan of the offerings revealed nothing costing more than ten quid. No matter what Abby ordered, she was fairly certain she could handle it without embarrassment. There was a special that evening on a plate of assorted starters for sharing, and so Jordan ordered that and then selected one of the few remaining tables inside, which sat beside a window with a view of the canal.

"So, where is this dance club you're taking me to," Abby asked.

"Well, it's not exactly a club. It's more of a floating pavilion where bands play and people can dance." She stiffened in anticipation of disappointment. After all, here she was trying to entertain a princess on her one night out in London by taking her to a free concert after buying her an appetizer special at a cheap café instead of springing for a real dinner. But to her surprise and relief, the expression on Abby's face was one of delight.

"A floating pavilion? That sounds magical!"

"You can see it out the window, if you look just over there." Jordan called her companion's attention to a spot on the other side of the water where hanging lanterns and fairy lights twinkled in the trees. It was magical looking indeed, part of a network of floating platforms, green spaces, and walkways that connected to form a park in the middle of the canal.

"I can hardly wait. Do you know what band is playing?"

Jordan shifted in her seat. She'd looked it up earlier, and the news she was about to deliver could either go over really well or really badly, depending on precisely what Abby had been picturing when she'd said she wanted to dance. "It's a local swing group. You know, like big band-era stuff."

Abby's eyes grew bright and shiny. "Big band? I love that!"

Jordan smiled in relief. "You do? Do you know how to dance to it?"

"A little bit. There were some old Art Deco clubs in Los Angeles where I used to hang out right after college. How about you?"

"My grandmother loved to jitterbug. She taught me when I was a little girl."

"Aw, that's so sweet. I would have loved to have

seen a tiny Jordan doing the jitterbug with her grammy."

"Well, I doubt I've improved much in twenty-five years. You ready to go find out?"

The band was already playing when they arrived, the wooden floor of the pavilion filled with couples dancing while others milled around on the green spaces or bought drinks at the bar on the far end. Some of the dancing couples swayed back and forth awkwardly on the sidelines, possibly the ones who hadn't gotten the memo about the nature of tonight's music and were expecting a rock band. Others had clearly turned out specifically to show off their footwork, and were jumping and jiving with great enthusiasm in the middle of the dance floor. Some of the women were even dressed similarly to Abby, in full-skirted dresses and vintage hairstyles, so that far from standing out in her somewhat unusual attire, the princess blended in completely.

They'd just found a spot on one edge, close to where the dance floor ended in a safety barrier, with the water from the canal lapping against the pavilion several feet below, when the tempo of the music shifted, and the band began to play a gentle, mellow tune that was made for a slow one-step.

"I'm not sure about what they were doing before," Jordan said, gesturing toward one couple that had been showing off some particularly impressive moves, "but I think I can handle giving this one a try. Would you like to dance?"

"I thought you'd never ask," Abby responded with a coy smile that sent a shot of heat straight to Jordan's loins. It was far from the first time that day that she'd experienced the sensation, and yet it still put a hitch in her breath each time it happened.

Dancing was not high on Jordan's list of favorite activities, and she'd chosen the location for the evening based solely on Abby's request, yet as she took the princess's slender hand in hers, she felt a rush of exhilaration at the prospect of holding her in her arms on the dance floor. The fingers of her right hand tingled as they closed around Abby's, her left arm circling her partner's incredibly tiny waist. She ran her index finger along the narrow leather belt, and an image formed in her mind of running her fingers instead along Abby's bare skin. Jordan shut her eyes tightly, urging the thought to pass. *You're not on a date,* she chided herself. *This is an assignment.*

It had been like this all day, ever since they'd kissed in Kensington Gardens. That single moment had broken down her defenses. Standing at the top of St. Paul's dome, Jordan knew she had asked the perfect questions for her story. The problem was, she hadn't even been thinking about the story when she'd asked. It had been a conversation, not an interview. She'd made the biggest mistake a journalist could possibly make. She'd failed to keep a proper emotional distance between herself and her story. Jordan looked down at the way Abby was nestled against her. Emotional distance? There wasn't even physical distance between them anymore.

Her arms stiffened slightly, and she shifted her body so as to put a few inches between herself and Abby's chest. She tried not to remember that she'd seen that same chest in all its naked glory just that morning, and failed miserably. Telling herself not to think of Abby naked was like telling herself not to think of a pink elephant. If only her job weren't riding on this story, this evening could go so differently. Abby liked her, Jordan could tell. And as for Jordan—well, clearly her journalistic integrity had been shredded to ribbons. But was it just a physical attraction for Jordan, or was there something more going on? Abby moved closer, and it was all Jordan could do not to groan from the sheer torture of it. And even as she squirmed from arousal she couldn't act on, she knew it went much deeper, and that she was on the brink of serious trouble and heartache.

The song came to an end, and before Jordan had a chance to lead Abby off the floor, a woman approached them with the unmistakable look of someone hell-bent on striking up a conversation. Her vintage attire marked her as a regular. She wore checkered trousers with wide cuffed legs held up by suspenders over a crisp white dress shirt, with short-cropped hair and bright red lipstick. "Hello, ladies! I couldn't help but notice you dancing just now. Do you come here often?"

In theory she was addressing them both, but her eyes were firmly fixed on Abby, and Jordan raised an eyebrow at the stranger's cheekiness. Had she really come over here to hit on Jordan's date? Well, not actually her date, but this woman had no way of knowing that. "This is my first time here," Abby offered, which was much nicer than the *sod off* that Jordan had wanted to say. Of all the British phrases she'd picked up in her time in London, that one was a real favorite. She couldn't tell if Abby was just being polite or if she was encouraging the woman. Jordan didn't care. Either way, it rankled.

"I'm Lucy," the woman said, extending her hand. "Would you like to dance?"

She looked to Jordan, who simply shrugged. She wasn't going to tell Abby what to do. "Sure. I'd love to."

Abby flashed Lucy one of her warmest smiles as she took the woman's hand and allowed herself to be led a short distance away. It was like a knife to Jordan's chest to watch Abby walk away like it didn't matter. Like *she* didn't matter. She wanted nothing more than to storm out onto the dance floor and pry Abby from Lucy's arms.

"I need a drink," Jordan muttered under her breath, her eyes narrowing.

There was a flash of light in the distance that reflected off the shiny surface of the dance floor. It caught Jordan's attention and kept her thoughts from going darker. There was no camera in sight, and the baseball cap from earlier had been swapped for a fedora, but she knew the man lounging at the bar had to be Max. She had no doubt he'd managed to keep up with their crazy antics the whole day, snapping pictures like a pro. He was fulfilling his end of the bargain, but would she be able to complete hers?

"Buy me a drink?" she grumbled by way of a greeting.

"Sorry, gave all my cash to someone earlier today." He was holding up what looked like a phone, casually looking down at it as if checking some texts, but as she took up position beside him, she could see that he was busy shooting video of Abby being spun in dizzying circles by her new friend. "Oh, wait. That was you."

"Come on, Max. I know you have a tab going." She had no patience for his games right now.

He gave her a sidelong look before lifting his free hand to motion to the bartender. "Fine. But only because you're brilliant."

"Gin and tonic," she said to the bartender, then turned her attention back to Max. "Brilliant, huh? Tell me more."

"Encouraging her to dance with that other woman."

"Lucy?" Jordan snorted. "Bitch. I'm considering breaking her knee caps when the song's over."

"Nah, it's a smart move. Princess on the town,

enjoying the London nightlife with her new girlfriend. What a story this will make!"

"Hey!" Jordan wasn't sure why the word girlfriend, in particular, had provoked her, but it had. "I thought I told you, Max, I'm not exploiting the bisexual angle. It wouldn't be right."

"Wouldn't be right? You're writing a glorified tabloid exposé, and you're worried about what's right? Come on. Romance sells, and it's not like we can use *you*. This Lucy chick is a godsend."

"What do you mean?" Jordan bristled. What exactly was Max implying? Didn't he think she was good enough for Abby? She was better for her than Lucy, that was for *damn* sure, even if Lucy happened to be a better dancer. "What's wrong with me?"

"An undercover reporter tricking an unsuspecting princess into a lesbian love affair? You'd look like a cad."

Something sounding like a cross between a growl and a cough issued from deep within Jordan's throat. It all sounded so ugly when he said it. "There will be no affairs, lesbian or otherwise. Got it? My story is about the hopes and dreams of a princess. I'm keeping it classy. Did you get any good shots today?" she asked, hoping to change the subject.

His face lit up. "So many, although I'm not sure I'll be able to walk tomorrow after the brutal pace you set. There's one shot I got of her with the telephoto lens when you were up on top of the dome at St. Paul's that I swear might win me a Pulitzer."

"As you were so quick to point out earlier, it's a glorified tabloid exposé. I don't think they give Pulitzer's for those."

"Ah, come on, Jordan. You said you were keeping it classy."

Jordan sighed. The truth was, she had no idea what she was doing. This day had filled her with confusion. Spending time with Princess Abigail was supposed to be an assignment, an easy path to a job-saving story, and yet as the day went on, Jordan's emotions were turning her into a mess. Her objectivity was beyond redemption, and if the sudden pang of jealousy she'd felt when Lucy had cut in was any indication, she was dangerously close to falling into—not love, certainly, but something too close to it for Jordan's comfort. *Less like falling,* she scolded herself, *and more like jumping in head first. Like an idiot.* If she wasn't careful, she was going to get all tangled up before this assignment was done.

"So, is this it, then?" Max asked. "Last night with Her Highness?"

"What?" Jordan frowned. "Oh, yeah. I guess so. I don't know."

"How much of my money do you have left?"

"Not much, mate." Jordan slugged him lightly on the shoulder. "Why, you offering more?"

"Not bloody likely. But here." Max pulled out his

wallet and removed an assortment of oddly sized bits of paper. "I stopped by my flat on the way here and grabbed these, in case you can use them."

Jordan rifled through the stack of tickets and vouchers she held in her hand. "Two tickets for the Tower of London, a voucher for a free river cruise on the Thames. What's all this?"

Max shrugged. "Moira's brother was supposed to come for a visit a few weeks ago and had to cancel, but she'd already bought all that. I don't even know what all's there, but I've got tomorrow free, and I thought some photos of her with the crown jewels would be good for the story."

"Thanks, Max. I think I'll be seeing her home tonight, but if not, I can definitely use these."

The song ended, and Max melted into the crowd. Moments later, when Abby found her at the bar, Jordan was there alone. She was still seething over the Lucy incident like a raving maniac, but with supreme effort, she forced her mouth into what she hoped was something resembling a normal person's smile.

"Want a drink?" she offered, inwardly shocked at how well she'd pulled off a casual tone.

Abby, her cheeks flushed from dancing, nodded eagerly. "Whatever you're having."

The bartender put it on Max's tab, and Jordan didn't correct him. Served him right for pointing out the obvious flaw in her brilliant plan, that her objectivity was no match for a beautiful woman. But Max had the pictures, and she'd gleaned enough throughout the day to write the story, so maybe the next thing was to bring the evening to an end. Once Abby had returned to her royal life and was far away from her, maybe she'd be able to get the woman out of her system and regain her focus.

"You ready to go?" Jordan asked as Abby drained the last of her drink, which truth be told had been mostly ice. As an American, this frustrated Jordan to no end. She loved ice, and yet it was nowhere to be found in this country, except when it was taking up valuable space in an expensive drink that could have been filled with more alcohol instead.

Abby frowned, a mixture of confusion and disappointment playing out across her face. "Already?"

"We don't have to," Jordan backtracked, cursing herself as she did. *Way to cave, coward.* "I just thought maybe I'd better get you home. You were really worried this morning about not making them worry."

"Oh." Abby glanced in the direction of the dance floor, and it was clear that leaving was the last thing she wanted to do. Lucy waved from the crowd and Jordan's back stiffened.

"Unless you've made other plans, that is." She hated herself for how petulant she'd just sounded. It's not like she was being jilted on a date. Hell, if the princess went home with Lucy, Jordan should be doing a happy dance. Integrity be damned. That would be the story of the century for sure. Instead, it was all she could do to keep herself from stomping her foot at the prospect that Abby might prefer someone else over her.

"Of course not. Jordan, you don't think I have any interest in Lucy, do you?" Abby placed a hand on Jordan's arm, and the warmth radiated from the spot through the fabric of Jordan's blazer so that she could feel it on her skin.

Jordan snatched her arm away. "Hey, whatever."

"Maybe you're right. We should go." Abby's face was a study in hurt feelings, and Jordan immediately regretted her behavior.

"Abby, I'm sorry. I didn't mean it to sound like that. It's just..." Jordan fumbled for an excuse that would sound better than *I was insanely jealous watching you dance with another woman.* "Look, I'm just not a great dancer."

Jordan had hoped that would soften her up, but it did not. Abby's eyes narrowed. "Well, it was very good of you to bring me here when it's so *obviously* not your thing."

"You're not listening!" Jordan threw her head back in frustration. "All, I meant was, if you want to go back out and dance with Lucy, it's okay with me. This was supposed to be your night to have fun."

Abby's nostril's flared, and her eyes were pure black as she studied Jordan in silence. "You want me to have fun? Then come dance with me."

TWELVE

AS IF ON CUE, as Abby grabbed Jordan's hand, the band struck up a new tune with the sensual quality that marked it as a tango. Abby couldn't hold back her sly smile as she pulled Jordan onto the dance floor. She couldn't have planned the timing better if she'd had a million dollars on her to bribe the band leader. They had chosen the perfect song for seduction, which was exactly what Abby had in mind. That was once in a lifetime luck, the kind money couldn't buy.

"What's that smile for?" Jordan asked. Her steps becoming hesitant the closer they got to the middle of the floor, and Abby felt a thrill of satisfaction at the woman's nervousness.

"Oh, nothing. You know what? I think we can start right here." Abby stopped and took Jordan into a starting position that was appropriate for a tango, placing her right hand firmly on the small of Jordan's back and taking Jordan's right hand with her left, stretching that arm out to the side until it was fully extended.

Jordan rested her left hand clumsily on Abby's shoulder. "Hey, this doesn't feel right. I think you've got it backward."

"No, I've got it exactly right," Abby informed her sweetly, though she was pretty sure Jordan could hear the triumph underneath. "I'll be taking the lead this time."

Abby pulled Jordan closer, their bodies pressed together from chest to hip. Though Jordan was taller, Abby angled her head so she could look her in the eyes. She stepped forward with her left foot, and Jordan took a step back with her right. When Abby stepped forward with her right, Jordan responded by stepping back on her left. She repeated this a few more times, staying in sync with the music, then threw in a hesitation step to see what would happen. Jordan followed along without missing a beat, their bodies moving in perfect unison

"Nicely done." Abby fixed her with a smoldering look, hoping to show Jordan just how attractive she found her, but the conflicted look she saw reflected back in Jordan's eyes surprised her. "What is it? You seem troubled by something. You're not still thinking about Lucy, are you?"

"No...no, of course not."

"Because you have no reason to worry. You're a

natural at the tango." But even as she said it, Abby sensed that Jordan's hesitation went beyond a lack of confidence at being able to execute a few dance moves. Something else was going on. "What's really going on?"

"Nothing."

"You know, I had a dance teacher in high school who used to say that when you're dancing, it's impossible to lie."

"Your high school had dance classes?" Jordan smirked. "What kind of la-di-da school did you go to, anyway?"

"It was my gym class!" Though it was true that she'd gone to an exclusive private school, thanks to her father's money, Jordan's teasing made her feel the need to defend herself. "It was nothing special. Every high school in California offered classes like that."

"Well. California." Jordan said it as though the state alone had proven her point. "It's not exactly Omaha."

"Oh yeah? Well, what did you do for gym class in Omaha?"

"We played dodge ball, as God intended."

This made Abby laugh so much that it took a while for her to realize that Jordan had completely derailed her from her original train of thought. She spun her out with one hand, then spun her back in close. "I was *talking* about the truth, before you interrupted."

Jordan blinked innocently. "Were you?"

"I was," Abby replied with a curt nod. "I think you're hiding something."

"Am I?" Jordan blinked again.

"Yes. Stop doing that."

"Doing what?"

Abby's eyes narrowed. "Answering a question with a question."

"Was I?"

"Yes! You just did it again."

"I did?" When Abby let out a sound like a growling tiger cub, Jordan laughed heartily. "Okay, okay. Just one more question, a serious one this time, and then I'll stop."

The tempo of the music shifted, and Abby performed a hesitation step, then led Jordan into a shallow dip. "Fine. Ask away."

"Why do you care if I'm keeping something from you?"

Abby looked earnestly into Jordan's eyes. "Because whatever it is, you seem troubled by it. I like you, Jordan. If you tell me what's going on, maybe I can help. Goodness knows you've listened to me go on about enough of my problems today."

"Wait. You like me?" Jordan arched her eyebrow in that way she had, and like clockwork Abby felt her knees give way to the point that she stumbled, completely losing count of the rhythm. Jordan chuckled. "I think I'm liking this truth theory of yours. Let's test out another one. I want to know why you decided to stay out with me all day instead of going home after lunch. Is it just because you like me, or is there something else going on?"

Abby's stomach tightened, and she drew a nervous breath. "What do you mean, something else?"

"Now you're doing it."

"Doing what?"

"Oh, no. You can't beat me at this game, Ducky. I *invented* this game. Tell me why you ran away yesterday."

Abby took a few rocking steps to get them both moving in time to the music again. Then she sighed. "I didn't mean to run away. Really I didn't. I'd taken those pills and I was confused. You saw how I was. And then an opportunity presented itself, and I just kind of wandered away."

"Without a plan?"

"A plan? I didn't even have a wallet! No phone, no credit card..." Abby swallowed hard as it truly struck her how much trouble she could have gotten into if Jordan hadn't come along. "Thank you, for coming to my rescue."

"Don't mention it." Jordan gave a little shrug. "So that's it, then. You just wandered away because you could?"

"In part." Abby sighed, knowing it was more complicated than that, but uncertain how much she could share without Jordan knowing who she was. "Sometimes the duties I'm expected to fulfill can feel so stifling. I just wanted to get away from it all for a few hours. I didn't think it through beyond that."

"So, there was no big, blowout fight with your family, or—"

"Oh, no you don't," Abby warned as she led Jordan into a series of grapevine steps across the edge of the dance floor. "I know what you're doing."

Jordan blinked so many times that she was downright batting her eyelashes. There was no other way to describe it. "What am I doing?"

Despite herself, all Abby could do was laugh. "You know exactly what you're doing. You're trying to avoid telling me the truth about what it is that you're not telling me."

"I'm not sure I follow."

"You're following just fine." Abby glanced down at Jordan's feet, which were, in fact, right in step with her own. "Remember, when you're dancing, you have to tell the truth."

"And why is that? You never explained the theory behind why you can't lie when you're dancing."

"Because—" Abby tightened her grip on Jordan's waist, yanking her body toward her—"when you're this close to someone, if they are anything other than completely honest, you can feel it."

Jordan's feet slowed to a stop, no longer dancing. She loosened her grip on Abby's left hand, and her arm drifted to Abby's side. Abby rested her newly freed hand on Jordan's shoulder. "You're right. I do have something to confess."

They stood in place, so close that Abby could hear her suck in her breath and feel the other woman's heart pounding against her chest. "It's okay. You can tell me."

"The truth is..." Jordan let out her breath, slow and shaky. "The truth is that I actually already knew how to tango."

Abby's brain struggled to work out the meaning of Jordan's words, which weren't at all what she'd been expecting. "Huh? You said you hadn't improved in twenty-five years."

"That was jitterbug. I'm talking about the tango. I love to tango." Jordan grinned as she snatched Abby's right arm from her waist and took her into position, locked eyes, and then immediately set off, leading Abby through a set of steps that showed off enough complicated footwork to be the envy of many an Argentine.

Abby's heart raced as she tried to keep up with the intricate moves, and for the most part she managed. Jordan was an excellent lead. "How did you learn to dance like this?"

"There was only one thing my grandma loved more than the jitterbug, and that was a good tango." Jordan spun Abby twice in rapid succession, then stopped her perfectly in place. "When my grandfather's health failed, she needed a partner, and I was the tallest of the grandkids, so naturally, I was nominated."

As she talked, Jordan led Abby into another spin, sweeping her leg out as she came around so when she pulled Abby close to her, Abby's left leg ended up crooked at the knee, sitting high atop Jordan's thigh. Jordan lunged into a deep dip, and the muscles of Abby's inner thighs stretched to their limits as she was pulled into a half split. No sooner was she upright, but Jordan walked her through a wide circle and then halted abruptly so that Abby bumped into her chest before stopping, too. Jordan sought out eye contact, not letting her look away as she repositioned her arms for the next move. Then all of a sudden, Abby felt herself bending back, nearly falling except for the strong, firm hold of Jordan's arm across the small of her back. Jordan held her there for several counts, trailing her free hand lightly from Abby's collarbone, along her chest between her breasts, and all the way to her belly button before she lifted her back upright. Their eyes locked again, and Abby gasped for air as the music came to an end.

It wasn't just the surprise of Jordan's dance prowess that had left her breathless, it was the way her body had responded to Jordan's guiding touch with each new step. She'd never experienced anything quite like it before. Every spot where Jordan had touched her tingled. Between her legs, the stretched muscles burned, but in a way that felt so good, it left her wanting more. Abby could tell without needing a mirror that her face was flushed. It had suddenly become so warm that she quickly stripped off the light-weight cardigan she'd been wearing, panting as the cool night air hit her exposed skin. She'd been staring into Jordan's eyes the whole time, and they were filled with as much desire as Abby herself felt.

"I know you never danced with your grandmother quite like that."

Jordan smiled slyly and did not look away. "I may have picked up a few new moves along the way."

The intensity of their eye contact grew to be too much, until finally Abby looked away. As she did, her attention was caught by a man standing off to one side of the dance floor, where it met with a strip of grass. He wore a crisp, dark suit, which in itself wasn't out of place, but it was something about the way he stood, stiff and alert, along with the almost military precision of his haircut that let her know instantly whom he must be. He was angled in such a way that he couldn't see her, and she could only see one side of him, but she knew if he were to turn, a discreet pin emblazoned with the flag of her father's kingdom would be somewhere on his chest.

Abby shut her eyes, as if doing so might make her invisible. *Not yet,* she whispered inaudibly as she let out her breath. If there was one thing Abby knew in that moment, it was that she wasn't ready to go home. But it wasn't just her royal duties she was trying to avoid. She wasn't ready to walk away from Jordan. Not now. Not until she had a chance to see where things could lead. She sent up another silent plea to anyone or anything in the universe that might be listening and feel inclined to help. *Please, not yet.*

When Abby opened her eyes, Jordan was watching her with a look of concern. "What did you say?"

"Nothing. It's just, it's getting crowded. We should probably head out."

A deep crease formed between Jordan's brows. "You want me to take you home?"

"No." Abby shook her head. She pressed her lips together and looked up at Jordan, feeling oddly shy. "No, I don't want to go home."

Jordan's expression turned suspicious. "You're not hungry again, are you?"

Abby laughed. "No, although given how much I've eaten today, I can see why you thought that."

"Then..." Jordan swallowed, her face a mix of hope and fear. "Then, what?"

"I was just thinking maybe we could go back to your place."

Butterflies swarmed in Abby's stomach as Jordan studied her without speaking. When she did finally find her voice, it came out sounding squeaky, like a mouse. "My place?"

"For a while," Abby encouraged. "If you'd like." Her gaze swept down toward Jordan's chest, and then up again, her long eyelashes fluttering coyly. Surely Jordan knew that she was proposing she spend the night, right? She was positive the attraction was mutual. The way their bodies had communicated just now as they danced left no room for doubt. So why did Jordan look so confused?

There was another excruciatingly silent pause, during which Abby shot a worried glance toward the plainclothes agent, but he evidently hadn't spotted her and had begun to move in the opposite direction. She was safe for the moment, but they needed to leave quickly, before he had a chance to circle back. "Jordan?"

"Huh?" Jordan blinked twice, looking startled. Then finally, she answered, "Um, sure. Why not?"

Abby let out a relieved laugh and grabbed Jordan by the hand, walking briskly from the dance floor and across the grass, toward the exit. As acceptances of propositions to spend the night together went, Jordan's may have lacked finesse, but for right now, it didn't matter. They were safely on their way, unseen, and Abby had at least one more night of freedom to enjoy, and someone to enjoy it with. What more could she really ask for than that?

THIRTEEN

THERE HAD BEEN little doubt in Jordan's mind what Abby was suggesting. It was the most dangerously tempting proposition she'd ever received, and though the response that left her brain had been a polite but firm no, thank you, it had sounded a little different by the time it reached her lips.

Why not?

It was all Jordan could do to keep from stomping her feet as they walked toward the canal path. *Why not? My God, when did you become such a fool?* There were a million reasons why not. Hadn't they been running through her brain on an endless loop all day? They had! She'd just chosen, repeatedly, not to listen. And now here she was, a journalist about to spend the night with the subject of her story—a princess, no less —like it was no big deal! She deserved to lose her career.

The music from the pavilion followed them for a while, gradually growing fainter as they went until there was nothing to be heard except for their own footsteps on the gravel and the lapping of water against the edge of the canal. The darkness had an inky quality, especially along the towpath where there were few lights, and while Jordan had made this walk alone a thousand times, having Abby with her made her suddenly aware of every shadow. The silence took on a menacing quality. Even the narrow boats that lined the canal, which usually looked so quaint during the day, were more sinister in the moonlight. Jordan's heart beat faster with each step, and she couldn't shake the feeling of being followed.

Beside her, Abby was scanning their surroundings with obvious unease. Without warning, she clutched Jordan's arm and pointed to a sprawling green space to their left, where a shadowy figure seemed to crouch beside a bush. "What's that over there?"

Jordan tensed, then let out her breath as she realized that the human shape she was looking at was little more than a jacket and trousers on a stake, stuffed with straw. "Relax. It's just a scarecrow. That's a community garden in there, and I'm guessing that must be where someone has planted a vegetable plot."

"Oh." Though she sounded relieved by the answer, Abby's eyes, nonetheless, continued to dart all around as they walked. She looked terrified.

What were you thinking, dragging Abby through a

place like this? True, it was the most direct route between the pavilion and her flat, but the canal could be an unsavory place at night. A little farther ahead, Jordan eyed a young man who lounged against a lamppost, certain he was selling drugs. This was definitely no place for a princess. Silently, Jordan took Abby's hand and quickened their pace. For the next fifteen minutes, Jordan didn't say a single word, her focus split between getting Abby away from the canal safely, and berating herself for bringing her there in the first place.

With every step, her mind was more made up. As soon as they reached the flat, she would take the last of Max's money and order Abby a cab. It was the only responsible thing to do. She was in no position to keep a crown princess safe, let alone the risk she was taking with her career, and her heart, if Abby stayed the night. It was settled. She was sending her home. Only when they were through the front door did Jordan finally breathe a sigh of relief, but she was surprised to see a deep frown creasing Abby's brow.

"I guess I'll just get my things," Abby said, with more than a hint of anger in her words.

"What? You're leaving?" This should have been welcome news. Hadn't she just decided that was for the best? It was exactly the turn of events that Jordan needed, offering safety for Abby and a way out of the professionally and morally compromising mess she'd gotten herself into. Which is probably why her first instinct was to talk Abby out of leaving, because her instincts since meeting this woman had been absolutely worthless. "But you just got here."

"First, you don't care if I dance with someone else." Abby's eyes were narrow, her lips pressed into a thin, almost invisible line. When she spoke, her voice had the eerie calm that came with simmering rage. She'd held up one finger as she said the word first, which clued Jordan into the probability that there were more points to come. When she held up a second finger, a knot formed in Jordan's stomach. How long was this list likely to be?

"Then you wanted to leave the pavilion. Then you agreed you wanted me to come home with you, only you didn't say two words to me the entire walk back. It's okay. I can take a hint."

"No. That's not what was going on."

"Really? I think it is. And I'd like for you to call me a cab." Abby pulled open the satchel that Jordan had been carrying throughout the day and pulled out the plastic bag that held her tiara. "I don't want to forget this again. Stupid thing. If I hadn't forgotten it earlier, you wouldn't have had to put up with me all day when it was clearly a burden for you." Abby sniffled but didn't bother to try to clear away the tear that streaked down her cheek.

Jordan was overtaken with a rush of panic. Tears were not something she was equipped to handle. Jordan would do anything, absolutely anything, to make it stop. "Come on now, Ducky. I promise I wasn't trying to ignore you."

"Well, you sure did a good job of it for not trying." Abby blinked, and more tears started down her glistening cheeks. "I don't get you. You've been hot and cold all day. Every time I really think we have a connection, you pull away."

"We do have a connection." There was no point in denying it, to herself or to Abby, so Jordan didn't bother to try. "I don't know where it could possibly lead, or the best way to deal with it, but it's there."

"Where it's going?" The creases in Abby's forehead deepened alarmingly. "How to *deal* with it?"

Jordan cringed to hear her own words coming from Abby's mouth. "That didn't come out the way I wanted it to. I only meant, you're just visiting London. You might get away with staying here tonight, but the clock's ticking for when you have to go back."

"It's not like I'll cease to exist, you know. I'm going back to work, not on a one-way mission to Mars." Abby began to fiddle with the bag that held the tiara. She pulled it out and set it on the tea cart, then twisted the plastic bag into a series of knots. It was a habit Jordan had noticed earlier, Abby's need to fidget when she was nervous or excited. Judging by the state of the bag in her hands, her mental state was one of extreme agitation.

"What are you suggesting, exactly, a long-distance relationship? We've known each other for all of twenty-four hours." Even as the words hit her ears, Jordan had a feeling she would regret saying them.

Sure enough, a fresh round of tears made their way down Abby's cheeks. "I don't know what I'm suggesting. I'm not thinking clearly. You're right. This is completely impossible, and heading nowhere, and I should go."

Abby contemplated the tiara, turning the glittering object over in her hands as she spoke. With the bag, which had been holding it, a wreck, and no place else to put it, she stuck the thing on her head and took a step toward the door. With that single step, Jordan was overtaken with a rush of panic. She hadn't been certain of many things in her life, but she knew without a doubt, that she couldn't let the woman walk out that door.

"Abby, please, don't go." Perhaps it was Jordan's use of her real name or just the urgency in her voice, but doubt played in Abby's eyes.

"I don't want to go." Her voice was small, and the tears on her face shone as brightly as the diamonds in her hair.

"You don't have to," Jordan assured her. It was stupid, and reckless, and would probably lead to professional ruin. She didn't care.

Jordan moved toward Abby, and Abby fell into her arms. Jordan stroked the back of Abby's neck, where the once neat chignon had come completely undone. "Please don't cry. You can stay as long as you like."

"Are you sure?" Abby snuffled against Jordan's shoulder, her words mixed with hot breath and tears. "You really don't want me to go?"

"Of course, I don't want you to go." As far as Jordan was concerned in that moment, she never wanted Abby to leave. Jordan eased Abby's head from her shoulder, cupping her chin between her hands. Abby's eyes shone, and Jordan's own eyes began to burn with unshed tears. "I've been in London for years, and today was the best day I've ever had here."

It was the truth. In fact, not only was it the best day she'd ever spent in London, it was quite possibly the best day she'd ever had, period. Try as she might, she couldn't remember another one that could compare. And the rapid pounding of her heart left little doubt that Abby was the reason why. What more did she need to know than that?

An instant later, their lips met, soft and sweet. Jordan wasn't sure who made the first move. She didn't care. All her thoughts were lost in the kiss, all her worries gone. Her job, her visa—what did it really matter? All she knew was that when Abby's arms were around her, it felt as if nothing in the world could ever go wrong. She didn't want the feeling to end.

Still deep in the kiss, Jordan reached out one hand and freed the Murphy bed from its cupboard. For once, it descended into position without any issues. Jordan took it as a welcome sign to continue. She slid her hand along Abby's side along the smooth cotton lawn of her dress until it was beneath the red cardigan, easing it off Abby's shoulder. Abby moaned as it slipped from her arm, and she quickly freed her other arm and let the cardigan fall to the floor. Jordan's blazer followed shortly thereafter, landing in a messy heap. She unbuttoned her pink silk blouse, then pulled off her trousers, and let them join the blazer on the floor. There was no question it would all have to be dry-cleaned after this, but that was a small price to pay. She stood in a pair of light blue cotton bikini underwear and a bra made of soft, neutral-colored T-shirt material. She wasn't one for fancy underthings.

Jordan shivered as the chill of the air hit her exposed skin. It was one of the things she hated about the basement flat, how cold it was even long after days had started to grow warm. "Is it too cold in here for you?" she asked as her fingertips traced the tiny bumps of gooseflesh along Abby's arms. "Come closer and I'll keep you warm."

Abby wrapped her arms around Jordan's waist, her fingers splayed across the naked skin as she ran her hands slowly up Jordan's back. She rested her head on Jordan's shoulder as Jordan found the zipper at the back of the yellow dress and inched it down. Abby stood still as Jordan unfastened the gold buckle on the leather belt, and then the dress dropped, adding to the growing laundry pile at their feet. Very carefully, Jordan lifted the tiara from Abby's head and placed it on the tea cart.

Jordan had seen Abby's body before, just that morning, in fact, but the circumstances were very different now, and she couldn't stop herself from taking a moment to admire her thoroughly. Abby was mostly naked, with just a borrowed pair of underwear, strikingly similar to what Jordan wore, as her only covering. Her skin was pale as ivory, with just the slightest hint of the California tan she'd once had remaining across her shoulders and chest. Jordan traced her finger along the faint ghost of a strap-line at her shoulder, which emphasized the fact that she wore no bra. If she'd been wearing one when she'd run away, it had been left behind in the dressing room of the burlesque show. It didn't matter. She had the perfect size breasts, full enough to give her an alluring curve at the bust, but small enough that she didn't strictly need the support.

Jordan trailed her fingers farther down the imaginary strap, over the swell of Abby's breast, and circled her delicate nipple, which hardened beneath her touch into a small pink pearl. Their eyes locked, and Jordan moved in for another kiss. Her attention wrapped up in exploring Abby's lips with her tongue, Jordan lowered them onto the mattress a little more clumsily than she'd intended. Their bottoms bounced on the edge, and it was at this moment that the Murphy bed chose to let out a loud warning snap. "Damn it!" Jordan cursed in a rough whisper. She eased herself a few inches to the center, then sprawled out on her side, and when the bed didn't protest, Jordan let out a shaky laugh. "I think it's okay."

Laughing as well, Abby slid to the center and stretched her body out beside Jordan's. She turned her face toward her and kissed her lips softly. Jordan lost herself in the moment, aware of nothing but the intoxicating feel of Abby's mouth on hers, their bodies sliding gently against one another in a constant, steady rhythm. But when Jordan went to place her leg over Abby's, the Murphy bed quickly reminded her who was boss with another deafening snap, like a branch breaking off a giant oak.

"Jordan?" Abby's voice trembled. "I don't want to end up in the wall again."

Jordan muffled her frustrated scream with a nearby pillow. "I hate this bed."

Instead of expressing her own frustration or anger, Abby surprised Jordan with a chuckle. "Don't take this the wrong way, but is this the first time you've brought a woman back to your apartment?"

Jordan looked at her steadily, arching an eyebrow. "Like, ever?"

Abby laughed some more. "No, that's not what I meant."

"Because believe me, I'm aware that I've handled this whole evening so smoothly that it would be easy for you to make that mistake." At that moment, Jordan wanted nothing more than to curl up in a ball and die of embarrassment, but she feared how the bed would respond if she tried it.

Abby placed a calming hand on her shoulder. "Jordan, that isn't what I meant at all. It's the bed I'm questioning, not you."

"No, as a matter of fact, I haven't brought anyone back since I moved to this flat. That's not to say there hasn't been anyone. There've been lots. Tons." Jordan groaned the minute the words were out of her mouth. This was not going to go over well.

Abby gave her a withering look. "I think I liked your answer better before you added the words lots and tons, just so you know."

"That was just my ego talking. There haven't been lots. Or tons. For reasons," she muttered more to herself than to Abby, "that are painfully obvious at the moment." With a defeated sigh, Jordan eased herself off the bed, a chorus of suspicious noises coming from deep within its springs.

Abby rose, too, with a questioning look. "Where are you going?"

"To find us some pajamas."

"You're giving up, just like that?"

"This evening is clearly not going as planned. What else am I going to do?" Jordan gave the corner of the Murphy bed a kick. Maybe she should be thanking it, instead. If it hadn't been such a piece of junk, she'd be halfway to destroying her last shot at saving her career right now. She didn't feel all that thankful.

"I can't believe you're willing to let an inanimate object get the better of you." Abby eyed her bemusedly, and Jordan could feel the heat rush to her cheeks. "Stand clear for a minute, and let me try."

Abby grasped the mattress by one end and lifted it upright, giving it several determined shoves until it landed on its side on the floor. As soon as the platform was free of its weight, it sprung back into the wall. Supporting the mattress with her shoulder, Abby closed the doors, then let the bed fall to the floor. "There. Still want to give up?" All Jordan could manage by way of response was a shake of the head. Abby smiled. "Good."

The next thing Jordan knew, Abby had her flat on her back, pinning her to the mattress as she straddled her torso, both arms held solidly above Jordan's head by a hand pressed firmly on each wrist. Jordan gaped. *How the hell did this tiny woman get the better of me?*

"Jujitsu," Abby replied, as if able to read her mind.

"Another gym class at your fancy high school?" Jordan asked, with far more swagger than she felt.

"No, this was a little more recent." She didn't elaborate, but Jordan could guess that becoming a princess may have had something to do with her sudden interest in being able to protect herself. "Given my size, I needed to learn a form of self-defense where I could use my opponent's strength against them."

"I guess that makes me your opponent?" Jordan

quipped, not at all liking the idea of her strength being used against her.

"Hardly." Abby flashed a sexy smile. "More of a dance partner."

"Well, that's a relief, because I have some plans for us." Jordan made a move to roll Abby over so that she could be on top, but she barely managed to move an inch. "What the hell?"

Abby giggled. "Did I mention I was fairly good at jujitsu?"

Jordan wriggled in frustration, feeling about as mighty as a minnow on a hook. "Okay, you've made your point. Now will you let me move?"

"Why, so you can take control? I don't think so. As it happens, I have some plans for us, too." The look Abby gave her was one of pure seduction that sent a shot of searing heat blazing through Jordan's core. Even so, she had to give her argument one more try.

"Oh, come on, Ducky. Be reasonable."

"I'll be honest, reasonable has never been one of my top qualities. Especially in bed." Abby dipped her head, her mouth landing next to Jordan's left ear, her teeth soon nibbling lightly at the fleshy lobe as shivers raced up and down Jordan's spine. She stopped just long enough to whisper, "I'll be taking the lead for this dance."

Jordan sucked in her breath as Abby's body flattened against hers, her mouth moving down her neck, pausing to circle her tongue just above Jordan's collarbone at the sensitive spot where her pulse throbbed beneath the skin. Any remaining arguments, or indeed any coherent thoughts at all, were expunged from her brain. Every inch of her body cried out at once, begging to be touched by Abby's tongue with the same thoroughness that single point on her neck was receiving. Abby's body scooted down as her mouth moved lower along her chest, stopping when she could go no farther without releasing Jordan's arms.

Abby tilted her head until she could catch Jordan's eye. "If I let go of your arms, do you promise to behave?"

Jordan swallowed hard, nodding silently. She would promise whatever she needed to promise, just as long as whatever Abby had been doing with her mouth before would resume. Her eyes twinkling with amusement, Abby loosened the pressure on Jordan's wrists and slid her hands down the length of her arms, then cupped her hands beneath Jordan's shoulders. She gave them a squeeze, at first gentle and then with deepening pressure, her fingers kneading every trace of tension from the muscles until Jordan lay limply on top of the sheets. Only then did Abby continue her descent, hands first, followed by mouth and tongue.

She stopped at Jordan's right breast, cupping it into her palm as she teased the nipple with her thumb. Jordan inhaled deeply, a little surprised to realize that she'd been remembering to breathe so far. She watched as Abby closed her lips around her hardened bud, then shut her eyes to focus completely on the tendrils of electricity that radiated out from her breast and headed on a twisting pathway through her belly toward a spot hidden deep between her legs. It seemed almost as if it must be glowing, a visible roadmap just beneath her skin, because just moments later, Abby was following it perfectly, making the downward journey with her tongue.

What had started as a tingling became a throbbing inside her as Abby traveled relentlessly lower, her arms encircling Jordan's hips, her fingers now pressing into her buttocks with the same massaging motions she'd used on Jordan's shoulders. If she'd been relaxed before, she'd melted into little more than a Jordan-shaped puddle now. How she didn't just evaporate completely was a mystery. She was barely aware of Abby's head pressing low against her pelvis, or of her legs drifting apart in response, until the moment Abby's mouth reached its intended destination. In that instant, all of Jordan's bones returned to her body, holding her rigid as Abby's tongue made its first swipe across her sensitive folds.

The rest became a blur, a steady rhythm made up of fingers stroking, of tongue lapping, following a choreography that took their steps from subtle teasing to sublime torture, until the moment Jordan cried out as her body seized and shook with a release over which she had no control. She grasped Abby's hair, tugging her upward, reveling in the feel of her weight, slight as it was, on top of her. Her mouth yielded unquestioningly to Abby's, lost in their kisses. Only as the sensations of her body began to fade did Jordan's ability to think return. When it did, she was terrified.

Oh my God, what have I done?

Jordan's body continued to tremble, but the cause was no longer unbridled ecstasy but unadulterated fear. Being a journalist was all Jordan had ever cared about. She'd put that ahead of everything else. But tonight, she'd crossed the uncrossable line, compromised her integrity, slept with the subject of her assignment. Part of her wanted to blame Abby for taking control, but the truth was that in the heat of the moment, Jordan had yielded willingly. Without her career, how would she even know who she was?

Jordan's heart pounded valiantly under the stress of this question, the force of all that blood returning to her brain making the sound of a rushing river in her ears at it raced through her head. *Too little, too late,* she thought bitterly. Where had all that blood been a few minutes ago, deserting her brain when she'd needed it most, leaving it starved and prone to poor judgment. She squirmed, and Abby's body shifted on top of hers in response.

"Ready for more?" Sleepiness made her words heavy as she reached down with one hand and stroked Jordan's thigh.

"No, not for me." Jordan quickly pressed her hand

over Abby's, stopping her. "I'm really more of a one-and-done kind of girl. But...you?"

Abby yawned loudly, then burrowed her head against Jordan's shoulder. "So tired, and so comfy. I can't believe I'm saying this, but I think right now, what I really want most is sleep."

Abby's eyes had fluttered closed halfway through her sentence, and as she drifted into a light sleep, Jordan breathed a sigh of relief that at least she could put off the morally fraught issue of reciprocation. As for the rest of this mess she'd created, unless she could figure out a way to correct her mistake and salvage a headline-grabbing story from this disaster, Jordan's career at the *London Crier* was done for good. Yet even now, with Abby's head resting on her chest, their bodies rising and falling together with each tandem breath, there was a part of Jordan that questioned whether something that felt so perfect could possibly be a mistake.

FOURTEEN

"A HOP-ON, HOP-OFF BUS?" Abby looked askance at Jordan, which just seemed to further the woman's resolve.

"Yes. You'll enjoy it."

"But, it's so touristy."

"I know. And you're a tourist." Jordan held up an array of tickets like a fan. "Tower of London, a river cruise. There're a few other things in here, too. We have a whole day ahead of us, and I promised to show you everything London had to offer, so chop-chop."

"I don't know. It's just a tower. Wouldn't you rather..." She paused to clear her throat, looking suggestively at the rumpled sheets that surrounded her on the mattress on the floor. "You know, stay in?"

"Don't be silly. It's the Tower of London! You have to see it."

"But—" Abby sighed. A bus tour was about the last

thing she would have chosen to do this morning. She'd woken up with Jordan's naked body spooned against her, her chest against Abby's back and their legs entwined. To say she'd been incredibly turned on was an understatement. But Jordan had hopped out of bed moments later without so much as a good morning kiss, and when she'd emerged from the bathroom, she was already showered and dressed. Abby would never have suspected that when it came to sex, Jordan would take the concept of one and done to such an extreme. She had yet to decide exactly what to make of it. Should she be worried? Insulted?

"Fine." Abby assumed there could be could be no mistaking the huffiness in her delivery, even for a woman as seemingly clueless as Jordan. "We'll take the hop-on, hop-off bus. Let me go get ready."

Abby picked her dress up from where it had been tossed the night before. It was creased in the back from sitting and a bit of a mess overall from the hours it had spent on the floor, but it was clean, and given her limited options, it would have to do for another day. One more day. That's what she had decided on last night. She would give herself another twenty-four hours before even thinking about what to do next. One more day with Jordan, one more day in London, one more day where no one knew she was Princess Abigail.

She put on the clean underwear Jordan had provided, and looked at herself in the bathroom mirror. Standing there in plain cotton bikinis and no bra, she didn't look like a princess. Not even a little bit. She looked like a normal woman, whose life was all her own. She slipped on the yellow dress and smoothed her hair into a high ponytail, like any other American tourist might do. Today, she was just plain old Abby Mallard, about to go sightseeing with a charming and attractive woman who made her smile. What more could she want out of life than that?

"Here," Jordan said as they were heading out the front door. She handed her a floppy straw hat and a pair of large sunglasses with white plastic frames.

"What are they?"

"I think a previous tenant left these in the cupboard. They should be good for keeping the sun off on top of the bus."

Though Abby raised an eyebrow as she donned the items, privately she was willing to admit that wearing them was kind of fun. With her sunglasses and wide-brimmed hat, Abby felt like a movie star in disguise. When she settled into her seat on the top of the double-decker bus some time later, she wondered if anyone would recognize her. Would her father's agent still be looking for her today? She'd caught a glimpse of her name on a newspaper as they'd walked to the bus stop. No photo, thank goodness—there was a reason she kept the number of photos she provided to the media to a minimum—but the headline suggested that they were keeping mum about her disappearance and sticking to the story that she was ill. It had been over thirty-six hours since she'd wandered out of Kensington Palace, and Abby wondered just how much longer she could keep her whereabouts a secret.

As the bus approached the Tower of London stop, Jordan rose and made her way to the stairs. Abby followed. Once they were inside the grounds, Abby had to admit that Jordan had been right. This wasn't any old tower. The history was so thick in the air that Abby could almost see the ghosts of the past rising up from the ground. As they paused in front of Traitor's Gate, where prisoners had once approached the castle by boat, Abby could hear their pleas of innocence in her imagination. When she stared at the spot where Anne Boleyn had lost her head, it was all she could do not to cover her own exposed neck with her hands in sympathy. She shivered and pulled her cardigan closer to her chest, though the day was sunny and mild. She knew that times had changed, but this place reminded her of just how brutal monarchies could be. *And like it or not, I'm a part of it.*

"You okay?" Jordan asked, placing a hand on Abby's shoulder.

"Yeah, I'm fine." It was a lie, but it wasn't like she could easily explain the feeling she had of being haunted by her murdered royal ancestors. Jordan would think she was completely loony.

Jordan looked at her questioningly, but let it pass without comment. "Maybe we should go inside for a while. The Crown Jewels are nearby, and they're pretty spectacular."

Abby flashed as bright a smile as she could manage. "Sure. Who doesn't like jewels, right?"

The entrance was an arched doorway between two imposing towers. A guard stood sentry in a booth to one side, and though his uniform had the antiquated look associated with palace guards the world over, this one sporting the bright red coat and tall fur hat that made him look like an extra in a movie, the rifle that rested on his shoulder appeared to be both very modern and convincingly lethal. Abby's father's palace had similarly dressed guards, sporting similar weapons, and she had yet to decide each time she passed them whether they made her feel more or less at ease. She felt a twinge of panic as they neared the door, convinced that the guard would recognize her and stop her, but his unblinking stare remained stoically fixed on some point in the distance and she entered the building without incident.

To Abby's surprise, the first room contained no jewels at all, but presented pictures and histories of all the kings and queens on large placards. She knew she should care more than she did, given that they were distant ancestors, but she found herself stifling a yawn. So many serious faces. Did even one of them look happy? Actually, there was one, King Edward VIII. In his photo he wore a top hat and morning coat, and sported a wide, toothy grin. *It figures,* Abby thought.

Of all the people on display in this gallery, he was the only one who'd been smart enough to escape his fate. Abdicating for love. Was that type of thing still an option for a modern monarch-to-be? *Asking for a friend...*Abby glanced across the room at Jordan and felt heat rise into her face. It was much too soon to put a label on what she felt for this woman. They'd only just met, after all. But the possibility that it might become love couldn't be dismissed. If she went back to her father's kingdom, and the never-ending parade of so-called suitable bachelors that she was expected to meet, how would she ever be able to find out?

Abby felt restless, like the walls of the exhibition room were closing in on her. Jordan, however, was engrossed in reading the placards, so rather than disturb her, Abby wandered into the next room. It was dark inside, except for a film that was being projected onto the far wall. Abby moved closer to the center, and as she did, suddenly all of the walls were transformed into a giant movie screen. Her breath caught as a larger-than-life-size scene of the queen's coronation surrounded her from every side, and she felt like she was trapped in the middle of the crowd in Westminster Abbey.

The speakers buzzed, and the sound of trumpets shook the room. An archbishop, dressed in robes of cream and gold, began to speak, and though the crackling of the recording betrayed its age, Abby knew what was being said then would be exactly the same if it were happening today. An impossibly young-looking Queen Elizabeth sat on a throne. She wore a dress of pure white, with a purple robe lined with ermine covering her slender shoulders and a glittering crown of diamonds on her head that was larger than anything Abby had ever imagined. She was no expert on crowns, but her own tiara had been heavy enough at a fraction of this size. A crown like the one worn by the queen had to have been twenty pounds or more. She was surprised the young woman was able to keep her head from bowing under its weight.

The queen began to speak, but in Abby's head it was no longer archival footage she was watching, but her own future. It was her hand that held the coronation pen to sign the oath, and her name that was signed into an ornate, leather-bound book. She was the one being handed an orb and scepter, and around whose shoulders was placed a golden robe. The room spun and Abby closed her eyes tightly, but she could still feel the eyes of a thousand spectators watching her. Gasping for air, she raced from the room and collided with Jordan, who was just entering.

"What's going on?" Though the lighting was too dim to see very much, Abby could hear the alarm in Jordan's voice. "The room with the jewels is the other way."

"I just need some air. I'll be back in a minute."

She continued to the entrance, not stopping until she was outside and could feel the warmth of sunlight on her face. She closed her eyes and breathed in slowly, willing her heart to stop racing.

"Excuse me?" It was a man's voice, belonging, she assumed to one of the yeoman who conducted the tours of the grounds. Perhaps he'd seen her hasty exit from the building and had come to check on her.

"I'm fine," she answered without opening her eyes. "Just a little claustrophobia." It was a less complicated excuse than trying to explain how watching a coronation that had happened over sixty years ago had sparked an existential crisis by reminding her how unprepared she was to ever be a queen.

"I'm glad to hear it, Your Royal Highness."

Abby's eyes flew open. Instead of being dressed like he'd stepped off a bottle of Beefeater Gin as she'd been expecting, the man in front of her wore a crisply tailored dark suit. The only thing that gave away that he was not just a businessman passing through the Tower grounds on his lunch break was the flag of her father's kingdom that he wore as a tiny pin on his lapel. She'd seen him the night before, at the pavilion. Her father's agent had caught up with her at last.

She giggled nervously. "You must have the wrong person."

His gaze was level, unwavering. "I'm quite certain I do not, Princess Abigail."

Abby swallowed. There would be no fooling him. "What do you want?"

"To make certain you're safe, of course."

"I told you, I'm just fine."

"Good. Then you'll have no trouble following me out front. There's a car waiting."

He lifted his arm, probably to gesture in the direction of the street with the aforementioned car, but in her mind she saw instead a hand holding a crown. She could all but feel the weight of it on her head, her neck tensing as if about to snap. If she got in that car, there would be no stopping it. She held her ground firmly. "I'm afraid I can't do that."

"The countess is worried."

"I'm sorry to hear it, but that's not my problem."

"Your family is worried." There was a glint in his eyes as she hesitated, as if he knew he'd stumbled on the right approach to make her do what he asked. "Your parents are concerned for your health."

"They don't know I've run away?"

"No. Not yet. They think you fainted at the reception on Friday night. They know how stressful the prospect of this state visit was for you, going alone, and they are preparing to travel to London to be by your side for it."

"They?" Abby frowned. "You mean my mother."

"No. Both of them. Your father insisted on it."

Her heart clenched. "But he can't! The doctor warned him." That was the whole reason she'd made this trip alone, because her father was too weak to travel. Now he was taking a risk, and it was all her fault. "Tell him I'm fine. There's no need for them to come here."

"Forgive me, Your Highness, but your father is a difficult man to persuade. It would be better for everyone if you just came back with me now."

Abby thought of Jordan, waiting for her inside. She felt stretched thin, her heart being pulled in two directions at once. "I can't. Not yet. I just need more time." *Not that I have any idea what I'll do with that time, or how I'll ever manage to force myself to go back to royal life when it's over...*

"How much time?"

Abby looked at the man in surprise. Frankly, she'd figured she was about two seconds away from being handcuffed and tossed into a waiting van. She hadn't expected him to be willing to negotiate. "A week?"

He laughed. "Impossible. The official story from the palace is that you were overcome with travel fatigue yesterday and had to take the day off to rest. Your parents have been told it was nerves from the large crowd at the reception. We're already straining credibility by canceling your schedule for a second day. An illness that lasts a week will attract the attention of every news outlet on the planet. But I'm not unreasonable. I can give you until tomorrow."

"Tomorrow? That's totally unreasonable. Say I have the flu. That will buy a few days, at least."

"It isn't flu season."

"I don't care. Tell my parents to stay where they

are. Tell them I'm fine. I'll be in touch with you by Wednesday, I promise."

"Not Wednesday. Tomorrow night. And you won't be in touch. You'll be back at the embassy, ready to wake up in your own bed bright and early on Tuesday morning to resume your schedule, or your father will hear every detail of what you've been up to these last few days."

Abby swallowed. "What do you mean by every detail?"

"Your Highness, do you truly believe that you could just wander away from Kensington Palace and no one would look for you? Do you know how many surveillance cameras there are in this city, or how many special agents are working in the embassy? I've been tailing you since I spotted you buying that dress in the Portobello Road market on Saturday morning. I appreciate that you bought such a nice, bright color. It made my job much easier."

Abby ran her hand over the bright lemon and cherry fabric and groaned inwardly. What a terrible runaway she'd turned out to be. She tried to remember everything that had happened since Saturday morning. He knew about her dancing at the pavilion with both Lucy and Jordan, and about staying the night at Jordan's, though hopefully not everything that had happened between them. Mercifully, the secret of the burlesque costume she could take with her to her grave. She breathed a sigh of relief on that front, but she couldn't pretend that he didn't have the upper hand. "Fine. I'll be back in my bed by the time the sun comes up on Tuesday morning."

"And you should take this, Your Highness." He held out his hand, and immediately Abby recognized her mobile phone. "You'll need it to alert the embassy of your arrival so that they can escort you to your apartment, and also to get in touch with me if you encounter any problems between now and then."

Abby took the phone and slid it into the pocket of her dress, and as she did so, she heard her name being called from a distance. She turned her head, searching for the source, and when she turned back a second later, the man was gone, though she thought she caught a glimpse of his suit fabric in a tour group that was heading toward the exit. She heard her name again, and this time she saw Jordan approaching from the other side of the building that held the Crown Jewels. Concern was etched across her features, and Abby felt a stab of guilt, knowing she was the cause.

"There you are!" Jordan took the last few steps at double speed, closing the distance between them. "I got through the whole exhibit, but you never caught up. Have you been out here the whole time?"

Abby nodded. "I was feeling dizzy inside."

"Do we need to go back to the flat?"

Abby shot a surreptitious glance in the direction that the man had disappeared. There was no sign of him, nor of anyone else who might work for her father.

"No. I'm much better now. But I think I've had enough of the Tower for today. Bunch of stuffy royalty."

"Not a fan of royalty, huh? We still have the cruise on the Thames. How does that sound? Or would that be too much for you?"

"No. In fact, that would be perfect." In the event they changed their mind about grabbing her and stuffing her into a waiting van, Abby felt fairly sure that her father's men would at least hesitate to follow her onto a boat.

"In that case, shall we?" Jordan held out her arm and Abby hooked hers around it at the elbow, feeling a surge of giddiness at the romantic gesture. Whatever odd mood Jordan had woken up in this morning, it seemed to have passed, which boded well for the evening ahead. Abby patted her pocket, heavy from her newly-retrieved phone, with all of its contacts and accounts. If this might be one of their last evenings together, it needed to be special, and she was already beginning to form a plan.

FIFTEEN

THE TOUR BOAT at the end of the dock was not exactly a luxury yacht. There were fancier ones nearby, sleek and almost futuristic in their design, built for speed and style. The one that waited for them was more like a flat platform that was furnished with folding stadium seats, with a clear roof that could retract in good weather by way of a rolling mechanism similar to a garage door. Jordan surveyed it with an unmistakable sense of disappointment. As soon as she had the chance, she planned to murder Max. Why had he thought this would be a good idea?

"Sorry about the boat," Jordan mumbled as they boarded. "I know it's probably not what you expected."

"Don't be silly," Abby assured her. "I'm sure it will be fun."

Jordan studied Abby's face for signs of displeasure, but she seemed genuinely content. Jordan found it odd. Here she was a princess, and yet the woman had yet to throw a hissy fit, demand to speak to a manager, or wonder out loud whether people would behave differently if they knew who her father was. It was not, Jordan reflected, the type of behavior she'd been led to expect from the royals, and she could only assume that Abby was unique. Not all princesses would be this understanding in the same situation. Hell, she'd had more than a few girlfriends who *weren't* princesses who wouldn't have been this understanding.

Jordan found an empty row of seats and ushered Abby in. "Would you like the one closest to the water?"

"Thank you." Abby took her seat, crossing one leg over the other and treating Jordan to an enticing glimpse of skin before she had a chance to smooth her skirt.

"Can you save the one next to you for a minute? I need to find the loo."

"You mean the bathroom?" Abby shook her head with obvious amusement. "You and those British phrases of yours. I sure hope you like it here, because you really *won't* fit in if you ever go back."

"Yeah, no kidding." Jordan smiled weakly as she turned toward the rear of the boat. She spotted Max's baseball cap all the way in the back, beside a set of doors that, whether called a loo, a bathroom, a restroom, or anything else, led to an unsavory set of facilities that she was grateful she did not actually need to use.

"Max, what the hell were you thinking with this boat? You made it sound like it was going to be something nice," Jordan scolded once they'd slipped out of Abby's range of sight. "Are you sure this glorified raft is seaworthy?"

Max shrugged. "It was meant to be for Moira's brother. I wasn't exactly looking for a sunset cruise with champagne, now was I?"

"Well, congratulations, mate, because this is *definitely* not that."

"Look, it doesn't matter. What's important is that I can get some great shots from back here of her looking at the sights. And since you didn't get her in front of the Crown Jewels, you owe me that much."

Jordan grimaced. "Sorry about that."

"I went through the exhibit three times, you know. The guards were starting to give me looks."

"What was I supposed to do?" Jordan countered. "She didn't want to go back in."

"It's fine. Just make sure when you get off the cruise, you take a nice stroll through St. James's Park. I have a few ideas. Oh, and this." He reached into his pocket and handed Jordan a business card for an upscale restaurant located in the Shard building. "The owner owes me a favor for some publicity shots I took for their website a while back. Call that number, and tell them what time you'll be arriving, and they'll have a table ready, and dinner and drinks on the house."

"Thanks, mate."

Max smiled broadly, his eyes twinkling. "I should be thanking you. Do you have any idea how much this story is worth?"

"Other than my job?"

"Word on the street is several tabloids are looking for photos of the princess. Apparently, they're not buying the official story that she's ill. This could be way bigger than either of us dreamed."

Swallowing hard, Jordan shoved the restaurant's card in her pocket, but not without an accompanying pang of guilt. She knew the place, though it was well out of her price range for anything more than a cocktail. With dim lighting and a panoramic view of the city, it oozed romance. Taking her to dinner at a place like that would send all sorts of messages to Abby that Jordan had no business sending.

When she returned to the seat Abby was saving for her, she was greeted with a warm smile, which only made the guilt intensify.

"So, what are we going to see on this cruise?" Abby asked.

"Pretty much the same things we saw on our bikes yesterday," Jordan informed her, "but in reverse order. And possibly not going by you as fast."

"It was your idea to race," Abby pointed out.

"Oh, was it?" Jordan asked. She remembered the incident as being a bit more of a joint decision.

Abby nodded. "You're very competitive. It's something I've noticed about you."

"You're saying *I'm* the competitive one?" Jordan's eyes widened. *If that isn't the pot calling the kettle black...*

"Extremely."

"I see." The smirk Jordan had barely kept off her face was crystal clear in her tone. "And what else have you noticed about me?"

"Well, you're very considerate."

"Really?" Jordan registered surprise, having expected more of Abby's teasing instead of an honest answer.

"Yes, you are. You're always opening doors for me, and you've insisted on paying for everything yesterday and today. It's really sweet. Chivalrous, almost."

"Please, don't stop there." Jordan deadpanned, making Abby laugh. "Feel free to continue."

"Okay. You know a lot about the history of the city, and I can tell that you love living here. And..." Abby hesitated, her expression growing more serious, "I'm not sure why, but I have feeling you don't like your job very much."

For the second time in as many minutes, Jordan was taken aback by an insight she hadn't expected to hear. "Why's that?"

"Because you never talk about it. I dated this guy

in college—oh, wait. It's rude to talk about the guys I've dated in the past, isn't it? Or the women I've dated, for that matter."

"Of course not. Go ahead." Was she about to get a full rundown of the love life of Princess Abigail? The part of Jordan that would always be a journalist first and foremost wished she could take out a notebook and pen. This could be quite the scoop.

"Okay. Well, anyway, this guy, Ted was his name, and he worked for one of those companies that sells products at parties. Multilevel marketing, they called it."

"You mean, like one of those pyramid scheme places?" Jordan gave her a teasingly shocked look. "What kind of shady guys did you used to date?"

"Oh, don't ask. My only defense is that it was college. The point is, Ted loved his job. He talked about it all the time. When we were in the car for more than a few minutes, which was every day because this was LA, and the traffic was always terrible, he'd put on these motivational talks that the company would give him to listen to."

"That sounds like hell."

"Oh, it was. That relationship ended for a reason, believe me. Granted he was an extreme example, but I find most people, when you first meet them, like to talk about their jobs. Yet in the two days we've spent together, you've barely mentioned your job at all. So that makes me think you don't like it very much."

Jordan's shoulders stiffened. Abby had hit a nerve with that one, though not for exactly the reason she'd suggested. Jordan loved her job, but right now Abby *was* her job, and she wasn't liking that fact one bit. It felt disloyal. "You know, you haven't mentioned your job much, either."

Abby shrugged, and it seemed to Jordan that she'd also hit a nerve. "There's not much to say. It's a job."

Jordan let the conversation drop without further comment, but not without making a mental note of her sullenness. She'd assumed this whole time that Abby had ventured away from the palace on a lark, just wanting some fun in London, but now she wondered if there was something more to it. For someone who seemed to see the good in just about everything, even this rickety floating raft of a tour boat, the woman suddenly appeared deeply dissatisfied. It made Jordan wonder, why exactly had Abby run away? The answer to *that* would make an amazing piece of investigative reporting. It wasn't the type of story the new management at the *Crier* would want to print, and it would take her so long to write it that she'd definitely be kicked out of the country before it was done, but it would be a worthwhile piece of journalism—one that she could be proud of.

Beside her, Abby had gone silent and seemed to be staring at the churning water beside the boat. This brooding mood was unlike the Abby Jordan had come to know, and it worried her. "There's London Bridge,"

Jordan said, pointing to the landmark and hoping it might snap her out of her mood. Indeed, Abby perked right up, but her face clouded over the moment she looked where Jordan had pointed.

"That's London Bridge? That's not what I was picturing. Not at all."

It was possibly the first real criticism Jordan had heard from her over anything she'd seen so far. "It's been rebuilt a few times."

"But, which bridge is the one with the big towers?"

"Tower Bridge." Jordan hoped her answer had been delivered relatively snark free. It hadn't been easy, although confusing the two bridges was a mistake a lot of tourists made.

"Well, where's *that* one?" Abby wrinkled her nose, still petulant.

Jordan chuckled. "Behind us. Quite a way back, so you won't be able to see it."

Abby, who had started to turn in her seat, turned back around with a pout. "How did I miss it?"

"I have no idea. It's right next to the Tower of London. You should have been able to see it when we got on the boat."

"I can't believe I didn't notice."

"That's okay." Jordan tamped down the guilt and forced a smile. "You'll see it tonight at dinner."

"Dinner?" Abby's brow creased. "I didn't realize you'd made plans."

"There's a nice place in the Shard—you know, that

really pointy building on the other side of the river? It's got an amazing view, and I was thinking we could head over so we could catch the lights coming on at Tower Bridge." Jordan frowned. "What's wrong? You look disappointed."

"It's just that tonight, instead of going out for dinner, I thought maybe I could make you something back at your place."

"You know how to cook?"

Jordan realized how little she'd managed to hide her incredulousness when Abby responded with a look sharp enough to kill. "I'll have you know, I'm a very good cook!"

"Really?" Her surprise was genuine. It had never occurred to her that a princess would know how to do something as ordinary as that. "When was the last time you cooked?"

Abby let out her breath in a huff. "I don't get a chance much these days, but just to prove it to you, I'll bet you I can make a meal out of anything you have in your pantry right now." She paused, her eyes suddenly shifting as if she realized too late the trouble she may have wandered into. "You do have *something* in the pantry, right?"

"Yes, I have food in the pantry." Jordan stiffened defensively, but then her expression grew uncertain. "I have kale. And possibly some things in tins."

"Tins, you mean like cans?" Abby gave a quick eye roll. "You and the British words again. Speak American. As for their contents, can you be more specific? *Things* encompasses a lot of, well, things. Are we talking sardines? Spam?"

It was Jordan's turn to roll her eyes. "I think I have tomatoes, possibly some white beans..."

Abby's eyes shone with an unexpected amount of excitement at Jordan's pathetic list. "How about garlic? Oregano?"

"Maybe?" Jordan's head was starting to swim. Now the woman wanted spices, too? "Look, I've got about ten quid in loyalty points on my Tesco card. You can use that to fill in the gaps."

"That's very generous," Abby said with a smirk.

Jordan shrugged. "I don't do a lot of cooking. It really wouldn't be a fair bet if I didn't offer a little bit of shopping. But, what happens if you win?"

"Then we both have a nice meal."

"And if you fail? What do I get if I win?"

"Well now, I'm not sure." Abby arched an eyebrow suggestively. "Did you have something in mind?"

Jordan's stomach tightened and she laughed nervously. One minute she'd been talking cooking and was even about to congratulate herself on dodging their romantic dinner date. The next minute she'd landed in a minefield. Before she could fully process the trouble she was in, Abby held out her hand.

"Do we have a bet, or are you too scared I'll win?" The woman's expression was infuriating, absolutely bursting with competitive challenge, and it quickly became too much for Jordan to withstand. She felt compelled to take Abby's hand and give it a shake. "I have no idea what I'm actually getting myself into, and I know that I will probably live to regret it, but yes. You've got yourself a bet."

———

WHEN THE CRUISE ENDED, Jordan and Abby disembarked at Westminster Pier and headed in the direction of St. James's Park. Max had been one of the first to get off the boat. Jordan had seen him setting a brisk pace for the park where he would scout out an unobtrusive location before their arrival from which to observe and take photographs. All she had to do was lead Abby there. It should have been a simple task, and yet the closer they came to their destination, the heavier Jordan's legs grew. It was almost as if they were being weighed down by the betrayal. There was no way she could go through with it. Instead of taking a left toward the park, Jordan reached for Abby's hand and went to the right.

Jordan glanced at Abby, who, being unfamiliar with the layout of the city, hadn't seemed to notice the abrupt change in direction. "How do you feel about World War II?"

Abby looked puzzled. "As a war? I suppose it was a necessary evil..."

"I wasn't looking for a term paper. One of my

favorite places in the city happens to be just down the way, and I'd love to show it to you. I know you like the clothing and the music from that era, but I wasn't sure if the history of the war was something you'd enjoy."

"If it's your favorite place, how could I not want to see it?"

Abby smiled that special smile she had that made Jordan's tummy flutter and her cheeks flush, the one that made her feel like she was the only person in the world. Jordan walked the rest of the distance to the Churchill War Rooms as if her feet were hovering several inches off the ground.

The underground bunker from which Winston Churchill and his wartime cabinet had strategized the defeat of Germany in the Second World War was reached through a set of narrow glass doors nestled between an ornate stone staircase and an exterior wall of the Treasury Building, on the side that overlooked St. James's Park. A hoodlike structure had recently been built above the doors, and to Jordan, the dark metal and unusual shape had always made it look like what would happen if Willy Wonka's elevator and a Star Wars villain had a baby. In Churchill's day the sprawling subterranean command center had been topped with sandbags and reached through a plain steel door. The Germans had never worked out the significance of the site, and even now, most passers-by would never guess the vital work that had been conducted in the sprawling labyrinth below.

The Cabinet War Rooms had always fascinated Jordan. She liked to imagine what the city would have been like back then. In some ways, Jordan had always felt a profound sense of disappointment at being born too late. As far as she was concerned, there would have been no place more exciting in the world for a reporter than London during the war. Plus, this underground lair was one of the few places in London, aside from the city's many churches, where one could escape the noise of the city and its eight million inhabitants to indulge in some moments of quiet contemplation. It also had the appeal that she had a membership, and so their admission that day wouldn't put a further dent in her dwindling reserve of cash.

She flashed her membership card at the ticket counter, and then they descended the stairs that led to the Cabinet War Rooms. Their first stop was in a spot where a glass-covered opening in the wall revealed a room filled with conference tables set up to form a square. Red steel beams crossed the ceiling, from which antique fixtures hung. Even the fans that had been mounted to the wall to circulate the air had the distinctive look of another era. Every book and pen on the table dated to the end of the war.

"Nothing has changed down here," Jordan said in a breathy whisper, "since the last person to leave switched the lights off in the Map Room in 1945. Isn't that amazing?"

Abby nodded, and though she might not have been

quite as enthused over that fact as Jordan was, Jordan could tell from the way her eyes widened that it had made an impression. "It does look very old-fashioned. It's hard to remember sometimes how much technology has changed."

Jordan pointed to a model of a German bomb that was suspended some distance above their heads. "Look at the size of that thing. There were no smart bombs back then. The entire city was under constant attack from bombs like those during the blitz."

They continued to follow the tour route, walking along a hallway of whitewashed brick, punctuated every so often with dark wooden doors. Utilitarian hooks had been added here and there to accommodate hats and coats, but other than that there was no ornamentation. The ceilings here, too, were crossed with red steel beams. They stopped in front of a room filled with small wooden desks, each with a vintage typewriter on its top.

"Speaking of modern technology, this was the typing pool. Can you imagine the mountains of paperwork they used to produce down here, before flash drives and cloud storage?"

"It must have been deafening down here when this room was filled with secretaries typing."

Jordan smiled. "You know, I've always loved that sound. If I ever have a flat large enough, I'd love to buy an old typewriter."

"Really? That's kind of strange. I thought only writers wanted those clunky old things."

"Er, yeah." Jordan twitched as the observation hit a little too close to the truth for safety. "Did you know that the ones down here didn't make any noise?"

"You're kidding!" Abby laughed, any additional comments she might have wanted to make about writers conveniently forgotten.

"No! Churchill hated noise. He couldn't stand when people whistled in the hallways, and the sound of typewriter keys drove him nuts. They brought in special noiseless typewriters from America to use down here. Can you imagine sitting at these desks, working twelve-hour shifts? They had to sit in front of sunlamps once a week, to keep from getting sick, because some of them slept, ate, and worked down here without ever venturing outside in daylight."

"It would have been a real adventure, though, don't you think?" Abby's words were accompanied by a dreamy sigh, and Jordan couldn't help but laugh. Abby stiffened slightly. "What, was that an insensitive thing for me to say? I mean, I know there was a war on and people were getting killed. I only meant—"

"No, I think I know what you meant." Jordan felt the same wistful nostalgia herself, especially as her own business gave her a front row seat to witness the growing shallowness of modern life. "People had a sense of purpose back then, like they were part of something bigger than themselves. Not like now."

Down another narrow hallway, they came to a kitchen with an enamel-covered cast-iron stove. There were pots and pans hanging from hooks, and somewhat incongruously, a cheerful metal bread box, painted bright green, that would've been at home in a grandmother's kitchen. Across from the kitchen was the prime minister's dining room. It's formal mahogany table and chairs sat on a threadbare oriental rug. There was an antique sideboard and a tea cart. Paintings hung on the walls.

"You'd never know you were in a bunker in this room," Abby commented.

"Old Winston took his food seriously. He was not a small man. They say he was quite a sight, racing through all these corridors with his big belly jiggling beneath his siren suit.

"What's a siren suit?"

"It was kind of like those one-piece garments that mechanics wear. People used to throw them on before heading to the bomb shelters during a raid in the middle of the night."

"Can you imagine having to get out of bed in the middle of the night like that? I sleep so soundly, I think I would have snored right through an air raid."

"Uh..." A memory of Abby lying naked across her chest, snoring softly as she slept, flitted into Jordan's mind and raised her internal temperature about a million degrees. "I think they have one of Churchill's siren suits on display down here somewhere. We should go look for it."

Abby looked down the hallway, then back the way they'd come, her eyes wide. "I had no idea there was so much down here."

"A lot of people were employed in the war effort."

"I think if I'd lived back then, I would've been a spy."

"Really?" Jordan raised an eyebrow incredulously. "A spy. Do you speak German, or French?"

"Both, actually." Abby laughed as shock registered on Jordan's face. "Spanish, too. My father insisted, even hired tutors when I was young. I guess he thought it would be a good idea, just in case."

"In case of what?"

"Oh, you know, global economy, blah blah blah."

"Oh, of course." In fact, it took Jordan a few seconds to figure out what Abby had left unsaid. It made perfect sense that even before she'd become the crown princess, her father had wanted her trained to rule, just in case. The trouble was, Jordan had been enjoying Abby's company so much that she'd completely forgotten for a moment that she was a princess and not a regular person. "They wanted you to be able to run the family business."

"Yeah, whether I want to or not. I mean, no one's ever asked, you know? They all just assume, like I should be thrilled to do it. They've never bothered to see if I'd rather do something else."

"Like be a spy behind enemy lines."

Abby giggled. "Exactly! Although, I'm not sure. I might have enjoyed being a code breaker."

"I saw a movie about that. A lot of women worked as code breakers. Are you good at math?"

Abby made a face. "Terrible."

"I think you had to be good at math."

"You're killing my dreams. You know, I would've been happy as a typist. I'm pretty good at typing. That's a solid career choice."

"Kind of low-key, compared to being a spy."

"Low-key is what I do best." Abby's face darkened. "That's why I just can't understand why they think..." She shook her head. "Never mind. It doesn't matter."

At the end of the corridor was a tiny room filled with gray metal boxes. The boxes were covered with lights, knobs, and switches. Jordan's chest swelled with emotion as she studied the contents of the room. "Keeping the population informed during the war was so important that they built a broadcasting room for the BBC underground so that they could keep reporting during air raids. Covering the news back then was one of the most important jobs a person could do."

"Was it? You never did tell me; what would you have done if you'd lived back then?"

"During the war? That's easy. I would've been a reporter."

"Did they have female reporters during the war?"

"Of course, there were! Why, Martha Gellhorn is considered one of the best war correspondents of all time. And there was Ruth Cowan, and Dickey Chapelle, and—"

"You seem to know a lot about this for a chemical salesperson."

There was an odd expression on Abby's face, and it reminded Jordan too late of the fact that she'd already been waxing rhapsodic about typewriters like a lunatic. Was Abby beginning to realize that Jordan wasn't who she'd claimed to be? It was either suspicion on Abby's part, or paranoia on Jordan's. Either way, it made her heart beat faster. "What do you mean?"

Whatever the look had been, it faded as quickly as it had come. Abby shrugged. "Nothing. It's just that you've given this some thought."

The truth was, strong emotions overtook her every time she thought of the important role people in her profession used to play, before tabloids and celebrity blogs had taken over for real journalism. But she could hardly explain that to Abby, and it was better to change the subject completely. "Oh, I don't know. Just being silly. Come on, I think they have a special exhibit of wartime photos down that way."

Along one of the walls, a collection of photographs had been displayed of civilians helping the war effort from the home front. Abby stopped in front of one, which was a black-and-white image of a young woman wearing mechanic's coveralls and a cap, her elbows resting on a car's chassis as she peered at its engine. An older woman, smartly dressed and carrying a fur stole, looked over her shoulder. "What's this?"

"That," Jordan said, "is a picture of the queen."

Abby stepped closer, squinting at the older woman. "That's the queen mum! She looks so young."

"It is, but that's not who I was talking about. You see that young mechanic?" Jordan chuckled as Abby gasped in sudden recognition. "Of course, she was still Princess Elizabeth back then."

"Honestly, I never pictured royals doing any real work." Bitterness sharpened her tone, and it pierced Jordan's heart. "Besides, people only like royalty because it gives them something to gossip about."

Suddenly, Jordan thought she could see a glimmer of what had prompted Abby to run away. "Not back then. When people saw a princess rolling up her sleeves for the war effort, it inspired them. It made them feel like they were all in it together."

Abby gave a derisive snort." The only thing people seem to care about now is who they're sleeping with or what they're wearing."

The look of pain on her face was unmistakable, and Jordan pressed her hands to her sides to keep from reaching out and smoothing Abby's brow. "I don't think that's true."

"Really?"

Abby's tone had been doubtful, but something in her expression said she was holding out hope. Without a moment of hesitation, Jordan offered it to her. "Yes, really. I think princesses can still make a big difference in the modern world."

As a reporter on assignment, she should have stayed quiet. Jordan knew this. It was her job to take notes, not give pep talks. But when it came to Princess Abigail, Jordan was realizing that she had lost all objectivity. Worse than that, Jordan was falling for her. And in just a few more hours, they would be back at her apartment again, alone for the night.

SIXTEEN

ABBY STARED at the inside of Jordan's refrigerator in disbelief. She'd spent most of the trip back coming up with a suitable recipe for the ingredients Jordan had listed as having in her pantry. She'd had a certain image in her head of what she'd find upon arrival. This had not been it. She closed her eyes and opened them again, but the view didn't change. Every shelf inside the fridge was stacked with bags of leafy greens.

"I have to admit, when you said kale, I just didn't picture this much of it."

Jordan groaned as she poked a finger at one of the bags. "It was all a big mistake."

"How do you get eleven bags of kale by mistake?"

"Simple. I was trying to order one bag, and my finger hit the key twice."

"And the grocery store didn't question it?"

"I asked about that. Apparently, juicing has

become a big trend in London this spring. Mine wasn't even the largest order the delivery guy had seen that week."

Abby opened one of the cupboards, but it, too, was filled with kale. "Should I keep looking? Or maybe you can just break the news to me gently now. If I open every cupboard, am I going to find anything other than kale?"

Jordan's face squished in thought. "Try the one at the end."

Holding her breath, Abby opened the cupboard. It did not contain kale. Instead, there were several cans of questionable contents and age, their labels peeling and their shiny metal tops dimmed with a thick layer of dust.

"Oh, right. The things in tins. I know I teased you, but it turns out that was a pretty accurate description." She turned the first one far enough to see the picture on the front. A smile slowly started to spread itself across her lips. "Diced tomatoes. That's a good start. And I think I see white beans back there. It looks like you weren't completely lying about the state of your inventory after all."

"To be honest, I'd forgotten about the kale." Jordan's tone was apologetic. "It was just too traumatic."

Far from feeling discouraged, Abby's spirits soared. She knew exactly what she was going to do. "It's okay. I can work with this."

"Are you sure?"

Abby took a quick mental inventory of what she'd found so far: beans, tomatoes, and kale, plus an unmarked plastic container of something that, if she was lucky, would turn out to be Italian seasoning. She knelt to examine the small shelves on the refrigerator door, and while the selections she was met with were mostly either completely dried out or a little too smelly to take a chance on, she did manage to find a small jar of minced garlic that had never even been opened. With a satisfied nod, she rose to her feet. "Absolutely. I'm all set."

Jordan gave her a disbelieving stare. "Were we looking at the same kitchen just now?"

"You have so little faith," Abby scolded with a laugh. Then she paused. "There is one thing, though. You have a pan, right?"

Jordan's jaw dropped in feigned offense. "Do I have a pan? Now who's lacking faith?" She pulled open the oven door and reached inside, emerging with a large skillet clasped in her fist. She handed it to Abby with a sheepish grin. "Just don't ask me for another one, 'cause this is all I've got."

"One pan will do."

"That's it? Nothing from the grocery store? I've got ten quid in loyalty points just waiting to be spent."

Abby hesitated. She didn't need ingredients, but she did need Jordan to leave the apartment for a little while. "How far is the store?"

"Depends what you need."

Abby considered for a moment. She'd been planning this surprise since they got on the boat, but it would only work if she had the place to herself long enough to set it all up. "How about a bottle of wine to have with dinner?"

"Red or white?"

Abby answered with zero hesitation, "Red, naturally."

"Okay. Since you're going to the trouble of cooking, the least I can do is get us a decent bottle. I'll go the extra distance to the big store. It'll take about two hours, but I think it will be worth it."

Abby nodded. Two hours would be perfect.

After Jordan left to retrieve the wine, the first thing Abby did was to dash off a text with the address of Jordan's flat. The biggest benefit to having her phone back in her possession was that she had access to all of her online shopping accounts. It had only taken a few minutes to place an order from the boat and arrange for same-day delivery. In just a few minutes, she would have everything she needed to make this night as unforgettable as she wanted it to be.

In the meantime, she grabbed a clean cloth and wiped the dust off the cans, followed by the pan, and then all of the surfaces in the kitchen, just for good measure. It was obvious that this was not a space that saw frequent use, with the exception of the microwave, which was caked in the splattered remnants of everything from curry to Thai noodles and beyond. From the looks of it, it had experienced an entire United Nations worth of takeout.

Preparing the ingredients, Abby couldn't help but laugh. As much as she'd teased Jordan about her bumper crop of kales, she couldn't have asked to find a better ingredient. The Tuscan bean concoction she was about to make was a trusted standby from her post-college days, the one thing she could throw together after the longest of days with mostly ingredients she had on hand, even when time and money were tight. Her host might not enjoy cooking, but Abby relished the opportunity to make dinner, if only because it was the most normal activity she'd had the chance to do in a very long time. At the palace, her father employed a full-time chef, but more and more over the past several months, she'd missed taking care of herself, and it magnified her already considerable doubt that she would ever be fulfilled by the life she was expected to lead.

She turned the burner on low and set the skillet on top, drizzling the last few drops from a bottle of olive oil she'd at first assumed was empty. She twisted off the lid of the minced garlic jar with a loud suction sound, then spooned some of the contents into the oil, listening to it sizzle as it made contact. She added more ingredients then began to trace figure eights on the bottom of the pan with a wooden spoon, lost in thought until a knock on the door brought her back to the present. She turned the stove to low and covered the pot before going to the door.

"I'll take them from here," she told the delivery person, a young man who was slightly winded from having just carried four large boxes down the stairs. Once she'd signed for them and brought them inside, she rummaged through a kitchen drawer to find a knife to slice open the tape.

The first box contained a new set of sheets, a comforter, and pillows. She set those aside and tried the next one, which had the most important item, a large inflatable air mattress with built-in pump. She eyed the space on the floor that the Murphy bed mattress had occupied the night before. Jordan had put it on its platform and folded it back into the wall that morning, leaving an empty spot that was ideal for her needs. She unfolded the mattress and plugged it in, and just a few minutes later, there was a comfortable bed. She smoothed the sheets on top, their intricate pattern of aqua flowers immediately brightening up the place, and added the matching comforter and pillows to create a look that was every bit as nice as something she might find in a hotel.

She eyed her handiwork with satisfaction, and no small amount of anticipation. Every minute she'd been in Jordan's presence that day, her whole body had been humming. The slightest accidental brush of her hand sent flames leaping up from Abby's skin. Given the turmoil her life had been recently, she wanted nothing more than to allow herself the euphoric release that came with a night of passion. The night before had been an appetizer, but tonight would be the main course. Abby couldn't remember the last time she'd wanted anyone this much. It wasn't just a physical desire, though that was part of it. There was more to it than that, and before Abby could take the final leap she'd begun to contemplate, she needed to know if Jordan felt it, too. That's what tonight was about.

Once the bed was ready, she turned her attention to the other two boxes. The larger of the two contained a folding bistro table and two chairs, all made of light-weight aluminum in the same aqua color as the sheets. The last box contained a white table cloth and an assortment of candles. She quickly covered the table, and placed the candles around the room, and was just lighting the last of them when she heard the key jiggle in the lock.

"It smells delicious," Jordan called out as she entered. She froze in place just a few steps inside the door. Her mouth had fallen open, and she stared around the transformed room with an expression of complete shock that made Abby flush with pride. "I know I wasn't gone *that* long. How did you manage all of this?"

"Magic." Abby frowned slightly, suddenly concerned that Jordan might not appreciate what she'd done. "You don't mind, do you?"

"Mind? Not at all." Jordan shook her head, still

somewhat dazed. "I think it looks amazing. I just can't imagine how you pulled it off. Do you have a fairy godmother I don't know about? Or, do I?"

"No, I'm afraid we're both fresh out of fairy godmothers" Abby chuckled, relieved that Jordan hadn't been offended by her gesture. "I will admit, it took a little more work than I'd expected, and now I'm starving. Come on, let's eat."

Carrying a plate of food in each hand, Abby made her way to the table. Jordan had retrieved two glasses from a cupboard and was starting to turn a corkscrew into the top of a bottle of wine, that she'd pulled from the grocery bag. The cork came loose with a pop, and Jordan filled both glasses almost to the top. Abby took them from Jordan, handing one back after Abby had settled into the seat across from her.

"I have to be honest," Jordan said, after taking a bite of the mixture of kale and beans, "I had my doubts you could pull this off. I'm not afraid to say that I was completely wrong. This tastes amazing."

Abby took a bite, as well, savoring the familiar, comfortable taste of a meal she hadn't had in years. For just a moment, she was able to shut everything else out of her mind and pretend that she was the same fresh out-of-college girl who had lived on cans of beans while trying to make it on her own. Tonight, she was just a regular person, on a date with a spectacular woman, and she had something important she wanted to discuss.

"Jordan," she began, resting her fork on her plate, "I wanted to say thank you."

"Why?" Jordan asked, looking genuinely puzzled. "Is that what all this was about?"

"In part. Look, when we met the other night, it was under the worst possible conditions. I was a total mess. But you took care of me, gave me a place to stay, and you've been nothing but nice to me ever since. I've had the most amazing two days of my entire life, and the way things had been going for me lately, that was the last thing I expected."

"It's been my pleasure," Jordan assured her.

Abby closed her eyes, and in her mind she could picture herself as Jordan had first seen her, wearing a dress she didn't like, stumbling around in someone else's shoes, ones that would never fit. In that moment, she knew that she could never be Princess Abigail again. Meeting Jordan had changed her, and she could never go back. "You said something earlier to me, when we were at the War Rooms, and it's made me do some soul searching."

Jordan cleared her throat with a nervous laugh. "It did?"

Abby took a deep breath. She needed Jordan to understand. "When I was younger, there was this movie I used to love. In it, the main characters meet on a train, and they have one night to spend together before they have to go their separate ways."

Jordan pressed her lips together. "Sounds like a story we can both relate to."

"At one point in the movie," Abby continued, praying what she said next wouldn't frighten Jordan off for good, "one of them says to the other that if they had the choice to either get married right that minute, or never see the other one again, they'd choose to get married."

Jordan's eyebrows rose a fraction of an inch, but she maintained her composure. "Bold choice. So, what you are saying is that you're going to hold me to that marriage arrangement from earlier today. Did you manage to book St. Paul's after all?"

"No, of course not." Abby giggled nervously. "What I'm saying, though, is that I know we only just met, but if I had to choose right now to marry you or never see you again...well, I can't imagine never seeing you again."

"Yeah. Me, too." It was barely more than a whisper.

"The truth is, that family business I've been telling you about is a little more involved than I let on. But, I've come to a decision about it."

The space between Jordan's brows shrank, forming a deep crease. "You have?"

"Just today, in fact. And I wanted you to be the first to know. I've decided that I'm not going to take over the business after all."

Jordan's eyes grew to the size of saucers. "What do you plan to do?"

"I'm not sure. But I was hoping to spend more time with you while I figure it out." As Jordan's eyes approached dinner-plate size, Abby quickly added, "I'm not suggesting you support me, or even that I keep staying here. I have money, and skills. I can take care of myself."

Jordan looked pointedly from the new bed to the linen-covered table. "I have no doubt about that."

Abby stood from the table and cleared the plates, taking them into the kitchen and placing them in the sink. It was a strategic move, designed to give Jordan a moment to let all that she'd said sink in. When Abby returned, she walked past the little bistro chair and sat instead on the mattress. It was firm and sturdy, with not even a hint of squeaking. She patted the spot beside her and when Jordan joined her, she scooted closer until their bodies were pressed together from shoulder to thigh.

At first Jordan seemed tense, almost uncertain, but as Abby rested her chin on Jordan's shoulder and brushed her lips against her ear, she could feel that resistance begin to yield. With her left hand, Abby massaged along Jordan's shoulder blade. With an audible sigh, much of Jordan's tension seemed to melt away.

"That feels fantastic," Jordan told her, eyes closed and a half smile on her lips. "Please don't stop."

Continuing to press her left thumb into the muscles of Jordan's shoulder, Abby shifted her weight to her left knee, then swung her right leg over so that it rested between Jordan's legs. Abby took her high hand and brushed it along Jordan's back, upward from her waist to her shoulder, until she was able to rub both shoulders with the same circular motions. She leaned in closer, kissing Jordan's neck. Jordan gave an appreciative murmur, but still Abby could tell that something was holding her back. Jordan sat without moving, Abby straddling her thigh.

"So, what do you think?" Abby held her breath for what seemed like forever as she waited for Jordan to respond.

"Abby, there's something I should probably tell you."

"Is it something good?" Abby's stomach clenched. Had she spoiled it all?

"Not exactly."

Abby drew in a quick breath. She looked Jordan in the eyes. "Then it can wait until tomorrow. Everything can wait, except one thing. I just need to know, whatever this is between us, do you feel it right now, too, or am I the only one?"

Jordan closed her eyes. "You're not the only one. I feel it, too. I shouldn't, but I do."

"Then let's agree to something." Abby's voice was resolute. "This feeling that's between us? Tonight, that's the only thing that matters."

Jordan returned her gaze, unblinking, as another eternity passed between them. Deep within her eyes something wavered and finally broke, and Abby could sense the last barrier falling as Jordan gave in completely to the moment. She nodded. "It's all that matters."

Abby closed the distance, covering Jordan's mouth with hers. Jordan's lips were soft and sweet, tasting of desire and a hint of red wine. Without breaking the connection of their lips, she slid both hands along Jordan's shoulder blades, digging her thumbs into the muscles as Jordan's breath caught. Her hands continued their descent, traveling down the length of Jordan's back, then Abby slipped her fingers beneath Jordan's plain white T-shirt and stripped it off over Jordan's head in one swift motion.

The expanse of her broad shoulders was broken by plain white bra straps in a material similar to the shirt that had just come off. Abby smiled. The no-nonsense style suited Jordan. Abby grasped the back band with her fingers and with a quick snapping of the hooks, the bra was off in an instant, revealing Jordan's lusciously rounded breasts for Abby to admire in full. She circled one dark areola with her thumb, touching the tip of her tongue to her lips as she felt the nipple harden. Abby leaned in close to Jordan's neck, letting her lips pass along Jordan's earlobe and travel down her neck to her chest. She squeezed Jordan's breasts together, creating a deep cleft where she buried her face. She breathed in deep, awash in the spicy scent of cinnamon and black-berries that she'd come to think of exclusively as Jordan's own.

All of this Jordan let her do, but when Abby gave Jordan a gentle push to get her to lie backward on the bed, Jordan stopped her. Abby frowned. "What's wrong? It's okay, you can tell me."

"It's just..." Jordan inhaled deeply, letting her breath out in a rush. "The truth is, this is another dance that I just happen to know a lot of steps to."

"Oh, is it now?" Abby struggled to keep a straight face as she played along.

"It is." Jordan fixed her eyes on Abby, holding her gaze as if by magnetic force, until nothing seemed to exist in the entire world except the two of them in that moment. A tingling began at the nape of Abby's neck and traveled all the way down her spine. "And considering how last night went, I think it's only fair that this time, I get the chance to lead."

SEVENTEEN

IN THE SPAN OF AN HOUR, the tiny space of her flat had been transformed as if by a miracle from cold and impersonal to warm and inviting, but at the moment, Jordan only had eyes for the woman who had made it all happen. Though in reality she was a princess, Jordan wondered if Abby wasn't better suited for the role of fairy godmother, her very presence bringing magic and the promise of dreams fulfilled.

Jordan gazed into Abby's eyes, the midnight black of intensely dark chocolate. The reflection of the candles flickered and danced, drawing Jordan in deep. She leaned in and kissed Abby's neck. "You are so beautiful," she whispered, and was rewarded with a faint, pleased laugh. "But there's one problem."

"There is?"

"Yes. You're wearing far too many clothes."

Jordan went to work righting the situation, unzip-

ping the by now very familiar zipper of the yellow
dress. Abby stood and began to ease the top from her
shoulders, sliding it down her arms.

This one dress was still the only garment Abby
had, and Jordan was a little surprised that she hadn't
conjured a new one from wherever the bed and the
candles and the rest of it had come from. In a way,
Jordan was glad she hadn't. The dress was perfect for
her. Next weekend when the Portobello Road market
was in full swing again, they'd have to go and buy a
hundred more. Well, Abby would have to do the
buying. Jordan was flat broke. Was there something
more broke than that? If so, that was what she was
going to be, now that her career-saving story was a
bust. She didn't have a choice. There was no chance
that Jordan could write about her now, not without
Abby's knowledge and permission, and definitely not
for the *Crier*. To do otherwise would be exploitive, and
Jordan could never do that to someone she loved.

I'm in love with Abby.

Jordan gasped at the realization, and at the same
moment Abby's dress slipped to the floor to reveal
the beautifully sculpted form beneath. The body that
had been hidden was even more stunning than
Jordan had remembered. Her hands ached with the
need to touch, reveling in the feel of Abby's smooth
skin against her palms as they followed the indent of
her waist and the flare of her hips. Jordan hooked her
thumbs in the waistband of her borrowed cotton

underwear—they'd replace these, too, as soon as possible, and Jordan secretly hoped the new ones would be silky with a hint of lace. When this last bit of covering was removed, she planted one hand on each of Abby's buttocks, cupping the soft flesh as she pulled her off balance, guiding her as she tumbled onto the bed.

Jordan was half-undressed already, and she made short work of the rest of her clothing before settling down alongside Abby, stretching her own limbs and pulling Abby close so that every inch that could possibly touch was pressed together, molded together like two pieces of soft clay, thoroughly and deliberately, until there was no way of determining where one stopped and the other began.

Jordan tickled Abby's earlobe playfully with her tongue, nipping it lightly with her teeth in a move that elicited a surprised but delighted squeal. Jordan pressed her lips to Abby's neck, certain she could feel the pulsing of her blood beneath the surface. She traveled lower, stopping briefly at her nipples before continuing along her stomach. She'd pay them more attention later, but right now Jordan had a different destination in mind.

When Jordan reached her lower stomach, she flicked her tongue into Abby's navel. Abby's pelvis wriggled, her back arching in encouragement as her legs parted. Moving at the tempo of the most sensuous tango, Jordan dragged her lips across Abby's right thigh, then her left. As Abby continued to buck and thrust, she kissed her more.

Jordan's plan had been to take it slow, to torment them both to the point where they could stand it no longer, but by the second time Abby's thighs clamped her head in their vice-like grip, the plan was out the window. Jordan wanted her too badly to wait one second more.

Jordan's head burrowed deeper between Abby's thighs, her mouth seeking out the hot wetness of her sex. As her tongue darted across the bundle of nerves at Abby's center, she felt Abby's nails dig into her shoulder. It was reminiscent of the massages she'd received before, but more urgent, and with it came a moan of desperate longing that raised the temperature of Jordan's core to roughly that of a wood burning stove glowing red.

Jordan took Abby into her mouth, exploring her fully with her tongue before sliding a finger inside, tentatively at first until the accompanying moan that burst from Abby's chest urged her to thrust deeper, first one and then two fingers working along to the steady, rhythmic beat of Jordan's heart as it thudded against the walls of her chest like a drum.

Abby's hips thrashed urgently, her buttocks bouncing off the inflated surface of the bed as if it was a trampoline. Jordan's fingers met with no resistance as they slid in and out of her through the wetness, her tongue bursting with the tangy taste that belonged to

Abby alone. She could have stayed there forever, her face pressed between Abby's legs, surrounded by her scent, as she felt Abby's body arch and shake. As she coaxed Abby closer and closer to climax, anticipation built deep inside her own body, almost as if the connection between them was so strong that Jordan was experiencing it, too.

At last Abby cried out, her nails digging in so deep to Jordan's shoulders that they'd probably drawn blood, not that Jordan cared in the least about that. Abby's body froze, tensed as if she were made of steel, then finally relaxed into the once-crisp sheets, which now were rumpled all around them on the bed. When Abby's muscles were soft and supple once more, and her breathing had slowed to somewhere approaching normal, Jordan slithered her way back up to lay next to her, wrapping her arms tightly around her, soaking in her warmth. She'd never felt so close to another person before. It was both wonderful and terrible.

How would she break it to Abby that she was a reporter for the *Crier*? Correction, that she'd *been* a reporter for the *Crier*. After her failure this week, they'd never keep her on, and especially after she'd made such a big fuss about getting a deal in writing for delivering the exclusive on Princess Abigail. She'd be the laughingstock at the office, a cautionary tale to keep other reporters in line for years to come. But there was no question of doing an exposé now. She was in too deep. The runaway princess wanted to run away with her. She'd set out to write a story, but somehow she'd become the story instead.

As she continued to fret, a small sigh escaped her, and Jordan felt Abby's arms tighten around her, soothing her. Abby's fingers stroked her forehead and massaged her scalp, then traced a line along her spine. Jordan felt her tension begin to dissolve under Abby's touch. As Abby's hands ventured lower, circling her bottom and sliding along the crevice between her thighs, Jordan's thinking grew fuzzier. Abby kissed her and the last of her concerns melted away. The future was something she could think about later. As Abby's touch stoked the heat of her desire, Jordan knew there were much better ways to spend the night ahead.

JORDAN HAD YET to look at the clock, but she could tell from the amount of daylight managing to make its way through the basement window, and by the sound of traffic coming from the street above, that it was well into Monday morning. Beside her, Abby rolled and stretched, her blond hair sticking out at an unruly angle on her left side. Jordan tousled it, letting her fingernails drag along Abby's scalp and eliciting a contented sigh like that of a lazy cat.

"Do I have to get up yet?" Abby asked, not bothering to mask a yawn.

"Not if you don't want to. There's nothing on the agenda today, unless you want there to be."

"Hmm."

"What was that?" It was hard for Jordan to tell if the sound had come from thinking or more yawning. "Is there something you'd like to do?"

"Other than you?" Abby asked with a saucy grin.

Jordan laughed. "Naughty girl."

"Are you complaining?"

"Absolutely not. As far as I'm concerned, I don't ever want to get out of bed again, as long as you're with me." Jordan kissed Abby's forehead tenderly. "I've never felt like this before."

"I haven't either. And there's no place else I'd rather be than right here, with you." Abby snuggled closer and Jordan sighed with contentment. After a few minutes of silence, Abby spoke again. "I suppose we can't stay in bed all day, though, and I wouldn't mind a bath. Maybe I could pop my dress in the wash? I thought I saw a washing machine in your bathroom."

"No!" Jordan's horrified tone caught her by surprise. "If you value your dress, do not put it anywhere near that evil thing."

"Why?"

"For one thing, it takes nine hours for one load, and even then, the clothes are never dry. And they will smell like mildew forever. Plus, no matter how careful you are about temperature and color, everything comes out the same shade of Dickensian gray after one wash."

"I don't want to risk that."

"No." Jordan shuddered at the memory of her first and only time running it. "There's a reason I only wear white T-shirts and jeans. I can do an entire month's worth of clothes at the laundromat down the street for less than twenty quid."

"I guess I can make it last for another day, while I order a few things."

Jordan nodded. "A much better plan. You're welcome to take a bath, though."

Abby smiled. "That sounds nice. What should we do after that?"

"Totally up to you," Jordan said with a shrug. "Although I think the band from Saturday night is playing at the pavilion again, if you want to give dancing another go."

Abby grinned. "That sounds perfect."

Abby swung her legs over the side of the inflatable mattress and rose. She was still delightfully naked from the night before, and Jordan appreciated every inch of her without so much as blinking until she'd ducked inside the bathroom and shut the door. When Jordan heard the taps running, she sat up in bed and stretched, then switched on her laptop and pulled up her favorite daily news app. As the day's first video selection began, Jordan turned up the volume and balanced it on top of her desk before leaning back to watch against the towering pile of new pillows.

Jordan heard the squeak of the taps being turned

as the sound of flowing water ceased. It was followed by a soft splash, and if she closed her eyes, she could picture Abby settling into the water, her naked skin turning a soft pink from the heat. How had she gotten so lucky?

When this whole thing had started, Jordan had looked at Abby as an assignment, the key to job security and nothing more. But in less than three days with the woman, Jordan had come to see so much more, to the point that she was prepared to sacrifice all hopes of keeping her job or staying in London for a shot at a future with her. What that would look like, Jordan wasn't sure. Maybe they would move to California. Abby would go back to the career she had loved and Jordan could work on establishing herself as an investigative journalist in Los Angeles. It would be difficult, but with a little help from Abby, at least she knew she wouldn't starve.

Jordan's belly gave a nervous flutter. The truth of her occupation was a detail she'd yet to divulge. It might not go over very well. On the other hand, Abby hadn't exactly been forthcoming about her status as European royalty, either, so it wasn't like she was the only one with a secret. As long as she never breathed a word of the tabloid story she'd set out to write, Jordan prayed it would be okay. All the same, she knew she should confess as soon as possible. The secret was eating away at her, and she couldn't stand deceiving Abby any longer. She cared for her too much. Maybe she would tell her the truth tonight, just to be safe.

Jordan glanced at her computer screen, barely registering the news story that was playing there. Her thoughts were elsewhere, focused mostly on what entertainment she could come up with for the two of them that day, should they actually decide to put on clothes and leave the flat. Jordan traced her fingers over the wrinkled sheet beneath her and wasn't convinced that clothing or leaving the flat were necessary, but she wanted a backup plan, just in case Abby felt differently.

Taking a closer look at the rumpled bed, Jordan stood and smoothed the sheets, then picked up the discarded clothing from the night before. She bundled up the dirty laundry into a ball, carefully placed Abby's dress on the neatly made bed, and salvaged her worn t-shirt to pull on over her head for at least a nod to modesty as she worked. When she got to her blazer, the outline of a rectangle in the pocket caught her eye. Pulling it out, Jordan saw the name of the restaurant where Max had arranged for them to have dinner the night before. It was a reservation they hadn't kept, and though there was no question that Jordan preferred the plans they'd opted for more, it did cross her mind to wonder whether it was too late to cash in on the promise of a free meal tonight.

Don't be rude, Jordan chastised herself after only a moment of contemplation. Max had gone to a lot of trouble for this story, loaning her money and giving her tickets to take Abby all around London, not to mention pulling strings with his friends. Even harder than breaking the news to Abby about being a reporter was the prospect of breaking the news to Max that the multi-thousand-pound payout she had dangled in front of him was no longer in the cards. She'd pay him back, of course. Once she received her back pay from the *Crier*, she'd be able to settle up with Max, plus pay off the last of her obligations, and buy a one-way ticket to Los Angeles. Barely. Max would get his money back and be able to buy Moira her ring, but sadly, there would be no upgrading to a fancier stone. But if Jordan was lucky, Moira would say yes, anyway, and Max would be back to speaking to her before the year's end.

Jordan was still straightening up the flat when she heard Abby's muted footsteps coming from the bathroom. She'd expected her to retrieve her dress from the bed, but when she looked up from her work, she was surprised to find Abby rooted in place halfway between the bathroom and the bed. She was wrapped haphazardly in a towel, dripping all over the floor, and standing so still that she seemed to have been turned to stone.

Frowning, Jordan followed Abby's gaze to the laptop screen, where a reporter with an earnest face was delivering the latest news. Splashed across the top of the screen was the headline, "King Randolph Collapses on Tarmac during Surprise Journey to

London." Without warning, the same file photo of Princess Abigail that Jordan had received from Diane flashed onto the screen. Jordan's heart leaped into her throat. When she turned back to look at Abby, the color was slowly draining from the woman's face, leaving her roughly the same Dickensian shade of gray that Jordan had feared for her dress.

Jordan's first impulse was to lunge at the computer and turn off the news, but she refrained. It was no use. She had no idea how long Abby had been standing there, but however long it had been, it was long enough. Abby's secret was out, and with the shocking news she'd just received, Jordan knew that things would never be the same.

EIGHTEEN

THOUGH STEAM from the bath still rose from her skin, Abby's blood had turned to ice in her veins. On the laptop screen was her father's face. She couldn't hear what the news commentator was saying, but the headline told her all she needed to know.

King Randolph Collapses on Tarmac during Surprise Journey to London.

Her father wasn't supposed to be here yet. His agent was supposed to have kept him from making the trip. But Abby knew why he'd come. It was all her fault. Of course her father had come. The memory of losing his mother and sister was still so fresh. How could she think he wouldn't worry enough about her to put concerns for his own health aside? She'd gotten so wrapped up in her desire for a normal life, so intent on growing her relationship with Jordan, that she'd forgotten what was at stake. She'd forgotten to think of her family. But her father hadn't forgotten her. Instead, he had come all this way to check on her, against doctor's orders, and look what had happened.

Flashing across the screen were images that tore at her heart. Outside the embassy in London as well as her father's palace back home, the people of her country had gathered to light candles, to leave flowers, and to hold up encouraging signs that wished both her and her father a speedy return to good health. As the camera moved closer, she could see that some of those who had gathered had tears in their eyes. In that moment, she was struck by a profound truth. The monarchy mattered to her people. Like the young princess Elizabeth who had inspired her nation during wartime, the people of their kingdom looked to her father, and to Abby. It was worth more to them than scandals and fashion, after all, much more. And she'd nearly let them all down.

The chill of the basement air sent a shiver coursing through her, and all at once Abby became aware of her surroundings. The water that continued to drip from her body had formed a mini puddle at her feet. The towel she'd wrapped around herself was insufficient either to make her dry or to keep her warm, and as the gooseflesh rose on her arms, she was grateful to spot her dress lying on the bed. However, a stab of pure dread hit her in the belly when she belatedly registered Jordan on the other side of the bed, staring at her with eyes wide. At that very moment, Abby saw her own photograph looking out at her from the computer screen, along with the words, "Princess Taken Ill."

Abby dashed to the laptop, shutting the lid with a snap, but she knew it was too late. There was no way Jordan had failed to see the picture, or to recognize the resemblance between her and the woman on the screen. Her secret was out. She waited in silence, her towel dangling half open, a cruel reminder that everything she'd tried to keep hidden had been revealed. And yet, as the seconds ticked by, Jordan said nothing.

Abby swallowed, the sound of it so loud in the silence of the flat that it felt deafening. She tossed the towel aside and shrugged her dress on over her head, contorting her arms to reach the zipper in the back. This, at least, seemed to have the effect of rousing Jordan from her shock, as she quickly came to Abby's rescue and slid the zipper closed.

"I..." Abby stopped and swallowed again, her throat like sandpaper. Jordan stood behind her, out of sight, or else she doubted she would have found the power to speak at all. "I'm not sure about dancing tonight, after all."

Jordan sniffed, but didn't speak. Abby could feel Jordan's fingers fiddling with the zipper. She patted it down and then smoothed the fabric along Abby's shoulders. When she responded, it was with a single word, that hovered in the gray area between statement and question. "Okay."

Did she guess why, or did Abby have to spell it

out? She opened her mouth, but found she couldn't make the words come out. Instead, she turned to face Jordan, a plastic smile stuck to her face. "Maybe we should go for a walk?"

Jordan nodded, and then, apparently still in no mood to talk, she scooped up a pile of laundry and disappeared into the bathroom. Moments later, Abby heard the sound of water running. She paced back and forth across the floor of the small flat while she waited, her brain emitting an unintelligible hum that did nothing to help her figure out how to explain to Jordan what was going on.

As she walked, Abby felt a buzzing against her thigh. She reached into her pocket and found the phone she'd tucked away the day before still hidden among her skirt's folds. It vibrated as she pulled it out. When she unlocked the screen, there was message after message, each tagged as urgent. Her fingers trembled as they hovered a hair's breadth above the screen, but as hard as she tried, she couldn't bring herself to open any of them. The one from her mother brought the sting of tears to her eyes. She'd been willing to walk away, to leave her royal life behind, but she hadn't truly thought through what she would lose. Running away wasn't the answer.

When Jordan appeared again, she was fully dressed, once more wearing her trademark jeans, T-shirt, and blazer. She'd even put on her shoes. Just seeing her brought a fresh batch of tears to the corners of Abby's eyes. She blinked them back, willing them not to fall. Now was the time for resolve. But seeing Jordan standing there, no doubt suspecting but not yet having heard from her own lips what Abby had to do, broke her heart in two. No matter what she chose, Abby knew that she would lose. She couldn't make herself say the words.

"Where would you like to go?" Jordan's eyes were dark and searching as she sought to hold Abby's gaze. It was all Abby could do not to collapse in a heap on the floor. Perhaps it would be easier if she did, she thought, if she just allowed her body to disintegrate and join the puddle of bathwater on the floor. Puddles had no feelings. She envied them for that.

"Kensington Palace." She'd said it clearly this time, no beating around the bush or hiding her destination behind a desire to walk through the gardens. Jordan raised an eyebrow, clearly having noticed this distinction, but refrained from commenting.

Abby gathered her belongings quickly. It's not like she had much. The tiara she carried in a plastic shopping bag, along with the little red clutch that held her American passport, her ticket to a life she would never have again. Her phone was in her pocket once more. She'd turned the notifications off, and so it no longer taunted her with its buzzing. Her purchases from the day before, the bedding and candles, she left behind, along with her borrowed sunglasses and hat. The need for disguising who she was had passed.

They left the flat in silence. With each retreating step, Abby tried to commit to memory the feel of this place she was leaving behind. It hadn't been particularly nice, with its lack of sunlight and its persistent dampness, but she'd shared it with Jordan, and so Abby wanted to remember every detail. She took in the sights along Portobello Road, committing them to memory, as well. When they reached what she recognized as the turnoff for Ladbroke Square Garden, she still had the key tucked inside her clutch. She slowed her gait, reaching out to place a hand lightly on Jordan's arm. "How about a walk through that gated park we were in the other day, for old time's sake?"

As they turned to follow the new road, Abby kept her hand on Jordan's arm, and soon Jordan had tucked it into the crook of her elbow, pressing Abby's fingers close to her side. As they walked, Abby could feel each breath that Jordan took as the movement of her ribcage radiated through her fingertips and up her arm. She felt connected to Jordan in a way that was both elemental and intimate. Abby put her other hand on top of Jordan's forearm, clasping her fingers together as if holding onto Jordan's arm for her life. She never wanted to let go, but after a few minutes, they stood in front of the locked gate, and Jordan looked at her expectantly.

"I still have the key." Abby retrieved it from the clutch and unlocked the gate, then let it dangle for a minute by its loop of red silk ribbon. The afternoon sunlight glinted off the dull brass and Abby watched it swing, mesmerized. Then she held it out, and slipped the loop over Jordan's head. The key came to rest on her chest. "Here, maybe you should have this now."

Jordan pressed the key to her skin, as though pressing it to her heart. "I'll keep it safe and use it well, at least until its rightful owner reports it missing and they change the locks." She winked, and Abby giggled, her insides glowing. She wished the walk would never end.

The park was quiet. It was a Monday afternoon, and Abby figured that most of the key holders were probably at work, slaving away to be able to afford the mortgages on the properties that allowed them access to one of the park's precious keys. As they strode along the path, Abby took Jordan's hand, holding it all the way to the other side. Instead of letting go, she held on even tighter as they neared Bayswater Road and the jostling crowds threatened to force them apart. All too soon, the gate to Embassy Row came into view. Abby slowed to a stop, averting her eyes from the destination that waited for her.

"I think I'd like to go alone from here." Abby looked into Jordan's eyes, reading confusion that was quickly replaced with silent understanding. "Please, when I head to that gate, turn around and go back home. Don't stay and watch, okay?"

Jordan's brow furrowed. "But, why?"

Abby's eyes stung as she blinked rapidly, and there

was a slight sniffling sound as she breathed in. She couldn't bear the thought of Jordan watching her go, seeing the guards approach her and then letting her through, escorting her down the long road to her father's state apartments beside her kingdom's embassy. She knew that Jordan knew who she was and why she was leaving, or would certainly figure it out soon if she somehow hadn't caught on, but the prospect of having her watch as Abby gave up on the dream of their life together was just too much. Her voice cracked as she urged her once again. "Just promise. Can you please just promise me that? Turn around and walk away."

"You've got it, Ducky."

The pain on Jordan's face reflected the emotions in Abby's heart. Without a thought for the busy street or the crowds of people passing by, Abby cupped Jordan's face in her hands and kissed her. The sweetness of her lips turned bitter with the addition of Abby's salty tears, and she finally pulled away, then turned without saying goodbye, and walked the rest of the distance to the guard house alone.

ABBY WAITED at the door to her father's bedroom, her hand poised above the doorknob. She was frozen in place, unable to open the door because she wasn't sure what she'd find on the other side. The guards at the entrance to Embassy Row had stopped her for less than a heartbeat before they'd recognized who she was and whisked her into one of the waiting unmarked cars. No one had said a word to her about her father's condition, not at the guard house and not when she'd been greeted at the front door by her father's butler. Each person she'd encountered had been polite, but distant. She wasn't sure whether the reserved attitudes had more to do with deference to her royal station, or judgment of how she'd abandoned her family and put the king's health at risk. As far as she was concerned, she deserved none of the first, and all of the last.

With a deep breath, she turned the knob and pushed, but the door failed to open. She frowned, then turned the knob again, but this time gave the door a pull. It swung open. Despite the anxiety that gnawed at her insides, Abby stifled a laugh. *I'm as bad as Jordan with opening doors.* Just thinking of the dark-haired beauty who had captured her heart during the past few days shot a pang of regret and longing through her insides. When she approached the massive bed at the far end of the room, in which she could barely make out the outline of her father's profile amidst all the blankets and covers, the tears in her eyes were as much for her own acute loss as they were for the direness of his current situation.

"Dad?" Abby's breath caught as she drew near enough to take in the ashen color of his face. "Dad? It's me, Abby."

Her father's eyes fluttered open, and he smiled weakly. "Abby. I've been so worried about you. Your mother and I wanted to come just as soon as we heard you were sick."

Her eyes widened. "You were worried about *me?* Dad, you could have died!"

"Nonsense. I'm just dehydrated. I got a little dizzy from the flight and lost my footing, that's all. The doctor says I'm fine." He waved his hand as if swatting away her concern. When he made eye contact, the warmth of his expression squeezed her heart like it was in a vice. "It's you I'm worried about, child. So sick that you couldn't call your mother for three days?"

Heat burned in Abby's cheeks. Either he believed the story his staff had concocted about her health, or more likely, he knew that it was a bunch of malarkey but was saving her from embarrassment by playing along. If it were the latter, it wasn't working. She was mortified about the trouble she'd put him and her mom through, and she felt the desperate need to come clean. She grabbed the hand he'd waved at her before and clasped it tightly, then spoke before she could change her mind.

"I have a confession. I haven't been ill. I..." Abby's voice faltered and she drew a quick breath to steel her nerves. "The truth is, Dad, I ran away."

The ghost of a smile that teased the corners of his mouth told Abby everything she needed to know. Her father had known the truth all along. "These past months have been hard on you."

"That's not a good excuse." Abby's head drooped on her neck. "All I can say in my defense is that it started out as an accident."

"And after that?"

"After that, I—"

At that moment, the door to her father's chamber burst open with a loud clunk. Abby whipped around and saw her mother making a beeline toward her, her arms stretched wide. "Abby!"

Abby fell into her mother's embrace, and any chance she had of holding back the tears that had threatened her all day evaporated the second she caught a whiff of her mother's familiar perfume. "Mom. Mom, I'm so sorry."

"She's admitted that it was what we'd suspected," her father said. Her mother responded by tightening her embrace.

"I wasn't thinking, Mom," Abby sniffled through her tears. "I wasn't thinking at all. I didn't want you to worry, and I didn't mean for Dad to come here and make himself sick."

"Oh, Abby. We're you're parents. How could you not have expected us to worry?"

Abby's mother released her from her arms and helped her to settle into a chair near the king's bed. It was a massive, winged thing with upholstery so thick that when she sat down, Abby sank at least a foot as it swallowed her into its depths. She closed her eyes as she tried to make sense of the past three days.

"It was an accident, Mom, that's all. I got turned around, and my head was swimming from those pills that Countess Margaret gave me. I ended up outside and I just sort of kept going."

The king's expression grew stern at the mention of the countess. "I've had a word with her already about that. She had no business giving you anything without the doctor's say-so."

"Well, I might not have needed them," Abby countered, "if I were allowed to do more for myself. I'm tired of feeling like a bird locked up in a cage."

"Abigail." Despite his weakened state, her father's stern tone made her bristle. "You know we follow those protocols for a reason. It's important to keep you protected and safe. It's a miracle that this wasn't splashed all over the front page of every newspaper in Europe. Just look at how the media has hounded us all these past several months."

"Maybe they hound us because they know we're keeping secrets. Your secret engagement, your secret daughter. If I were in charge of public relations for the palace, I would have handled a lot of things differently. Your stroke, for instance."

Her father's face darkened. "We're not talking about me right now, young lady. We're talking about you. Specifically, you were going to explain to your mother and me why it was that you thought it would be okay to disappear for three days without a single word."

Abby pressed her lips together, her cheeks burning. "I only wanted to explore on my own for a little while. I was planning to head right back, only I got lost and confused, like I said before. If it hadn't been for Jordan, I don't know what I would have done."

"Jordan?" Her mother asked.

"She's a woman I met, who came to my rescue. Mom and Dad, there's something else I have to tell you." Though she was shaking from the inside out, Abby willed herself to tell them the rest. She'd made a decision, and they deserved to be the first to know. "I know it's only been a few days, but I think I've fallen in love with her, and I'd like to invite her to the palace so that we can continue our relationship."

Their response was stunned silence, which on a continuum of possible responses was somewhat less than what she'd hoped for but better than many of the alternatives. Abby watched, holding her breath, as her mother turned to look at her father, who in turn looked at Abby.

But what he said next was not at all what she'd expected to hear.

"My dear, we know all about Jordan Baxter. There's something you need to know, as well." He pulled the thick cord that was used to summon the servants, and almost immediately, the chamber door opened and the same plainclothes agent who had tracked Abby to the Tower of London strode in.

"Hank," her father said to the man, "could you please tell my daughter what you've learned?"

The agent bowed. "Yes, Your Highness. It's come to my attention in the course of my duties that Jordan Baxter, with whom Princess Abigail has formed a close association, is an investigative reporter for the *Londontown Crier*, a local newspaper that has recently been sold to a tabloid publisher from Australia."

Abby gasped. Jordan, a reporter? That was impossible. She was a salesperson, for her family's fertilizer business. Wasn't she? Abby recalled Jordan's fondness for typewriters, and the way she'd known the names of all those female reporters. Jordan being a reporter made sense, but if it were true, that would mean she had lied. There was only one reason a tabloid reporter would want to spend time with a princess.

Abby's eyes narrowed as she looked from her mother to her father. "Are you just telling me this because you think it's too soon, that I'm rushing into this relationship? Because I'd remind you that the two of you fell in love quickly, too, and look at all the years you wasted because people told *you* it was too soon and it would never work."

"I wish I could say it wasn't true, but I can't." Her mother stood by her side and rested a hand on her shoulder. "I'm so sorry, sweetheart, but Jordan Baxter is a reporter, and the organization she works for has just announced a huge bonus for proof that you were not ill during your London trip. We think this Jordan woman was sent by her paper to get an exclusive story on you. Now do you see why we worry, and try to keep you safe?"

The room spun and Abby shut her eyes. She'd been so worried that Jordan wouldn't forgive her for not telling her about being a princess. Instead, Jordan had been lying to her this entire time? She'd been such a fool. Unless there was another explanation. That had to be it, and she had a plan to find out. "I need to give Jordan the benefit of the doubt. I won't believe she meant to betray me without proof. Mom and Dad, will you trust me enough to help me find out the truth?"

NINETEEN

THE OFFICES of the *Londontown Crier* were located in a glass-fronted building a few blocks from Kensington Gardens. It had taken Jordan every ounce of strength to walk through them on her way into work that morning, and she'd left her flat twenty minutes early so as to take a route that did not involve passing within sight of the palace itself, or the gated entrance to Embassy Row. Even with that precaution, as Jordan stood in front of the building and watched the last few stragglers filing into the elevators beyond the security desk, her heart was heavy. The new management had called a staff meeting for ten o'clock, and it was the last place Jordan wanted to be.

She checked the time on her phone. It was a quarter to ten. With a sigh, she entered the building through the revolving door. She usually avoided these types of entrances, knowing that with her luck it was only a matter of time before she got stuck in one, but today she didn't care. Part of her even welcomed the final squash of glass panels that would put an end to her misery. The only thing worse than waking up in her flat alone that morning was the prospect of explaining to her new boss that the story she'd promised him was a total bust.

She made it into the building without incident, and avoided being sandwiched between the closing elevator doors for good measure, which put her odds for surviving all the way until she reached the meeting room depressingly high. When she arrived at the *Crier's* offices, an eager young intern was even holding the door open, removing the last possible obstacle between her and utter public humiliation. Why was her life so unfair?

The meeting room was packed with participants and humming with chatter as she sought out a seat as far from the front as possible. But as Jordan snaked her way through the maze of extra chairs that had been brought in for this all-hands-on-deck meeting, she felt the heavy weight of a stranger's hand on her shoulder. When she turned, she was face-to-face with *him*.

"Jordan Baxter," he said in his strong Aussie accent. "Good to see ya."

Jordan did her best to swallow down the bitterness that rose in her throat. "Uh, yes. Hi."

He flashed a crocodile grin. "I hear good things. I can hardly wait for your report."

Her stomach knotted as Jordan gave him a crooked half smile in response. "It'll be something, for sure," she muttered as he went off to corner the next unsuspecting journalist.

In the back corner of the room, Jordan found Diane, with whom she obviously shared a seating strategy. There was an empty spot beside her, and Diane patted the chair. "I saved it for you," she told Jordan, who sat gratefully. "How's that story of the century going?"

Jordan groaned. "Don't ask."

"Writer's block?"

Jordan shook her head. "Turns out, princesses are more elusive than I thought. I didn't get it after all."

Diane's eyebrows shot skyward. "Is that right? Because I got a message from that photographer friend of yours yesterday, Max, and he had a very interesting story to tell."

"Did he?" Jordan's laugh rang with disingenuousness. "Max is full of it. Always has been."

"I see. So, you didn't spend the weekend giving Princess Abigail her own private tour of London?"

"Do you know how ridiculous that sounds, Diane?"

"Interesting." Diane studied Jordan's face, making her squirm, but said nothing else.

"Why are you here, Diane? I thought you were leaving."

"Yes, well I haven't made it official yet. But how

about you? Without that story, I assume you've made up your mind to return to the States?"

"We'll see." Jordan's shoulders slumped. She'd been holding out hope for a miracle, but if one were coming, it needed to be quick.

From the moment the meeting was underway, it was an exercise in agony. One by one, as the bloggers who had been added to the staff introduced themselves, the sensationalistic new path the *Crier* would be traveling became more and more clear. When Jordan's turn came, any lingering doubt had vanished. There would be no miracle. She knew what she had to do.

The Australian grinned at her again, his resemblance to a crocodile becoming even more uncanny. "Jordan, the moment I've been waiting for. Tell us about this juicy exclusive you have in the works."

This was it. Jordan sat up straight in her chair. "There is no exclusive."

If she'd ever wondered what a disappointed crocodile would look like, now she knew. "What?"

"I thought I could get the story, but I was wrong."

"You're certain? Because you were fairly insistent on getting a signed contract."

"Yes. I'm sorry."

The new owner's eyes narrowed, his face hardening. "And what about the rumors that Princess Abigail wasn't sick after all, but had run away for a night out on the town, huh?"

Jordan shrugged. "As far as I can tell, they're just rumors."

"Is that right?"

"Have you seen any proof?" Jordan held her breath, but she could tell by his expression that he had not. "Well, there you go, then."

But the stubborn old man hadn't quiet given up hope. "What about the reports of Princess Abigail's miraculous recovery this morning, which just so happened to coincide with the arrival of dear old mum and dad?"

Jordan rolled her eyes. "You know, I know you're used to tabloids, so you may not know this, but at a real newspaper, we don't just believe every two-bit rumor we come across without doing some investigation first. It's called journalism."

Beside her, Jordan heard Diane give what could only be described as a gleeful snort. Everyone else kept quiet, but Jordan was pleased to see smirks on a few of her colleagues' faces. Maybe this place wasn't headed straight to hell, after all. Maybe some of these people would be ready to put up a fight along the way. It was almost too bad she wouldn't be here to see it.

Her new boss was less than amused. In fact, the Aussie's face had turned a mottled shade of red that made it look like the skin had been stained with beets. "Thank you for that insight, Ms. Baxter. Perhaps you could step down the hall right now and go talk to Janice about that."

When heads were on the chopping block at the *Crier*, it was Janice who wielded the ax. Jordan had it coming, of course. She'd just about begged the old coot to fire her. It still didn't make it fun. She trudged down the hallway, bracing herself for the encounter. The only bright side was that, based on the experiences of former colleagues who'd been fired, Janice would issue her final pay in cash on the spot. The old management had preferred to avoid the mess of disgruntled employees returning to the building, and Jordan assumed that new management might be similarly inclined.

"Jordan."

Jordan turned at the sound of her name and saw Diane walking toward her. "Hey, Diane. I guess I burned that bridge pretty thoroughly, huh?"

Diane chuckled. "Well if you did, there was just enough of it left that I managed to run across it, too, right before the last bit of flames."

"You quit?" Jordan held up her hand and her mentor slapped it for a high five.

"Told him exactly what he could do with my job, and it felt fantastic. Thank you for the inspiration." Diane's expression grew more serious. "I have to ask, though, was this part of your plan all along? Did you make up a long shot princess story just to reveal the Australian for the fool that he is?"

Slowly, Jordan shook her head. "The truth is, I could have delivered it. But you were right. This tabloid trash isn't me. When it came down to it, I couldn't betray Ducky like that."

Jordan froze as she heard herself say Abby's nickname. An odd look passed over Diane's face, but in the end, she simply nodded. "Good decision, Jordan. I'm proud of you. Now let's go pick up our pay from Janice, shall we?"

It took almost no time at all to wrap up the loose ends of her career as an award-winning investigative journalist for the *Crier*. As she boarded the elevator with Diane afterward, part of her was still in shock. She'd barely read the termination forms as she signed them, and she'd pocketed the envelope containing her final pay without so much as a glance inside. In the lobby, Diane placed a hand on her shoulder, stopping her in her tracks.

"I want you to take this, Jordan." Diane held out her own envelope, which she'd just received from Janice.

Jordan shook her head vehemently. "No, I can't."

"Please," Diane urged. "You've been my star reporter for the past five years, and I know how little I paid you for it. There's enough to get you back to the States, plus some extra to help you settle in when you're there. I insist."

Jordan took the envelope and put it in her pocket along with her own. She felt a tear slide down her cheek as her mentor drew her into a hug. "Thank you, Diane."

"One more thing. I know you're technically not my reporter anymore, but I have one last assignment for you, if you want it."

"Okay, tell me more." Always a reporter, some of Jordan's melancholy faded at the intrigue of a new assignment. That was always the way it went with her, and she had a feeling Diane knew it.

"This press pass for Princess Abigail's press conference arrived for you this morning. It's been rescheduled for tomorrow morning at the embassy. I think maybe you should go check it out, just in case there's any part of your story that was left unfinished."

"I don't have a story, remember?" The odd look was back on Diane's face, and Jordan was almost certain it meant that her mentor knew a lot more about what had transpired between her and the princess than she was letting on. Jordan's hand shook as she took the pass from Diane. "I'm afraid the story might be finished just the way it is, but thank you."

"You should go to it, Jordan," Diane reiterated. "Sometimes even the best reporter can sometimes be surprised by how a story unfolds."

As she exited the lobby of the *Londontown Crier* for the final time, Jordan mostly felt numb. So many years of work, and what had she ended up with to show for it? *Your integrity, Baxter,* said the voice in her head. *You have your integrity to show for it.* Her phone buzzed with an incoming text. Jordan groaned. It was from Max. He wanted to meet up at the pub and was dying to hear how much they were going to make on the story. Admitting to her employer—correction, former employer—that there would be no story had been hard enough. Explaining it to Max just might break her.

***

MAX WAITED in their usual spot. The baseball hats and fedora he'd worn while undercover had been replaced with his trusty Royal Stewart tartan wool cap. As Jordan approached the table, the broad smile on his face made her spirits fall. Breaking the news to him was going to be about as enjoyable as kicking a puppy.

"Hey mate!" Max pointed to a pint of dark brown stout on the table. "Got you your favorite."

"Thanks." Jordan sat at the edge of the seat, balancing precariously as if ready to spring up and run at any moment. She left the pint untouched.

"So, what did the new boss say about the exclusive?" Max's eyes sparkled, and Jordan wondered how many pints he'd already finished off while waiting for her to arrive. "Did he give you a promotion? No, never mind that. Just tell me how rich we're going to be."

"Max, I don't know how to tell this to you, buddy, so I'm just going to go ahead and say it." Jordan eyed the dark pint, cursing the sense of loyalty that kept her from consuming her unearned reward. "There is no story."

"Sorry?" Max tilted his head to one side. "What do you mean there's no story? Of course there's a story! Or wait. Do you mean you're going to sell it to a competitor for more money? That's brilliant!"

"No, Max. I'm not going to sell it for more money. I won't be writing a story."

"But, there has to be a story to go with my photographs." Max looked genuinely confused. "I can't just publish them as is."

"I know you can't, mate." Jordan sighed, reaching into her pocket for the envelope she'd received from Diane. Jordan squinted at the bills and did some quick mental arithmetic, subtracting out just enough to cover the cost of the plane fare home. "That's why I'm going to give you this. It's twenty-five."

"Jesus, Baxter! Twenty-five thousand?" Max's eyes and jaw vied for which could open wider. He became agitated, bouncing in his seat. "I never dreamed it would be that much. Moira's about to get the biggest engagement ring you've ever seen!"

"No, no Max." Jordan placed a steadying hand on his shoulder, pushing him back down into the chair. "Not twenty-five thousand. It's two thousand five hundred."

Max's face crumpled. "I don't understand. Word on the street was that the going rate was at least ten, and that was for a lot less than what we had. Did someone else get the scoop?"

"No. No one got the scoop. Including the *Crier*. There is no scoop."

"How can there be no scoop?" He still wasn't getting it.

"I can't do it, Max." Tears welled in Jordan's eyes as she thought of Abby. "I thought I could, but it turns out it's not always open season on princesses after all. Not when you get to know them. Not when you..."

"Not when you fall in love with them?" If the words alone hadn't done so, the look on his face told her that he'd finally figured it out. But instead of anger, she was surprised to see understanding as well, and maybe a touch of respect. He sighed. "Well, I did say you should keep it classy."

"I'm really sorry, mate. I know you were counting on the money."

"It's not the money. Sure, I would have liked to have bought Moira a nicer ring, but it won't be the end of the world if I don't."

"Unless she says no," Jordan quipped, attempting to lighten the mood.

"Well, yeah, then I'd have to kill you, naturally."

"I'd expect nothing less."

"But what about what this story meant for you, the prestige? I still say it could have been Pulitzer material."

"Not a lot of prestige in tabloid gossip."

"Then what about your job, not to mention your visa. What will you do now?"

Jordan wished she had an answer, but inside her all she felt was a yawning emptiness. She shrugged. "Not a clue."

Max reached into his bag and pulled out a tablet. He switched it on. "Want to see some of the photos?"

"Sure. That would be great." Jordan smiled wistfully. She probably shouldn't torture herself by looking at them, but she missed Abby's face.

Max looked at the screen and chuckled. He turned it around to show her the photo of Abby on the dance floor at the pavilion. Her head was tossed back in the middle of a laugh, and though Jordan was fairly certain the person she was dancing with was Lucy, her face was hidden from view. "I love this one. I was thinking for a caption, maybe The Princess and the Polka."

Jordan groaned. "That's terrible." As she flipped through the pictures, her chest grew heavy and her shoulders drooped. "I can't believe she's gone."

Max gave her a sympathetic look. "No plans to see each other again?"

"No. Well, unless you count the press conference tomorrow morning."

"Yeah, good luck getting in. It's invitation only."

Jordan reached into her pocket and pulled out the press pass. "You mean, this invitation?"

Max stared at the pass, his mouth open wide. "How did you get that?"

"Diane. It says it'll admit two. Wanna come as my plus-one?"

His eyes lit up. "Seriously? I'd be able to capture some amazing shots."

Jordan gave his shoulder a playful slug. "You bet. Considering what you've done for me the past few days, it's the least I can do."

Max downed the last of his beer and rose to leave. He pointed to the untouched pint. "I've got to get going, but you might as well drink that."

"You're sure? I don't deserve it."

"You're forgiven, which is more than I can say for you if you let a perfect pour like that one go to waste."

"You're the best, mate, you know that?" Jordan picked up the glass and raised it in salute before taking a sip.

"And don't you forget it," he replied. "I'll meet you at the embassy tomorrow morning at eight."

TWENTY

ABBY PEEKED through the door into the embassy's Great Hall, trying to steady her nerves. The room was long and narrow, about as large as the King's Gallery in Kensington Palace, and every inch as grand. It was on the first floor of the embassy and had a grand collection of paintings and sculptures from some of the most notable artists of their kingdom on permanent display. Right now, the room was silent, filled with rows of empty chairs. Soon, those chairs would be occupied by a select group of reporters who had been invited from around London to attend the press conference that she and her father would hold together. It was their first such event, and butterflies fluttered around inside Abby's stomach at the thought.

Although she was nervous about it, the press conference had been her own suggestion. As her father's strength had returned over the past two days, they'd spent quite a bit of time talking about the kingdom. After so many months of feeling like the only thing her family wanted from her was to play dress-up in a tiara and high heels, Abby was as surprised as she was pleased to discover that her father respected her experience in public relations and wanted to hear her ideas. She'd given him more than a few, and there were plenty more where those had come from.

In truth, there was more riding on this press conference for Abby than anyone would suspect. Though the guest list was made up almost entirely of trusted reporters from some of the top news agencies in the world, she'd also included on the list a certain assignment reporter whose photo on the website of a local tabloid rag had appeared shockingly familiar to her. Whether Jordan would come, and what she would say to explain herself and her actions if she did, were still very much up in the air, and were the sources of the majority of Abby's current anxiety. Only time would tell.

"Your Highness?" It was Countess Margaret.

Abby backed away from the door she'd been looking through and faced her lady-in-waiting with a certain sense of satisfaction at the memory of her mother and father putting the woman soundly in her place. They'd reached the mutual conclusion that a woman of Abby's age did not require the services of a chaperone any longer, and Abby doubted that the countess would be bossing her around anymore. "Yes, Margaret?"

"I've come to inform you that the woman from the market would like to put the finishing touches on your hair." It couldn't exactly be described as grumbling, but it was obvious the countess did not relish her diminished role, nor appreciate Abby's newfound confidence as crown princess.

"The woman from the market? I think you must mean my new stylist. I do hope you're making her feel welcome." The warning in Abby's tone was veiled but unmistakable. The countess's snootiness would no longer be tolerated.

"Of course, your Highness." The countess bowed her head respectfully. Abby let the matter drop, assured that she and the countess were now on the same page.

Abby made her way down the hall to the spare office that had been set up as a makeshift dressing room. Her new stylist, whose name was Francine and who had until yesterday been the proprietor of a market stall on Portobello Road that specialized in vintage clothing, waited for her inside. She'd been easy enough to track down. Her father's agent, Hank, had already done a complete profile of the woman and her business after Abby had stopped there to shop. All that had remained was having someone from the palace reach out to her with the offer to become Princess

Abigail's full-time stylist. Francine had jumped at the chance.

Francine clapped her hands together when Abby entered. "You've gone with the creamy- yellow Givenchy, I see. An excellent choice."

"They were all exquisite, Francine, but this one called to me."

Abby smoothed her hands over the A-line dress she'd chosen for the occasion. Like the cotton lawn before it, this one had a full skirt and a thin belt that accentuated the waist, but its delicate lace fabric gave it a much more elegant look. The straight horizontal neckline made it appropriate for the formal occasion, while the bare shoulders and playful button detail along the low-cut back made it just a little bit daring. Countess Margaret had nearly required smelling salts when Abby had tried it on that morning, deeming it completely unacceptable, and Abby wasn't embarrassed to admit that may have influenced her final decision.

"Here, let me add a little spray to that chignon." Francine reached out with a comb and smoothed Abby's stray hairs into place before giving it a generous spritz of hair product. It did a fine job, but unlike the goop her previous stylist had used, it did not make Abby feel like she was ready to go on safari with her hair doubling as a pith helmet.

Abby looked in the full-length mirror that had been brought into the office for her use. She couldn't hold back the delighted laugh that bubbled up inside her. For the first time since becoming a princess, she truly believed that she looked and felt the part. Her dress was perfect. Her creamy ballet flats were as comfortable as they were demure, and she'd be able to stand for hours in them if the need arose. Her only jewelry, a simple pair of pearl earrings, was understated but sophisticated.

The best part was, there was no tiara in sight. In fact, the moment she'd returned, the plastic shopping bag that she'd used to transport the priceless Gamberini tiara halfway across London had been whisked away. Abby wasn't sure where they'd taken it. It could be safely stowed in an underground vault overseen by magical goblins for all she cared. She hoped not to see it again for a very long time. With any luck, it would not make another appearance until her wedding day, which was something she was far from thinking about just yet.

Wedding day? I have to find out if the woman I've fallen for is planning to betray me first.

Ah, love. There were so many little details.

A short time later, Abby was once more standing at the door to the Great Hall. Her father stood beside her this time, resplendent in his dark blue uniform with its gold braid on the epaulets and cuffs, a sash of light blue silk draped diagonally across him from shoulder to hip. Scores of medals glittered regally on his chest. He looked healthier today than Abby had seen him in a while, and she attributed that, at least in part, to the frank conversations they'd begun to engage in during the past two days. Now that she'd started to communicate honestly with her family, Abby felt confident it would continue. She planned to do everything she could to relieve her father's worries so that he could make a full recovery.

Just before the door opened, her father took her fingers and gave them a squeeze, accompanied by an encouraging smile. For those few seconds, though he might look every inch a king, he was just a regular dad, cheering her on. As Abby entered the room, the first thing she noticed was that the Great Hall was no longer quiet, and the chairs were no longer empty. Instead, the air buzzed with the anticipatory hum of dozens of reporters who were waiting for them to appear. Abby entered the room first, and it went eerily silent as soon as her presence was noticed.

As Abby made her way to one of the two chairs that had been placed on a raised dais at the front of the room, her stomach did flip-flops. Only after she was seated and had taken a few calming breaths did she dare to look out across the room. She glimpsed Jordan in the front row, with her friend Max seated beside her, but avoided eye contact. Instead, Abby dug the fingers of one hand into the heavily carved arm of her chair, holding it with an iron grip. Her heart fought to escape her chest, but on the outside, she maintained the illusion of calm as though she'd been a princess her entire life. Now that she had truly set her mind on being the type of crown princess that her family and her kingdom could be proud of, she was determined to succeed.

After her father gave a prepared speech to welcome the reporters and update them on his and his daughter's health, the floor was given over for questions from the reporters. From the middle of the room, a man rose and identified himself as a reporter for the *Times*.

"Princess Abigail," he began, "what do you say to rumors that you were not, in fact, ill, but were out and about in London? There were social media reports of people spotting you on trains, in restaurants, dancing at outdoor pavilion—"

Abby interrupted him with a hearty laugh that she hoped emphasized the absurdity of the notion that a princess would be caught dancing at some random outdoor pavilion. "Did they mention who my dance partner was supposed to be? I'm curious if it was Bigfoot or Elvis." The crowd laughed, and in her imagination, Abby did a happy dance. She was off the hook. "This type of rumor goes to illustrate something that I've recently been discussing with my father, which is that without open access and honest communication between the palace and the public, rumors run rampant. As some of you know, I have a passion for public relations, so this is a shortcoming we'll be working hard to improve in the coming months and years."

The questions shifted to policy matters after that, until finally one of the embassy staff announced that it was time for the press conference to end. This was the moment Abby had been waiting for, and she rose from her chair, hoping no one could tell how much she was trembling. "Excuse me, but before we go, I'd very much like to meet some of the members of the press."

"That's highly unusual," said the startled-looking aide.

"Perhaps just those in the front row, then." Abby had, of course, seen to it that Jordan and Max scored front row seats.

"They've not been fully vetted, your Highness," he argued.

"Indeed. Well, sometimes, you have to have faith in people, don't you think?" Abby's gaze traveled across the front row, stopping as her eyes locked with Jordan's. It was the first time she'd dared to look at her. Now that she had, it felt as if every other occupant of the room had melted away, so that it was only the two of them. "I trust that faith will not be unjustified."

The aide led her to the front row, beginning with the reporter on the far right. Abby shook hands and made small talk with each person as she moved down the line, but a part of her brain was always counting how many more steps before she reached Jordan.

"Mr. Sinclair, how lovely to meet you." *Six to go.*

"Yes, Ms. Jameson, I do believe that children are the future of this planet." *Three left.*

At last, there was only one to go.

The man with the familiar ginger beard put out his hand. "Max MacGregor, fashion photographer."

"How do you do, Mr. MacGregor?

He held out a manila envelope. "I was hoping I could present your Highness with an exclusive set of commemorative photographs of your visit to London."

Abby opened the envelope and peeked inside. The photo on top was of her and Jordan doing the tango at the pavilion on Saturday night. It was right at the moment where Jordan had dipped her backward, and the smoldering look they shared was unmistakable. She looked pointedly at Max. "What a remarkable set of photos. I'd say they're somewhat valuable, are they not?"

"Yes, they probably are. As it happens, those are the *only* ones in existence. My gift to you."

Abby nodded regally, though under different circumstances she would have flung her arms around the Scotsman and given his ruddy cheek a kiss. "Thank you. Your generosity is humbling."

Abby slid a few inches to her left and was face-to-face with Jordan. The anxiety she felt inside seemed to be reflected back at her from Jordan's pinched and chalky face. Though dressed nicely in black wool trousers and a pink silk blouse, both of which Abby recognized and knew she must have had dry-cleaned especially for the occasion, it didn't escape her notice that the woman looked like she hadn't slept well for days. Half of her was sorry to see it, but half of her was glad. Despite the luxury of her room in her father's state apartments next door, her best night of sleep in recent memory was on an air mattress on the floor of a small basement flat on Portobello Road. On some level it was good to know she wasn't alone in that.

"Jordan Baxter, your Highness. Independent journalist."

"Independent?" Abby raised an eyebrow at this introduction, an action that nearly made her laugh because it was Jordan's signature move, and one that had clearly rubbed off on her from their time together. "That's interesting. Are you not affiliated with the *Londontown Crier?*"

Jordan's pale cheeks flushed pink. "I was, in fact, until very recently. I'm between jobs at the moment."

"I see."

Jordan cleared her throat nervously. "May I also say, Princess, that what you said about having faith in people? I very much believe that your faith is not unjustified."

The corners of Abby's lips twitched as she struggled to maintain her composure, the result ending up as a crooked smile instead of a toothy grin. "I'm so very glad to hear you say that, Ms. Baxter. Perhaps in time such faith will be rewarded."

The aide nudged Abby along the line at this point,

and though she was far from ready to go, she didn't
wish to make a scene. She met the final handful of
reporters in a complete daze, her mind too busy
replaying every detail of her encounter with Jordan to
manage anything more than politely going through the
motions of saying hello.

She returned to her spot on the dais with a
profound sense of relief. She'd needed some assurance
that Jordan wouldn't betray her, that the feelings
between them were more than a carefully plotted trick.
The photos in her hand, not to mention Jordan's
haggard face, were all the proof she required. As she
and her father rose to depart, she looked her father
directly in the eyes and gave a single nod. It was the
signal they'd arranged. The second part of the plan
could go forward. But would Jordan go for it? All Abby
could do was wait, and hope that her faith would be
rewarded.

TWENTY-ONE

WITHIN SECONDS of the press conference ending, Abby and the king were gone. The rows of chairs in the Great Hall emptied quickly, each reporter hoping to be the first to post their story to their respective news sites. Jordan remained rooted to the floor, her eyes fixed on the chair where Abby had been. Only when Max nudged her with an elbow to her side, did she reluctantly turn her head away.

"You want me to stay?" Max's brow was etched with concern.

"No, I'll be fine." More than anything, Jordan wanted to be alone.

No you don't. You want to be with Abby. It was true, of course. When it came to choices, Abby occupied the top slot, while being alone came in a very distant second. Still, Jordan had had gotten a chance to see her, and to tell her in some small way that her secret was safe. This wasn't a fairy tale and Jordan was pretty sure she didn't have a fairy godmother waiting for her back at her flat, so that would have to be good enough.

Finally, she turned to leave. She'd worn her best work shoes, a pair of dressy loafers with a solid chunk of a heel that clicked as she walked along the marble floor. The sound of her steps echoed all around her. The Great Hall seemed to stretch on forever, with paintings in gold frames and sculptures on stone pedestals as far as the eye could see. With each step, she fought back the tears that threatened to spill over her bottom eyelids like water bursting from a dam.

Though she'd been positive she was all alone, suddenly, there was a man walking beside her. Jordan turned her head and saw that he was dressed in an impeccably pressed suit, and wore the flag of Abby's kingdom on his lapel. He was the type of man who meant business, and never cracked a joke.

"Ms. Baxter, will you follow me, please." It was not a question.

Jordan swallowed hard, wincing as something popped somewhere in the vicinity of her ears or jaw. *This is it,* she thought. *This is the part where I am arrested and carted off to a dungeon for the rest of my life to protect the image of the monarchy.* She wondered if there was such a thing as a traitor's gate in Abby's kingdom, and whether they would row her through it in a boat before locking her up and throwing away the key.

The man led her through a doorway and down a long hallway. Unlike the Great Hall, this had the utilitarian feel of a typical office building. At the end of the hall was a set of stairs, which they took down one level to where a steel door blocked the way, armed with a combination keypad and scanner. The man punched in a code and scanned his hand, and the lock on the door clicked open. Beyond it was a tunnel with plain cement walls and floor. The walked in silence, Jordan's heart thumping. She wanted to ask where they were going, but was too afraid. She could only assume there would be an unmarked van waiting for her at the other end.

Instead, the tunnel ended at another stairway, and when they emerged on the ground level, the door opened to reveal what appeared to be the spacious entryway of a house. They went past the mahogany staircase and through a door into a room that appeared to be an office or library. Bookcases lined the walls, and there was a large desk of solid carved oak in front of a fireplace. As Jordan tried to figure out why she'd been brought to this place, the man who had led her there left, shutting the door. One moment she was alone in the room, but a moment later, a familiar voice sent her heart soaring.

"Jordan!"

While Jordan had been facing the other direction,

Abby had slipped through a door near the fireplace that blended perfectly into the wood paneling. Jordan wouldn't have known it was there except that at the sound of Abby's voice, she turned and caught it swinging shut. Still dressed in her creamy-yellow lace dress that she'd worn to the press conference, Abby strode across the room, her full skirt swinging gracefully. Before Jordan could react, Abby flung herself forward, gathering Jordan into an enthusiastic embrace.

"Don't take this the wrong way," Jordan said as Abby squeezed the air from her, "but what am I doing here? Actually, let's take a step back. Where am I?"

"Hank didn't explain?"

"Is Hank the one I thought was taking me to prison for the rest of my life?"

"Oh, Jordan, I'm so sorry." Instead of letting her go, Abby held her even tighter. "I know he's a little scary, but I couldn't exactly drag you out of the Great Hall myself, could I?"

"I'm still unclear on why I needed to be dragged from the Great Hall at all." Jordan filled her air with lungs as Abby finally released her.

"Oh my goodness, of course. I don't know where my brain is." Abby was talking a mile a minute, her hands fidgeting with her skirt in that way they did when she was nervous or excited. "I'm sorry. I've completely forgotten your question. What was it you wanted to know?"

Despite her confusion, Jordan's first impulse was to laugh. "Let's start with where am I."

"This is my father's London apartment."

Jordan raised an eyebrow. "This is not an apartment. I know. I've lived in plenty of apartments in my life. This is an apartment the way those giant mansions the Rockefellers and Vanderbilts built are summer cottages."

Abby laughed. "I suppose you're right. But in my defense, it's a lot smaller than our palace."

Jordan whistled. "I'd love to see *that*."

Abby's expression turned pensive. "Would you? Because that's kind of what I wanted to talk to you about."

Jordan pressed her front teeth into her bottom lip. "I don't understand."

"Look, Jordan, obviously I've figured out that you're a journalist. And you know that I'm a princess. And I also know what you did for me just now, back in the Great Hall, and what it cost you."

"You do?"

"Maybe not entirely, but I can guess. You had the scandal of a lifetime on your hands. I know how tabloids work. That had to be worth a fortune. Instead, you're out of a job."

"To be honest, it was a job I'm not really cut out for. Don't get me wrong, I love being a journalist, but staying at the *Crier* would have meant betraying your trust. I couldn't pretend that our time together didn't mean anything to me, Abby. I couldn't pretend that *you* didn't mean anything to me, because you do."

Abby nodded. "I feel the same."

"YOU DO?"

"I DO." For a moment they were both silent, and Jordan gazed into Abby's eyes as if spellbound. A hint of a cloud passed over Abby's face. "But what will you do now?"

Jordan sighed. "I don't know. I need to be a journalist. I need to write. It's all I know."

Abby's eyes sparkled merrily, like she had a secret she was bursting to share. "You know, my father's agent, Hank, gave me a file he'd put together on you the other day. He included some of your published articles. I read them, and they're good. Like, really good."

Jordan blushed. "Thanks."

"The thing is, I'm going to be overseeing palace communications and public relations when I return home, and one of my priorities is to make the monarchy more accessible to the public. Which is why I'd like to hire you."

"Wait." Jordan blinked, uncomprehending. "You're saying you want to offer me a job?"

"Technically, my father does, but yes. We'd like to

invite you to write a series of in-depth articles on the House of Gamberini."

"To make you look good?" Jordan asked suspiciously.

"Not at all. You'll have complete control over the content of what you publish. Like I said, I've read your work and I have complete faith that you'll be fair and honest. That's all we expect."

"So, what, you want me to move from London and—"

Abby's face clouded. "I know it's asking a lot."

But Jordan grinned. "Actually, it's a godsend. The *Crier* was sponsoring my visa. The way things are right now, it was going to be almost impossible to find another sponsor, so I thought I was looking at a one-way ticket to the States."

"If you decide to accept, you'll have a generous salary, an apartment near the palace, and complete access to anything you need to do your work."

Jordan's eyes darted around the luxurious library. "When you say apartment, are we talking your definition of the word, or mine?"

Abby laughed. "Probably somewhere in between. I can get you pictures, if you'd like."

"That's okay. I've seen your decorating ability. If you think it's nice, that's good enough for me."

"There's one other thing. Since you'd be living nearby and we'd have the chance to see each other regularly..." Abby hesitated, biting her lip, "what with the connection we felt when we were together and all..."

Jordan knew where this was going, and though it was a tempting offer, maybe the most tempting she'd ever had in her life, she felt her brow furrow. "I'm not saying I think this will happen, but what happens if after a little while, when the whole whirlwind dies down, we realize that things between us just aren't meant to be?"

"Then they aren't meant to be."

Jordan shook her head. "No, I mean, what happens to the whole offer? You know, the generous salary and the apartment, and—"

"I had faith in you, Jordan, so now I hope you can have some in me. You giving the two of us a chance has nothing to do with the job. That's yours, no matter what. And you'll be working for my father, not for me, so I won't be your boss or have anything to do with that. But I also want to say, for the record, that I think what we have together is the real deal. I wouldn't have brought you here if I didn't think you were the one."

Abby placed a hand on Jordan's arm. Even that slightest touch sent a surge of electricity through her and sent the world around her spinning in the best possible way. How could she say no to that?

"I trust you, Ducky. And I would love to take the job. And more than that, I would love to give us a chance, and see where things might lead, because, for the record, I think you might be the one, too."

Abby let out a squeal and caught Jordan up in an embrace. As Jordan felt herself surrounded by Abby's soothing warmth she marveled at the turn her life had taken. She'd thought that real life could never be like a fairy tale, and yet somehow she'd had the good fortune to find a real-life princess and personal fairy godmother, all rolled into one.

TWENTY-TWO

ONE YEAR LATER...

Abby stared at the pile of gowns on her bed, experiencing a potent mix of awe and dread. Francine had outdone herself this time. Each piece was more exquisite than the next and Abby would love to wear each and every one, but would there really be time to wear all of these on the trip? After all, she was only going to London for a few days. From the look of things, she'd be spending most of her time getting changed.

"Could you hand me that schedule again?" Abby turned to address Jordan, who was standing on the other side of the bedroom, sorting through a stack of research notes she'd left on Abby's desk. Though they each still kept their own apartments, Jordan stayed over several nights each week, and liked to keep her work close by in case inspiration struck.

Jordan crossed the room, holding a printed sheet of paper in her hand. "Here you go."

Abby took the schedule, but not before pulling Jordan in for a kiss. Their lips came together, soft and tender. Even after a year, kissing Jordan never failed to send a shiver down Abby's spine and leave her wanting more. In truth, it led to something *more* about as often as not, though sadly the wardrobe on Abby's bed would put a crimp in her desires today. At least until her bags were packed.

"Can this be right?" Abby squinted at the schedule. Every minute of the day was accounted for in excruciating detail. "This is going to be terrible. I don't even know why you're bothering to come."

"But I thought you loved London." It was impossible for Abby not to pick up on the hurt in Jordan's voice.

"I do," Abby assured her hastily. "It's one of my favorite places, and don't get me wrong, I'm glad you're going. I'd be lost without you."

"You would?"

"Of course I would. I love you, and I love every minute I spend with you. I guess I just kind of dreamed that someday we'd go back to London together and be able to explore it like we did last year. This," she shook the schedule in her hand, "is not going to be that kind of trip."

"Really?" Jordan's face softened into a sweet smile. "You love me?"

"Of course I do, you nut. I tell you that every day."

Jordan grinned. "I know, but I do enjoy hearing it. For the record, I love you, too."

"God, I hope so," Abby joked. "I went through a lot of trouble to bring you here."

Jordan studied her with an intensity that made Abby feel like everything around them had gone still. "Tell me, do you really want to spend the weekend exploring the city like we did last year?"

"More than anything." Abby sighed. Though she'd grown accustomed to her role as crown princess over the past twelve months, and had come to love her father's kingdom and its people as her own, she'd be lying if she said she didn't sometimes miss being able to come and go as she pleased, like she'd once been able to do.

"What if I told you that you could?" Mischief twinkled in Jordan's eyes.

"Then I'd have to say you were joking. Just look at this monstrosity of a schedule." Abby shoved the paper into Jordan's hands. To her surprise, Jordan tore the paper in half without so much as a glance. "Jordan!"

"I have a confession." Whatever it was, Jordan didn't look repentant. In fact, she looked immensely pleased with herself. "This schedule is a decoy."

"What are you talking about?"

"The whole trip, the state visit. It's a ruse. I asked your father to help me plan it as a surprise, sort of an anniversary trip. After all, it's been a year since we met. I thought we should celebrate."

"You mean, we're just going on a...vacation? Like a normal couple?" Abby looked unbelievingly from the ripped paper to her girlfriend's face, then started to laugh. "I should have known you'd get my father involved. The two of you are as thick as thieves these days. I don't stand a chance."

"He and I both agreed that you needed a few days away. He's even agreed that we can go incognito, as long as we have a small security detail nearby."

"You mean, it's going to be just the two of us, wandering around London?" Abby could hardly believe her ears. She and Jordan had plenty of privacy at the palace, but after a full year devoted to public life, she'd almost forgotten what it was like to walk down the street or pop into a pub without an entourage. "Where do we even begin?"

"I had a few thoughts on that," Jordan said. "I hope you don't mind."

"Of course not. I know you still miss it sometimes. We have beautiful mountains and some amazing ski resorts here, but none of our cities can compare to London."

"Can I quote you on that, Princess Abigail?" Jordan teased, pretending to pull out a notebook and pen to take notes.

"Absolutely not. That was strictly off the record, and you know it. Now, what do you have planned?"

"Well, for one thing, you won't need any of these." Jordan waved her hand at the pile of gowns. "Your bags are already packed, and I've included a floppy garden hat and sunglasses, for old time's sake."

Abby nodded approvingly. "Smart."

"I thought we'd go back to my old neighborhood and some of my favorite places. There's a museum I'd love to take you to, and we can take a walk through Holland park. I thought we'd have lunch at this great pub, and maybe take in a movie in Notting Hill."

"Sounds magical." Abby paused. "But tell me, did you book us a basement-level cave with a Murphy bed, too. You know, for old time's sake?"

Jordan cringed. "I thought I could do a little better than that. I've secured a place overlooking Ladbroke Square Garden. And, look." Jordan fished a red ribbon from around her neck, which had been hiding beneath her shirt. On the end was a key. "I still have the key to the garden."

"But if they've changed the locks?"

"So what if they have? We'll just jump over the fence."

"Jordan," Abby warned.

"What?" Jordan batted her lashes, which by now Abby had learned meant that she was plotting trouble. "Oh come on, how do you think I got in there last time?"

"You broke into the garden?"

"Yes, but only after you stole a key from an old

lady, and coins from the fountain, if my memory serves me right."

Abby felt her cheeks grow warm. "But I was so hungry. I just wanted a donut."

"Ah, Ducky, aren't we a perfect pair of criminals?" Jordan asked.

"Or maybe we're just a perfect pair." Abby wrapped her arms around Jordan and clasped them tight, knowing with all her heart that she had truly found the one, and that whatever the future held, they would face it together.

THANK YOU FOR READING!

Hi there!

Miranda here. I can't thank you enough for deciding to read my book today. There are two things I absolutely loved about writing London Holiday. First, it is an homage to my favorite classic movie, Roman Holiday, which I got to rewatch several times as I decided how to update the story and setting to give it a modern lesbian twist. And second, I actually got to sit London as part of the research for this book, where I had a chance to tour the city with my good friend and fellow lesfic writer TB Markinson. I really hope you enjoyed it!

When I started writing my first book, *Telling Lies Online*, as a project for NaNo (National Novel Writing Month) in 2015, I never imagined it would eventually lead to me making a living as a full time writer. It was a lifelong dream of mine to do so, and I am so thankful to readers like you, because without you, I wouldn't be where I am today, doing what I love most.

I've written over a dozen novels now, and I like to think I've learned a little more with each one. I continue to publish new books every year. Some are lighthearted, low-heat level romantic comedies. Others are sizzling, dramatic contemporary romances. I try to offer a little something for every reading mood.

I hope you'll sign up for my mailing list by visiting www.mirandamacleod.com/list so we can keep in touch. You'll receive a free copy of *Telling Lies Online* for subscribing, and have the chance to participate in monthly sales and giveaways, plus find out when new books are on the way.

You'll also be the first to hear my behind the scenes stories, like the time I had a bottle of wine explode in my cupboard while doing research *Accidental Honeymoon*. Or the time I attended a paint and sip class in preparation for writing my medical age-gap romance, *Hearts in Motion*.

What can I say? This writing thing is *serious* business, that apparently often involves wine.

You'll also get updates on all the ways my two kittens, the Sisters of Chaos, are helping me by sitting on my laptop or knocking my pens onto the floor. Wine and cats. What could be better, except maybe books?

Happy reading!
Miranda

ABOUT THE AUTHOR

Originally from southern California, Miranda now lives in New England and writes heartfelt romances and romantic comedies featuring witty and charmingly flawed women that you'll want to marry. Or just grab a coffee with, if that's more your thing. She spent way too many years in graduate school, worked in professional theater and film, and held temp jobs in just about every office building in downtown Boston.

To find out about her upcoming releases and take advantage of exclusive sales, be sure to sign up for her newsletter.

Let's be in touch!

mirandamacleod.com
miranda@mirandamacleod.com

Printed in Great Britain
by Amazon

58322689R00189